What People Are Saying About Miriam Allenson's Books

"Miriam Allenson writes with heat, heart, and humor."

–Gina Ardito, author of the Calendar Girls Series

"Miriam Allenson writes characters that leap off the page and into your heart, bringing love and laughter with them."

–Nancy Herkness, best-selling author of the Wager of Hearts series

"By the time I reached the end of the book, I knew that this was one that would be going on my re-read shelf."

–Karen Laird, Shade Tree Book Reviews

"Hilarious, sexy, heartwarming…a fabulous debut! Miriam Allenson hits it out of the park in her debut novel FOR THE LOVE OF THE DAME. Sofia and Car are proof that when opposites attract, sparks fly."

–Lisa Verge Higgins, author of Senseless Acts of Beauty

This book is dedicated to Charles Stuart, King of England, who apparently had so many children, it was hard to count them all

When The Duke Finds His Heart

A Billionaire Dukes Novel

Miriam Allenson

Publishing History

Print edition published by MS Allenson & Associates,
© 2021
Cover design by Rhubarb Crew
Formatting by Lisa Verge Higgins
Editing by Gina Ardito and Paula Gardner

ISBN13: 978-1733850148

CHAPTER ONE

It was icing on the cake, the cherry on top, the perfect ending to a totally imperfect, crazy long day. The room Livvy had reserved at London's Hotel Elgar wasn't ready because the toilet was leaking.

"I am so sorry," said the clerk, all blond hair and soulful eyes. "When the water leaked into the room below, we knew there was a problem in yours. But no worries. It will be taken care of shortly."

"Don't you have another room you can put me in?" asked Livvy, trying to keep the whine from her voice.

"Oh no, miss. We are full."

Eyes gritty from lack of sleep on the long, hellish flight across the Atlantic, Livvy drooped against the reception desk. She rubbed the spot just above the bridge of her nose where a drum corps was practicing for a concert. "How long will it be before the work's done?"

With an annoying chirpiness, the clerk said, "Give us fifteen minutes."

Livvy had been gaslighted enough in her life to recognize a con when she heard one. "Is that an approximate 15 minutes, or an actual 15 minutes?"

"We don't know that, do we?"

Livvy sighed. "Is there a place in the hotel where I can get a drink?"

"Oh, dear, I'm so sorry. There isn't." Miss Chirpy looked sad, but then perked up. "There is a club down the street. They have a lovely bar. And if you go, we'll put your luggage in your room so it will all be ready for you when you return."

It took Livvy about a second and a half to decide. If she couldn't have a pillow, a blanket, and a bed, it would have to be a bar and a brandy. The question was did she want to go after the bar and the brandy in the dark in a city she didn't know? Could she manage it, with the drum corps making a home for itself in the center of her forehead?

The meeting with the Duke of Brompton, the one she'd come to England for, was tomorrow morning at eleven o'clock. It would be best to prepare for it with a good night's sleep. A drink would help with that. So, yes, she would take a walk down the street. Then, one drink later, she'd make the return trek, and her room would be ready. If the hotel gods were smiling.

What could go wrong?

She got the answer to that the moment she stepped inside Club Chaos and was hit with its gibber of drums, deafening war of guitars, and banshee wail of vocals. She almost wilted. But she'd come for a brandy, and she would have one. Like she knew it would, the thing went down sharp and heated. "Okay," she muttered, barely hearing herself over the cacophony. "Time to get yourself back to the hotel."

Except the brandy was really good, which made her think there'd be no big deal about having another.

Looking the way of the bartender, she raised her hand in mute request for a refill. In the light from the hooded lamps that dangled down over the bar, it was clear to Livvy he hadn't noticed her and wouldn't, not while he was busy hitting on a woman with turquoise hair.

With burning eyes, she stared at the strobe-lit dance floor, where what seemed like all the humans in London were bumping and grinding, sometimes in sync with the music, more often not. She sent the bartender a doleful look, but he was still working it with his lady friend. Livvy could have knocked her glass against the bar until it shattered. In Club Chaos no one would hear, maybe not even the tall, skinny dude standing two barstools away.

What a weirdo he was, wearing a suit to a club and shoes with tassels. Wrong clothes maybe, but she had to say, with his long, thin face, blade of a nose, square jaw, and close-cropped hair, he was kind of hot. If you liked the medieval monk type.

Movement distracted her. A woman with blond hair halfway down her back sauntered by on a pair of black, stiletto-heeled boots. She wore a white tee shirt that someone had scooped the front out of right down to her nipples. Her skin-tight, black leather pants accentuated her...everything. The woman slowed, tossed her mane, and smiled at the man with tasseled shoes. He smiled back. Until he caught Livvy's eye and the smile disappeared into a frown.

After a beat, Livvy lifted a hand to her face and patted her mouth and chin. Had she slobbered on herself? She looked down at her shirt. No slobber there. So why the frown? The light came on. Of course. He wouldn't like it that she'd caught him eyeballing a woman with her boobs hanging out.

The drum corps gave way to a thousand-piece orchestra playing the 1812 Overture, the version with cannons. Livvy stared at the dance floor where the bumping and grinding went on. Stared only. Because now all she could see was that self-righteous frown.

"Jerk," she muttered. "Monk."

He placed the short, stout glass he'd been holding onto his bar stool.

As its rich, amber liquid jumped to the beat of the drums eating up the room, she leaned toward him and yelled, "Can you move your drink?"

Monk Man inclined his head in her direction and left it where it was.

Had he heard her? She tried again. "It would be a bad thing if it went over and it spilled on me."

"It won't."

"He speaks," she muttered and took a sip of the watered down remainder of her drink.

Livvy's brain cycled through all the possibilities for the attitude. Maybe he'd had a bad day, or he was thinking about a knotty problem with no solution. Maybe he was drowning his sorrows in drink and just wanted to be left alone. Or maybe females offering him judgment was not his jam.

"Total jerk," she said between her teeth. Then, because the condensation from melting ice cubes made it slippery, the glass squirted from her hand and clunked down on the floor near Monk Man's left foot.

Livvy gasped. She hadn't meant for *that* to happen.

He straightened away from the bar, snatched his glass off his stool, stepped out of range, and glared.

She gave him her most serious eyes-only mea culpa.

He glared some more.

All right, then. Mea culpa rejected. She pressed her lips together. She would *not* laugh.

The monk's glare grew darker. He turned toward the bartender and raised an arm, which brought the bartender running.

"Yes, sir?"

Monk Man snapped his fingers. "Towel, please."

Faster than a speeding bullet, the bartender flipped one over to Mr. Monk, who dropped it onto the floor. With the tip of one tasseled loafer, he wiped up the mini-spill and kicked the ice cubes under the overhang bottom of the bar. Then, dropping the towel onto the bar, he gave Livvy a look that was easy to read: go far away from here, maybe take a boat ride down the River Styx.

More laughter threatening, Livvy managed, "Sorry."

She got a pissed-off nod in return.

Now that he wasn't slouched against the bar, Livvy saw he was taller than she'd thought. She didn't like standing next to mega tall men. They made her feel…well, short. Standing next to this one, annoying as he was? Not so bad for some weird reason. And he wasn't skinny. He was lean and kind of rangy and well put-together. She gazed at his hands. And his long fingers. She appreciated a man with nice hands. And long fingers. "How did you do it? Get the bartender's attention. I haven't been able to forever. I wanted another drink."

He bent to pick up her glass. He set it on the bar, snapped those lovely, long fingers, and the bartender was back. "Refill for the lady." The bartender hurried to do what he was told.

Livvy nodded at Monk Man and she caught a glimpse of his hard and stony, light-colored eyes. That unblinking stare went right through her in an odd, sexual way.

Before she could think what *that* meant, her drink arrived. She took a gulp and her head went upsy-daisy. Lips against her glass, she giggled. "You're kind of nice. Are you a prince?"

If disapproval had gradients, his deepened. "No." He turned back to the dance floor.

Okaaay. Maybe not so nice. Speaking of which, she hoped the Duke of Brompton was nice because if not, this trip to England was destined to be a total dud.

She made a sound that was part pain and part frustration.

Mr. Monk frowned. "Beg pardon?"

She gave him a little shake of her head. Like she would tell anyone, let alone a stranger, what she was thinking. Anyway, it was too late when he looked away and just stood there in his dark, broody aura. He braced one foot on a rung of the barstool he no longer used as a table—thank God—drink dangling from his fingers. He was so *noli me tangere*—touch-me-not—that Livvy knew she should ignore him.

Except, as it often did with her, perversity took over. "I should have said thank you for mopping up the mess I made. And apologized for it getting on your shoes."

He acknowledged her with a duck of his chin.

"Do you have a shoeshine guy I can call?"

That got his attention. Like she could call the baffled expression on his face attention.

She pointed. "Liquor is hell on leather. I'll pay him to polish your shoes."

"No need."

Livvy sidled closer.

"How do you stand the noise? We're being assaulted by bad decibels."

No answer. Well, what could she expect? The guy was *noli me tangere*. She would have given up. If she hadn't seen that little twitch of his lips.

He was entertained, was he, but wasn't going to show it? Dude was not getting away with that. "How's that Brexit thing going? Could you guys have figured out a better way to commit suicide? And what will you do with all those euros you have in your pocket?"

No visible reaction. But she was getting to him. She could feel it in the air.

"I mean, all your politicians, have any of them ever heard of unintended consequences?"

He half turned toward her. "I rather think none of us knows the long-term impact of Brexit."

I rather think… Good God, he had a *Downton Abbey* accent. And she felt encouraged to tease him some more.

"You know, now that your politicians have divorced Europe, you're going to need passport control. Maybe under the White Cliffs of Dover."

Another twitch of his lips.

"Here's why I'm interested. I just dropped in from across the Pond, although why you Brits call the second biggest body of water in the world a pond escapes me. Anyway, I need to know things because I might be here for a while."

She dropped one hand to her side, crossed her fingers, and sent good vibes to the Duke of Brompton, wherever he was, tonight.

Monk Man pressed his lips together. His eyes were smiling even if his mouth wasn't. "Quite."

She beckoned him to come closer and he did, filling the space around her. That was crazy because he wasn't one of those muscle-bound, football player types. He was more track and field. "What's your opinion? Do you think Harry and Meghan will be back and if they do come back, where will they live? And here's another thing. Can you guys cut them a little slack? They want to be normal."

His eyes—she still didn't know what color they were—smiled some more. "Quite."

"Is quite your only word?"

"No." Said with a twinkle in his now not-stony, kind of awesome eyes.

That little bit of shine was all she needed. She jumped up on her stool so she could be more in his face, which she wasn't, because his face was still miles above hers. "Maybe if the Queen forgives them, she'll give them their own house. Maybe they want a palace. Your palaces, in case you didn't know, are like big hotels with plumbing issues." Like the plumbing issue in her not so big hotel. "Or maybe they'll need to wait for another palace to become available."

He folded his arms across his chest and shifted a bit toward her. "Perhaps."

"Which brings me to another thing. Soccer. Yeah, I know. You call it football. The biggest rivalry, is that Manchester United and Arsenal? Inquiring minds would like to be made whole."

His eyebrows hiked straight up. "What?" His mouth curved upward in pleasure. It stunned her. He was no medieval monk man, not even a Cassius, long and lean and definitely not murderous. With his shiny, light eyes, long nose, and a mouth that was trying so hard to be hard but failed? Maybe he wouldn't make *People Magazine's* Sexiest Man Alive issue. That would be the world's loss.

"Damn, you're hot," she blurted. "I—I mean, damn, you're tall."

"I have noticed that when I look in the mirror, the tall part."

"You're a lot taller than my brother-in-law."

His smile ticked down. "Is that good or bad?"

"There's nothing good about my brother-in-law."

He nodded and looked back at the dance floor.

Livvy made a fist and punched her knee. What had made her mention Kyle? Like she'd let him spoil this moment? Good that she hadn't mentioned her father. That would have been total spoilage. "You know what's wrong with all the people in here?"

He cocked his head in her direction.

"They're auditioning."

"For…?"

"A zombie movie."

And then he laughed. Laugh lines framed his mouth and his eyes and he was perfect in his suit, perfect in his tassels, perfect.

"What's your name?" she asked, leaning closer. If she leaned any more, she'd fall and he'd have to catch her. And wouldn't that be more perfect?

"My name is Jack." He lifted his stool and put it down behind him. Now there was nothing between them but air. "What's yours?"

She knew better than to give up her real name to a stranger, hot as he was. "Princess Leia."

One eyebrow came up. "Right, then. Where is your lovely, white robe and your droid?" His *Downton Abbey* accent melded with his smooth, baritone voice and made Livvy think about dark places.

His smile played with the corners of his mouth. "Do you need someone to save you from Darth Vader? Shall I be the one to do that?"

"There are two Darth Vaders in my life. Could you?"

He raised one eyebrow. "Yes, I can. Save you, that is. Who shall I be? Luke or Han?"

"I'm kind of a Han girl myself."

He shifted closer. The bottom of his suit jacket grazed her jean-clad knees.

"Then I'll be Han."

"I'm guessing this…" She fingered one of his suit's pocket flaps… "says you came straight from your office."

He took a sip of his drink and swallowed. Her gaze fixed there, at the base of his throat. What would happen if she touched him there? Would his skin be hot? If she cupped a hand to the side of his neck, would she feel the thrum of his pulse? Would it be running as fast as hers?

"I didn't come straight from my office." His intense eyes studied her. "Does my suit bother you?"

With fingers operating without direction from her brain, she grazed over the silky wool of his lapel. "Your suit is really fine."

"I'm pleased you like it. As for why I'm wearing it, I was at a meeting."

"Did you drive from there in your Millennium Falcon?"

"No." He raised one hand and smoothed his fingers over the thin cotton of her shirt. "I don't care for clubs."

She felt the impression of every one of his fingers and the heat of his hand through to her skin. Her heart beat heavy and hard. She pulled on his jacket, bringing him closer. "But you did it anyway. Came here. To Club Chaos. Why?"

"Why?" The Cassius look was back. But then it went away and, the outside of his thighs brushed up against the inside of hers. "Because I didn't want to miss meeting you."

"That is such a line," she whispered and her private parts woke up.

"It is." With unblinking pale eyes, he stared into hers. "It has the added benefit of being true."

"Nice," she whispered.

"I believe some American person of note once said that. Although I might be indulging in a bit of hyperbole."

"Are you trying to impress me with your recollection skills?" She wanted to slide a hand from his jacket to the placket of his shirt and all those cute little buttons, up to that place that beckoned her, where she could touch the exposed skin at the base of his throat.

He removed the glass from her nerveless fingers, reached behind him, and placed it on the bar.

"Would you like to dance?" He slid a hand up her leg to her hip, and she took in a sharp breath. The way he looked at her, she knew. He was asking for permission, and it had nothing to do with dancing.

His forefinger painted circles across the muscle just above her knee. The little bit of light in the club's stygian darkness—relieved only by the staccato throb of the strobes—accentuated the glow of skin on his high cheekbones.

"Yes," she said. "Will it work?"

His mouth was a weapon that had been shaped by the devil. It softened the severity of his face. "I can assure you it will. In any way we want it to." He raised her right hand to his lips. Turning it, he placed a kiss in the center of her palm, the heat of his breath bathing her skin. Her eyes threatened to roll back in her head.

She wanted to touch the neatly-cut hair at the back of his neck. She wanted to unbutton his shirt and press her hands against his naked chest. "I shouldn't tell you this, but you're kind of catnip-ish."

One eyebrow twitched. "Is that a word?"

"Yes, it's a word."

"I've never heard it before."

"I might have made it up," she said. "I'm a word person." She stared at his mouth and its profligate, lower lip. Would it be smooth and soft? Would it be warm or cool? Would it feel like satin? Would he… She squirmed on the stool's hard seat.

"I'm a word person, as well," he said. "I publish books."

A warning bell sounded. "That's a coincidence. I'm a writer."

"If you write the way you speak, I imagine your writing is quite charming."

She pulled back, everything in her cooling. "You're kidding."

Faint surprise curled one eyebrow upward. "Why would I be?"

Because he didn't know about her Darth Vaders who laughed their heads off thinking she could write a book, let alone get it published.

"The book I'm writing isn't finished," she hedged.

"Ah, you're an author-type writer. Lovely." His gaze roamed over her. She felt it touch her breasts, rise to her face, to the crown of her head, and then zero in on her mouth. Her own mouth tingled. "I am."

"Then keep on working until it is."

"Sure." She nodded. The whole conversation had taken on a surreal quality. "Are we two strangers having a moment?"

He dropped both hands to rest on her knees. "We aren't strangers."

Livvy didn't know if her head spun from the vertigo of drink, the intoxication of his fingers, or the feel of his hard body crowding up against hers. "If we're not, what are we?"

"That's the mystery of it," he murmured, his lips close, his hands moving up her thighs to glide slowly over her hips. "I love a good mystery. Don't you?"

"Maybe that's another line," she whispered and began to slide off her stool.

He braced her in his arms. "Steady on, my girl."

"I can do that." Except she wasn't sure that was true.

His lips close to her ear, he murmured, "You're not what I thought." He insinuated a hand beneath her hair and massaged the nape of her neck. "And now, I'm rather interested in knowing more about the woman who wants to discuss Brexit, royals gone astray, and zombie movies."

"Really?"

"Really." His lips hovered over her cheek just at her hairline, the heat of his quiet exhalations bathing her ear. "Just a word of caution, if you plan on staying with us. The euro was never our currency. Good Lord, why use them when we have the pound?"

She closed her eyes and took in the scent of him, all cedar and something. "Rule Britannia."

As his lips skated across her cheek, he shifted his hands from her hips to her knees.

She lay her head against his chest and felt the thump of his heart. "This is probably crazy. I want to take off your clothes."

"Not here, I hope." He palmed her knees apart and took a step between them to press against the juncture of her thighs.

The skip and spin of words spooled out around her. She squinted up at him. "Am I safe with you?"

"Dear Princess. Rest assured. You are."

Heat began to flicker everywhere across her body. "That's good."

He drew back mere inches. She stared up into the mysterious color of his eyes. "Would you like to come with me to my hotel?"

His ascetic features sharpened up lean and hungry. "Where is it?"

"Right down the street."

He slid his hands into her armpits, his palms pressed against the sides of her breasts, and lifted her off her stool.

"The toilet—the loo—surely it's been fixed."

He didn't ask what she meant. Or maybe he hadn't heard, because now with her hand in his, he pulled her through the crowd.

As they neared the exit, dark gave way to light. The cacophonous noise dimmed.

He brought her to a halt, turned, and at last she saw. His eyes were blue, a deep glacier blue. Like Iceland.

"Are you sure?" His gaze wandered her face. He was giving her an out. She could use the broken toilet as an excuse, no harm, no foul. Surely, no foul.

A fleeting thought about tomorrow's meeting with the duke tickled the part of her brain where good sense lodged. She ignored it. "I'm sure. In fact, I'm doubly sure."

A smile melted the Icelandic blue of his eyes into something more like Tahiti. He bent from his great height, took her face in his hands, and brushed her lips with his. He tasted like whisky.

This time it was she who took his hand. She started toward the door and stopped. A stray thought lodged in her brain. "I've heard sometimes it just happens."

He frowned. "I beg your pardon?"

She stood on tiptoes, hooked one hand around the nape of his neck, and pulled his face down to hers. *This*, it whispered. *Him.* She silenced it. "Ignore me."

CHAPTER TWO

J ack Anstruther was trying to drown himself in a glass. Not that he would because he never did, no matter how bad it got, because then he lost control and he never lost control. Well, he had done, today, when he'd lost it spectacularly.

It had begun as all Jack's staff meetings did. But then the discussion about the sale of Anstruther Media Group, *all* parts of it, grew heated. Max Honeywell, Jack's heretofore steady and reliable marketing officer triggered it. He offered up his point—civilly enough to begin with—listened to Jack's counterpoint, listened to the others who spoke—interrupted them, his voice growing louder—and then hammered away at the position he'd taken to begin with. At which point everything fell apart.

Don't be an effing idiot, Jack, Max shouted, his face red, a vein standing out down the center of his forehead. *Sell it,* Max raged while everyone else looked on, shocked into silence. *What difference does it make when you're selling Browne the rest of the company? Let Chalcott House go. It will never be anything but a shadow of what it was. Browne will do what you refuse to do: wring maximum profit out of it, something you could have done long ago.*

So he'd stood by the bar, nursed his whisky, and thought about Max and how to sack him. If not for Princess Leia, he might have come up with something. He might even have come up with the reason for Browne's sudden push to buy Chalcott House when he knew full well Jack wouldn't sell.

But the princess had been determined to catch his attention. He was now no longer thinking about Robert Browne, a man he'd come to detest. And he'd put aside trying to decide if Max figured into Browne's plans.

What he was thinking about was what the princess looked like under the white shirt and the snug jeans that shaped her thighs and hips.

She pulled him to a halt and gazed up at him. "I can see my breath."

His body grew hot and tight.

Eyes half-closed, she said, "It's frigid cold and frostbite is next."

The light from a streetlamp picked out streaks of red running through her glossy, dark brown hair. "Do you think so?" He wanted to graze his fingertips over those streaks of red, to see if they were touched with pixie dust.

She wasn't classically pretty. Her mouth was too small, her eyes too big, her chin too narrow, her cheek bones too sharp. She was too short for him. But in her eyes—green or hazel, he couldn't tell which in the minimal light—lurked sparks of humor that snapped and shone, depending upon whether she was teasing him or getting ready to say something outrageous. She made him laugh. These last years, the number of times he found reason for true laughter was slim.

"I do and if you don't take care of me, Jack, my fingers will turn black and fall off." She wiggled the fingers of one hand in his face. "That would be a bad thing. I type with these fingers."

As he took her hand in his, he thought about her fingers and where she might make use of them on him.

What would he touch first after he undressed her? What would the thick mass of her hair look like spread over a white pillowcase? "Don't worry. I'll make sure you don't lose a single digit," he said, his voice hoarse.

"That is so—" She took a shuddery breath. Lifting her hand from his, she ran a finger across his lips and, feather-light, down the front of his neck. "—so sexy."

He wondered if somewhere nearby there was an alley where they could detour and he could unbutton and unzip her jeans and burrow one hand inside to start what he intended to finish in her hotel room.

She mumbled something unintelligible.

"Say that again?"

Expecting a saucy answer, he wasn't prepared for her to lose her balance. He caught her before she could fall.

"Oops!" She giggled. "Maybe I shouldn't have had that second drink. I am so…"

The flames engulfing him died to a smolder. She was drunk. He sighed. There'd be no white pillowcases with Princess Leia tonight, not for him. "Lovely girl, have a care."

She stood up straight. "Sorry. Nightmare day."

For the first time, he noticed the rings beneath her eyes and felt a pang of sympathy for her. She did look exhausted. "What made it a nightmare?"

"When you board your plane at 9:15 at night in Newark—that's an airport in New Jersey right across the river from New York City."

"Yes, I know." One arm around her shoulders, he urged her on and they began to walk again. Rather, *he* walked, she stumbled.

"Then they say there's a delay and then they say it will be soon, and then they say it won't be soon. It's already midnight when they say, so sorry, but there won't be any soon, at least not soon," she warbled.

"We need to bring in another plane because this one might crash into the Atlantic. Nobody wants that."

Though his body still hummed with need, he managed a smile. "That would be terrible for all concerned."

"So, eventually they put us on a new plane and we go buh-bye Newark and here I am, in merry old England." She threw out an arm and missed a step. "Ta-da!"

He braced her up and eyed the hotel, still two blocks away. Where before he'd been thinking about being in her bed, now he hoped he wouldn't have to carry her the rest of the way. "That does qualify as a nightmare."

"Total." She turned toward him and he wound both arms around her. Not for any other reason, mind, but for her comfort. Her slight body was warm and pliant and she leaned against him as if she belonged, and he liked it. Still, Princess Leia was jet-lagged, knackered, and drunk. His loss. He made it a practice never to shag a woman who wouldn't remember the following morning what she'd done the night before. They'd had their moment. Sometimes one didn't get more than that.

She came to a stop. He looked down into her upturned face with its smile, so appealing in its lopsidedness.

"You know, I'll have to check. But I'm pretty sure Charles is almost as tall as you."

He frowned. "Who's Charles?"

An odd combination of emotions chased themselves across her face before she blinked them away. "Oh, just a guy."

"Is he why you've come to the UK?"

"Not really."

What kind of answer was *that*? He started them walking again. "Is your Charles a Brit?" *A lover?*

With each step she took, she leaned more heavily against him. It had become all but impossible to move her in a straight line. "Kind of," she said.

Irked, he said, "Where are you meeting him?"

"I don't remember, but I have the address in my luggage, and why are you so annoyed?"

"I'm not." He was. About Charles, whoever the wanker was.

On her face was a new smile, this one dreamy, as if she'd remembered something that delighted her. "You know Rotten Row?"

"Of course."

"The William of William and Mary built it. You know, king and queen, the Glorious Revolution. He wanted a short cut from Kensington Palace, where he lived to St. James Palace, where he worked. So, he built one and called it the Route du Roi. And then, guess what? Because you Brits can't pronounce French words, you made Route du Roi into Rotten Row."

He chuckled. "How do you know that?"

"I'm a fount of inconsequential knowledge." After a beat, she added, "Some people say it's a parlor trick."

"It's not a parlor trick." The person who'd said so was an idiot.

She slid both hands beneath the flaps of his suit and pressed her palms against his shirt. He felt the imprint of each of her fingers on his chest. He wished she wouldn't do that.

"So, my hotel, there it is. Only a half block away." She canted her head in the direction. "The Hotel Elgar. It's named after the guy who wrote Pomp and Circumstance." She began to sing off key. "La la-la la la…. High school graduation."

"I'm not sure that was the use Elgar had in mind."

She gave him her witchy smile. "I was kidding."

"I know." He touched the corner of her mouth and its plump, lower lip. Cautioning himself to remain in check, he said, "I'm familiar with the hotel. It's where I held my meeting today."

"If *you* held it, *you* must be the boss man." She dropped her head back on her neck and her shining, brown hair swung back and forth behind her in slow motion.

He wanted to ghost a hand over it. He wanted to tangle his hands in it. He wanted to… He couldn't. Leaning down, his lips close to hers, he whispered, "I am."

"Are you the solitary kind? Do you play your cards close to your chest?" Her lips parted in a way that told him she would welcome a kiss.

His scruples began to fade. "I do. I prefer it that way."

"Have you always?" she whispered.

He had, since that time long ago when he realized if he wasn't careful about every step he took, his family was going to lose the little that was left after the disaster. "Yes. Always."

She skated a finger across his lower lip. He felt her touch there and everywhere. "Bingo," she whispered.

He forced himself to remember the thread of conversation. "What do you mean?"

She closed her eyes and pressed her teeth into her lower lip. He took in a centering breath, hoping it would serve as a counterbalance to his John Thomas, hard as a rock inside his trousers.

"When I first saw the way you stood with that drink in your hand, I thought yeah, that guy spends too much time alone with himself."

Her lower lip glistened. She'd stopped biting it. Now, he wanted to. "I'm not lonely."

Eyes still closed, she shook her head. "I said alone, not lonely. And you don't smile much."

Jack didn't want to be analyzed. Certainly not by this woman, a stranger really. His body cooled. "I smile."

Shaking her head, she said, "No, you don't, but it's okay. Can I ask you a question?"

Did he want her to? Jack didn't like questions asked by strangers. "Ask me," he said, wary.

"Where do you live?"

He relaxed. "I have a house outside of London, in Berkhamsted, and a flat in Kensington."

"Where do you park your Millennium Falcon?" she asked.

His driver, Henry had borrowed the Millennium Falcon—car—to visit his daughter who lived in north London. "In the car park in Kensington. At my flat."

"Kensington. I remembered. That's where my meeting is tomorrow."

"May *I* ask a question?"

"Why not? I…" Her voice faded away. "Sorry, what?"

Chalcott House's offices were in Kensington. In Somerset Mews. "Where in Kensington is your meeting?"

A look of confusion imprinted itself on her face.

He sighed and started them forward again. "Let's walk on."

Another few steps and she was leaning more heavily against him. He savored the feel of the one small but lovely breast his hand was pressed up against. Once more, he reminded himself. This was off limits.

She stopped and put her arm around his waist. A scent of some sweet flower rose from her beautiful hair. And then, she twisted and hooked her fingers into the waistband of his trousers.

Bloody, bloody unfair.

To divert himself, he said, "So, Princess, do you know how to get to your meeting tomorrow?"

"Not to worry. And stop calling me Princess. My name is Livvy."

He frowned. "Livvy. Isn't that a shortened version of Olivia?"

"'Course it is. What else would it be?"

Was it possible? With everything he'd brooded over today—Max and his outrageous behavior, Robert Browne and his unwelcome interest in Chalcott House—he'd forgotten about tomorrow's meeting with that persistent American woman, Olivia Sterling.

After wearing him down with her incessant emails and texts, he'd told her if she came to England and could convince him, he'd give her what she wanted: access to his library at Brompton Court so she could complete her research for a book she was writing. Was it possible this was that Olivia Sterling? It had to be.

How strange the universe was. To meet his tenacious American correspondent in a club of all things, a place he might otherwise never have gone to, and to find out she was as provoking—and yes, funny—in person as she was in the ether. "Well, then, Livvy Olivia. Do you have a surname?" There was always a chance she wasn't Olivia Sterling.

"You ask some really dumb questions." Her voice was scratchy with annoyance.

"Indulge me." His step was light, his head lighter.

"Okay, then. It's Browne. Livvy Browne."

He froze.

"Why are you stopping?"

Because there was a part of him that wanted to deny what he'd just heard.

"It's just a little farther to the hotel," she said just before her knees gave.

He wanted to let her fall. Someone would find her. But the street was deserted. He couldn't do it. He had no choice. He lifted her into his arms.

"Oh, great. Being carried. So nice."

Not nice. Not at all.

"Anyway," she mumbled. "I've got a car picking me up tomorrow morning at ten-thirty. Do you think that's enough time to get me where I'm going by eleven?"

He barely felt the weight of her. He barely felt anything. "I don't know."

She snuggled her face against his shoulder. He thought about nudging her face away.

"The address. I remember. It's 10 Somerset Mews. I'm meeting with the Duke of Brompton."

There. More proof.

"Do you know him?"

"I know him."

"You do? What's he like?"

"I'm not sure I can say."

"Well, that's a cop out," she said, voice muffled. "You sure you don't want to give me a heads-up on the guy?"

He stared straight ahead at the hotel's marquee. "Tell me. What's your father's first name?"

She raised her head a drop and looked at him with bleary eyes. "Why do you want to know that?"

He wouldn't meet her gaze. "Answer me."

A frown rippled across her forehead. "I don't want to."

Of course she didn't. "Do it anyway."

She dropped her head back onto his shoulder. "It's Robert."

That confirmed what he would do next. He would take her to her room. Lay her down on her bed. Walk out. And then he would decide how, tomorrow, he would tell Olivia Browne—she who was the daughter of venture capitalist, Robert Browne—that he would not give her permission to search his library for the exact thing that would help her finish her book.

She and her father might have thought it a clever stratagem to plant her at Brompton Court. No matter how remote it was to his life, it was still his property. Did Browne think she could somehow help pressure Jack to sell him Chalcott House?

He didn't know. But when it came to business, Jack believed in playing to win. He believed in taking smart risks, and he believed in professional integrity.

He did not believe in coincidences.

***

Being carried was so romantic, but it wasn't comfortable, though the books said it was. As Jack took his long paces—he was so tall, long paces would be his thing—she was jolted back and forth. If she could have formed a thought and then sent a message to her mouth to say it, she would have asked him to be less bouncy. She pursed her lips to shape the words. Nothing came out.

Besides, there were other things about her return trip to the hotel that she liked very well. The feel of being in Jack's arms and the sleek muscles of his not ninety-eight-pound-weakling body. "Gym," she whispered.

"What?" He kept walking. Faster.

Gym made sense to her brain, which was operating on low power.

She loved his cologne. Very cedar-ish. She wondered if he was for sale. He could make a fortune bottling himself. She nuzzled her nose and mouth against his shirt. Pure aromatherapy.

His skin was hot against her forehead where she mashed it against his throat. He could plug himself into an electric grid and reduce everyone's heating bill.

She nudged her chin against the placket of his shirt where it was still buttoned. How she wanted to unbutton him. Only she couldn't. Her chin didn't have opposable thumbs.

It was odd to be carried on a street in London in the middle of the night. She wanted him to carry her forever. It felt good. The weirdest thing… it felt like someone cared for her.

Jack shouldered his way into Elgar's lobby. He didn't care what anyone thought of him carrying a woman into the hotel. The blond-headed clerk behind the reception desk—who recognized him from the many times he stayed overnight after meetings—certainly didn't share her opinion, just gave him the key to Olivia's room. Inappropriate that. He'd speak to her after he got rid of his burden.

As he rode up in the elevator with the woman in his arms, he wondered how his security people had failed to determine that Sterling wasn't her true surname. They'd traced her to northern New Jersey, where she volunteered at a local library and worked as a server in an Italian restaurant. She'd been truthful about one thing at least. She was a writer. She wrote a blog and a column for a small newspaper.

In the column she wrote—under the name, Sterling—there was nothing that gave his investigators pause. He'd read some of them, himself. They were funny.

When she'd begun her electronic assault six months previous, he'd read the first email with its request for access to Brompton Court, his estate in Lincolnshire. Then he deleted it. She sent him four or five more, which he also deleted. Until curiosity got the better of him and he read another.

> Dear Your Grace, I get that you think I'm some woman with too much time on my hands, but I want to write a biography about your ten or sixteen times grandmother. Word is she kept diaries and they're in your library. It will be very helpful to my writing if you would let me in so I could read them.

That was what she wanted, was it? Again, he stopped reading her emails. But one morning, after they kept coming, curiosity again got the better of him.

> Dear Your Grace, maybe I'm addressing you wrong? Maybe that's why you haven't answered me? Would you like me to call you Dear Duke instead of Dear Your Grace? I'm okay with either.

He hated his title and hardly used it, though he couldn't help but smile at her nonsense.

When the next email came, he read it right away.

> I've been studying Chalcott House's catalog and I'm afraid you would not publish your grand-mother's books (You did know she

wrote four of them, right?). If you
read any of them, you'd be horrified.
Dear Duke, your grandmother wrote
erotica.

And he laughed.

From that point on, he looked forward to her
daily messages. After six months of accumulated
emails, and then of all things, texts, he knew he
needed to meet Olivia Sterling. At the very least, he
could decide why he found her so appealing, even if
just from her words. Now, he wondered how he
could have allowed himself to be so fooled.

Tapping the key card against the entry pad, he
opened the door, stepped across to the bed, and put
her down. She flopped over on her side away from
him.

She was so tiny, seemingly fragile. How stupid
was that thought.

He turned to leave when she lifted her head.
"Cold," she muttered and curled up in a ball. Tremors
ran through her body.

He reached for a blanket folded up on one of the
chairs and spread it over her.

For a second or two, she was still, but then threw
the blanket aside and he saw she still wore her boots.
On a hard exhale, he cursed himself for a fool,
reached down, wrenched one off and then the other,
and dropped both on the floor next to the bed.

Her mouth opened a drop. A tiny snore escaped. If she knew she snored, would she write about it in her blog?

She sat up and looked around, her hair wild, her shirt riding up and exposing a swath of pale skin at her waist. "Jack? Where am I?"

He placed both hands on her shoulders and nudged her down. "You're where you shouldn't be, Olivia Browne."

Confusion clouded her eyes. "I don't understand."

He pulled the blanket up to her neck. "Go to sleep."

He watched her for a long moment. Olivia Sterling. Olivia Browne. Princess Leia. He didn't know what she might have been to him if she hadn't lied about who she was. That was over now and he knew what he'd always known. He needed to remain vigilant against those who would destroy his interests. Most important, he had to guard against those who would destroy his family.

The universe wasn't strange. It was a fucking bitch.

CHAPTER THREE

Livvy opened her eyes. Light filtered into the room from beneath the drapes. She bolted straight up. Fumbling for the hotel's boxy radio-alarm clock, she turned its face toward her.

It was ten o'clock. She'd overslept.

Throwing herself out of bed, she tripped over her boots and staggered to the bathroom. Only when she felt the chill of the tile on the bottoms of her feet did memory come whooshing back.

Last night. Club Chaos. Liquor.

Jack.

She stared down at herself. She was wearing what she'd been wearing. Except not her boots. Well yeah. She'd just tripped over them. She braced herself on the sink's vanity, moaned and knew. Jack had taken off her boots.

Everything in her came to attention. Goose bumps. Hair follicles. Neurotransmitters. Had he—? Had she gone along with—?

She hoped it wasn't what she was imagining. Because if it were, it meant two things. She'd had sex with a stranger. And she couldn't remember enjoying it.

She pushed away from the vanity, reached into the shower stall, and twisted the knob into the on position. She stripped out of her clothing and kicked it aside. Stepping under the cascade of hot water, she washed accumulated travel dirt from her body and flexed her private parts. They didn't feel used.

She poured a generous amount of shampoo onto her head and scrubbed like it would help her fill in the blanks in her drink-saturated, jet-lagged brain. After rinsing twice, she wrenched at the knob hard enough it should have come off the wall. She couldn't remember much from last night. Well, except for the part where Jack carried her in his arms. That was… she sighed…amazing.

Though she hadn't met the man before last night, she'd more than gotten the sense he wasn't the type so hard up for sex he'd have it with a woman dead to the world. She shook herself out of her head trip and swiped a towel over the mirror so she could see enough to blow-dry her hair. Now was not the time to think about last night. She had a meeting she couldn't be late for.

Once the duke had given her the go-ahead to come to England, she'd worked hard to come up with her pitch. Which she needed to review right now. She'd concentrate on the diaries, of course, though she'd throw in a little about how much she knew about Jessamine and her family. Which was a ton.

Maybe if it came up in conversation, she'd mention Caleb, Jessamine's brother, or James, the first duke, or James's son, who ended his life with his head in a basket, poor guy.

She would *not* bring up the financial scandal the current duke's father got sucked into that made a big splash in London's gossipy newspapers. That would be a total non-starter and she was not into self-destruction. Whatever he said, she'd take her cues from him.

She plopped down on her bed. After yanking up first one knee-hi, then the other, she threw on her white silk blouse with the mock turtle collar, and the black pencil-thin trousers that hit her just at the ankle. She stood and rushed into the bathroom.

It would have been nice if she could have known what the duke looked like. All she'd been able to find were a few grainy pictures. One was with him and Marybeth McKenzie, Chalcott House's star author of the Red Dragon Saga. In it, he wore a solemn face and a full beard. He towered over the much shorter, all smiles Marybeth.

Standing on her tiptoes—why were these hotel mirrors always so high—she applied her mascara. She paused, still holding the slender wand and studied what she saw. Pale skin, puffy eyes—today bloodshot hazel—all from late night drinking with a dreamy man. She made a face. She would not think about last night.

She finished putting on her makeup and slid into her flats. Then, grabbing her purse, she told herself to pull it together. Today was the day she'd worked toward for months. Succeeding at it was part of her master plan. She was not going to screw it up fantasizing about a man she'd never see again.

It was 10:57 when Livvy leapt up the three shallow steps to the front door of the tall, narrow building, numbered 10 Somerset Mews. She paused and took several deep breaths before stepping across the threshold. It would not be cool to throw open the door while panting like a dog.

To the woman sitting at the desk against the far wall, Livvy said, "Hi. I'm Olivia Sterling. I have an eleven o'clock appointment with the duke."

The woman stood. "He's expecting you. Please follow me."

She followed the receptionist into a short, uncarpeted hallway. Livvy took a deep breath. "Chin up, girlfriend," she whispered.

The woman opened the door at the end and stepped aside for Livvy to enter. Without a sound, she closed the door behind her.

This room was tidy and spare. There was a sideboard with framed pictures on it and strangely a mini-punching bag on a stand in one corner. There was a lustrous, deep blue and green area rug beneath her feet and a dark wood desk with two chairs in front of it. Three tall, narrow windows with off-white mini-blinds drawn halfway down covered the far wall, and a man—not some random man, because who else would it be but the duke—stood, hands folded behind his back, looking out those windows.

Livvy took in an instant impression of lean build, well set-up shoulders, the suggestion of a fine ass beneath the single-vented jacket, and equally fine, narrow waist and hips, and height. The duke of Brompton was one tall man. He was as tall as Jack.

Pressing her lips together hard, she reminded herself not to think of the excellent specimen of man she'd met last night when all she needed from this particular man was for him to be an excellent means to an end.

He still hadn't turned. She wondered about protocol. When you entered a room and a duke didn't seem to know you were there, were you supposed to announce yourself? Stamp on the floor to let him know he wasn't alone? Clear your throat, maybe? Cough? She coughed.

He turned. Livvy blinked to clear her vision. But her vision was perfect and she knew it. "Jack! What are you doing here?"

He raised one eyebrow. "I should think that was obvious, Miss Browne."

"That's not my—" She took a step back. Her shoulders hit the door she'd just come through. Truncated thoughts flew around her head like bats caught in scalding sunlight. She flailed around for something to say, until she managed, "What happened to your beard?"

"I shaved if off." His eyes were the Icelandic blue that went with his monk face, more remote now, if it was possible, than when she'd first seen him in Club Chaos.

"I…I…" Her mouth was desert-dry. "Why didn't you tell me who you were?"

"Ah. An interesting question, considering the trajectory of our relationship."

"The trajectory—"

"Why didn't *you* tell *me* you're Robert Browne's daughter? And why, in all the many times you contacted me, did you call yourself Olivia Sterling?"

Because if she'd hadn't, he would never have let her near him. "It…It's my mother's maiden name."

He raised an eyebrow. "An interesting answer and rife with lack of candor. I do not care for deceit."

Unpleasant heat burned her cheeks. "The thing is, I thought you might not—" She licked her lips. "Because you're selling your company to my—" She tried for something…anything…to get a grip. "And he's not—" She exhaled sharply. "When did you know?"

Jack…the duke…came around to the front of the desk, closing the distance between them until they were inches apart. He unbuttoned his suit jacket. "Not right away."

Her back pressed hard against the door, she fixed her gaze on the minute movements of his long fingers as they slipped the buttons from the button holes. "When did you?"

"Last night on the way back to the hotel. You told me yourself."

"I did?" The last button came undone. Swamped by his overwhelming closeness, she sidled away from the door and toward the wall. "Why are you unbuttoning your jacket?"

His eyebrows twitched, the effect altering the sternness of his features. "I'm about to sit." He tipped his head in the direction of the two chairs behind him.

She hesitated a long moment. Then, on noodle legs, she stumbled toward one of the chairs and dropped into it before she could embarrass herself by splatting on the floor. "I don't remember telling you."

He sat a lot more smoothly than she did. "I'm not surprised. You were drunk."

"Yes, I was," she admitted and felt her face flush. "Last night, I overindulged."

The flintiness in his blue eyes softened and then hardened again.

She folded one clammy hand against the other. "So, who are you really? Are you Nigel, the Duke of Brompton, or Jack?"

"I'm both."

Livvy's head throbbed. "How do you get Jack from Nigel?"

"I have three given names and a surname: Nigel Alastair John Anstruther."

"Well, Jack makes sense, then, since it's a perfectly acceptable nickname for John. And Nigel and Alastair aren't exactly what you'd call popular names." Her toes curled inside her shoes. First she couldn't put two words together, and now she was insulting his parents' name choices? Good job.

"Perhaps."

Livvy gripped her messenger bag. Desperate, she tried to think of something smart to say, because not one thing she'd planned came to her mind. "You have an interesting family."

"Do I? I don't suppose it's any more interesting than yours."

She couldn't let herself rise to that barb. "I meant your historic family. Jessamine. The reason I'm here."

She inched forward on her chair and clutched her messenger bag to her chest. "Here's the thing. I need to know if my real last name is going to keep you from letting me into your library."

***

Jack supposed he should admire her tenacity. Before, when he'd turned around, her skin had paled to ash and her eyes widened in shock. Though she'd regained some color, her knees were locked together, and she held onto that damn bag like it would serve as her protection. Her body language—he'd become a student of body language of late—said she was shielding herself against him, not that it would do her any good. He was moments from escorting her out of his office.

On the other hand, it might be a distraction to hear her make her case. He folded one leg over the other. "If you think you can convince me, by all means, try."

"Do you know what a value proposition is?" she asked.

Of all things she might have said, this wasn't it. However, in the six months since she'd burst into his life, if only electronically, she'd never failed to surprise him. "I do."

She leaned forward, her gaze animated, if guarded. "I get it. You don't think writing a biography about Jessamine is all that important. That's okay. But when I'm searching the shelves in your library looking for her diaries, there will be something in it for you, too."

He raised an eyebrow.

"You care about your library," she said.

She was wrong about that. Along with every other part of the building, he despised the library at Brompton Court.

"I plan on treating your library with respect."

Some variation on that sentiment was in every email and text she sent him.

"It doesn't matter that I've never been in it. I know it's got to have centuries' worth of books that are worth saving."

The publisher in him knew old books deserved to be saved. He nodded and that had her sitting even further forward. She'd come to this meeting armored in professional dress, a high-necked white blouse, black trousers and flats and he found himself still wondering what she looked like if she weren't wearing any of it. He shifted in his chair to refocus his wandering mind.

"I volunteer at my local library—I love books by the way. When I was a kid you would never find me without a book in my hands." She got a far-off look in her eyes. "You might say books saved my life."

She blinked and took a breath. "Anyway, a couple of months ago, I took a class in preservation techniques. I know what to do and what not to do with old books. You can be sure I'll only touch your books with clean hands." She held up her hands, their backs to him. "Clean hands save books. Clean fingernails, too. And gloves."

He flexed his jaw against a smile he wouldn't show her.

She wiggled to the edge of her seat. His gaze fell to her hips. He'd wanted to touch those hips—naked hips—do things to her body, last night, that—"Continue."

"I promise I'll look at every book in your library and flag the ones you should save."

Her hair, shining this morning in the light coming in from the windows, shifted on her shoulders. His fingers twitched. He'd badly wanted to see her hair spread across a pillow, to anchor his hands in it as he—

She was going on and on and he was having a hard time hearing.

"—organize them by date and by category: fiction, non-fiction, first editions, letters, pamphlets, and anything else I find. For as long as you let me be there, I'll be your personal librarian, I'll—"

He began to sweat, and held up a hand. "Enough of your value proposition."

She went silent.

He gentled his voice even as he kept his heart hard. "Did he send you?"

Her skin paled again. "He most definitely did not."

Of course she would know he referred to her father. "Why should I believe you?"

"Would I be sitting here if I'd told you my last name was Browne?"

Ignoring that obvious charge, he said, "Your father and I are entering an exceedingly tense part of our negotiations. Things are not going well at present."

She frowned. "Because…?"

"He's decided he wants to buy a part of my company I told him I wouldn't sell. My publishing company, Chalcott House. Did you know about that?"

Her hazel eyes glittered with intensity. "I didn't because we don't talk." She came to her feet. Her bag dropped to the floor. "Can I tell you a story about a briefcase? It will help you understand why."

Was telling him a story meant to soften him towards her? He couldn't see how that was possible, given that she was who she was. But there was the business of her fascinating him…beguiling him…a thing he didn't understand. More fool him, he wanted to hear her story. He gave her a reluctant nod.

"It's about what he and my mother named me. Not so much my mother, because she wasn't in the picture even when she was, and then they divorced when I was five and disappeared from our lives altogether. Anyway, it was mostly him, the Pater Familias." She paused. "That's Latin for head of the family."

"I know Latin. I have a public school education."

"Yes. I knew that about you." Her eyes widened. She looked down at her feet where her oversized bag lay. "Sorry. I looked you up, okay?" She plucked her bag from the floor. "Anyway, my sisters are named Sheryl, Stephanie, and Sylvia. When I was seven years old, the Pater Familias told me, in not so many words because after all I was only seven, why I wasn't a Sarah or a Susan. He'd wanted three kids. Me being number four? I was a mistake. No way was I about to get one of those S names he favored."

Jack had three sisters. Each one had been loved for herself from the moment of birth. Olivia hadn't been wanted and worse, Browne told her. Son of a bitch, to do that to his own child. Still, he wasn't about to soften towards her because her father had treated her badly. "What does a briefcase have to do with that?"

"I wanted to show him I was worth an S name even if I didn't have one. One night—he wasn't home—I took a nail and scratched a message on the inside flap of his designer leather briefcase so the next morning, he'd see the heart I drew and inside the heart, 'Livvy' and know I loved him. He threw the bag away."

She began to fiddle with the clasp on her bag. "He said he should have known that I would do something dumb."

Her chin quivered before she firmed it hard enough that the tic went away. "Nothing I did or didn't do, I could never be in the same league as my sisters."

Browne had branded her with a letter. By so doing, he'd let her think she was somehow inferior. Unable to look at the glint in her eyes, Jack brushed a non-existent speck from his trousers' leg.

"Can you imagine, a seven-year-old kid, knowing she didn't have her father's love? Oh, I kept trying to prove he should love me, but I couldn't. Believe me I tried. Knowing this, do you think he'd tell me anything about his business I couldn't learn from the news?"

Her eyes glistened with just-constrained emotion. "If I did try to help him, that would legit make me a fool and I am not a fool. You only need to know I haven't spoken to him in a year since a family birthday party that I wouldn't have attended if I'd known he was going to be there. It was the last thing I—"

Her gaze dropped to the floor but only for a second before she lifted her head. "You don't need to know anything more about my family's dysfunction. You just need to know this. If Robert Browne wants me to help him shake you down, he better find someone else to do it. It won't be me."

Jessamine was a foxy lady.
When I get finished writing
her story, you're going to be
proud she was your ancestor.
Text, Livvy to the duke

CHAPTER FOUR

The story was a breathtaking example of cruelty. Jack could understand how she might have hardened herself against Browne for making her feel worthless. But he'd known liars whose practice to deceive was legendary. He wouldn't allow himself to soften towards this woman who might well be trying to worm her way into his life to find out his secrets to, once more, try to win her father's love. "Then, you've had no contact with your father for the last year?"

"I don't know how many ways I can say it." She blew on a strand of hair that had fallen onto her cheek. "How about this? I am not his Trojan Horse."

Trojan Horse. So over-the-top. He wasn't surprised. She'd been that from the beginning.

"Remind me again what your interest is in Jessamine Beresford and her diaries?"

"She's the mother of the first duke, she's—"

"That's a fact, not a reason. You said the diaries are going to help you. How?"

"When I find them, I'll have what I need to finish writing my book."

"Everyone thinks they can write a book," he said, aware that he was being cruel.

She flinched. "I know. I've been trying."

"Most people fail." That was true, as well. Out of kindness, he didn't ever speak so frankly to new writers. Fragile egos and all that. He'd made an exception in her case.

Nostrils flaring, she said, "I'm not most people."

"That is true."

She lifted her chin. "You want to know why? It's because she was amazing. She was Catholic gentry, a dangerous thing in those militant Protestant years. Equally dangerous, she was a supporter of the Stuart kings when her family supported Cromwell. She wrote pamphlets about how wrong Cromwell was for England and why they needed Charles Stuart back on the throne. She could have been executed for such treason. Instead she took it a step further and became a spy for Charles."

Jack folded his arms across his chest. "Go on."

"There's thought she might have saved Charles' life at one point when he was living in Antwerp."

If only he could believe her. He stuck a finger under his collar. It had grown quite warm in the room. "You tell an interesting story."

"From about 1654 to 1659, she traveled back and forth across the Channel, making the circuit of Europe's capitals. For what she believed in—him in this case—she willingly put her life on the line."

"Kudos are in order for my forebear." It wasn't warm in this room. It was hot.

She shot him a disapproving look. "She was honorable, and smart, and brave, and she didn't take crap from anyone. That's why."

He looked across at the thermostat on the wall. When had he turned it up so high?

Here she stood, chin thrust out, fire in her eyes, spine rigid, standing up to him, even though she might well be losing the thing for which she had come to England.

"One more thing; Jessamine died soon after her child was born. She never revealed who her child's father was. The diaries will tell me—"

"The diaries again." He clasped a hand to the back of his neck. He was sweating.

"Why aren't you the least bit interested in Jessamine's life?" She gave him an accusatory look. "Did you read anything I sent you about her?"

"I read it all." She was relentless. And perspiration had begun to melt the starch in his collar.

"Jessamine Beresford was a rock star. She was part of British history and her uterus—with a little input—was where the dukes of Brompton got their start. Are you going to say your own grandmother doesn't deserve her rightful place in history?"

"She's not my grandmother." For years he'd made sure never to think about anyone associated with Brompton Court. He'd included this historic figure until he couldn't avoid it because of this American woman's insistence.

She narrowed her eyes at him. "It's a figure of speech."

He came to his feet. "All right, enough!" He snatched his mobile off his desk. He'd expected her to wither in the face of his knife-cold anger. Instead, she was fire, passion, and backbone, and she was poking at something inside him he couldn't name. More to the point, she'd refused to show him any weakness, and he was about to reward her. "Go to Brompton Court. Find the diaries."

Her eyes widened.

Perversity coursed through him. "You have a month to do it. These are my terms. Do you accept?"

She nodded. Watchfully.

The damn bag she'd used like a shield slipped off her shoulder and caught in the crook of her elbow. Her lips parted. "I'm good to go? I'm in?"

"For a month. I suggest you leave before I change my mind." He keyed in a text on his mobile. "I'm telling my driver, Stebbins, to take you back to your hotel to pack your things, and then drive you to Brompton Court."

Her frown was comical. "R-Really?"

"Yes, really. I'm calling ahead to my housekeeper and telling her to prepare a room for you." Even as the words dropped from his mouth, he couldn't believe he'd said them. Goading her, because he was as annoyed at himself as he was at her, he added, "Didn't think about where you were going to stay once you got to Brompton Court, did you?"

Never taking her eyes off him, she backed toward the door. "I did. I found an Airbnb nearby. Now I can cancel my reservation and save a little money. Thank you for that."

Her father was one of the richest men in the world. Why did she need to save money? Oh, right. She didn't take crap—or money, either it seemed—from her father. "You're welcome," he grumped.

Cocking her head to one side, she studied him for a long moment. And then she said, "Maybe I was right."

He stiffened. Was she about to throw an insult his way?

"Last night I asked if you were a prince."

What was this? "And?"

"When someone is as nice as you're being to me, I think it's fair to say you really are a prince."

Pulling the door open, she stepped into the hallway. "Among men."

She began to close the door, but then swung it open again. "No, don't say it. You are." This time she closed the door all the way. Gently.

The sudden absence of sound froze him in place. Had she just sent him a parting shot? He strode toward the door. His hand hovered over the knob. He made a fist, and took a step back.

He stood motionless for long moments and then stalked out of his office into the anteroom. He wondered if she would still be there. She wasn't. Isabella looked up. "Sir?"

"I'm going out for a bit. I'll be at my sister's and then back for my meeting with Max. Don't call me unless it's urgent."

He stepped outside. He'd achieved success in business beyond anything he could have imagined at the start. In all his dealings, he never let his heart interfere. Today, because of his irrational attraction for Olivia Browne, he'd done it. Led with his heart.

A cluster of birds had taken up residence in Somerset Mews' trees. They were a noisy lot. Even so, above the cacophony he could hear her voice.

It's more than fair to say you're a prince among men.

Who spoke like that? *She* did. Olivia Browne…Sterling…Princess Leia. She weaponized words. He found it damnably fascinating. And so he'd sent her to Brompton Court. He knew where she was now. She couldn't surprise him by showing up somewhere else where he didn't expect her. He told himself he was doing what he always did: making logical decisions not rationalized ones.

He looked around and cursed. Or perhaps not. He'd told Stebbins to drive her up to Brompton

Court, which meant he was without a car. He called for an Uber.

Livvy levitated out of the duke's office. She raced across the cobblestones to the end of the street, where his driver and car waited. Throwing herself into the back seat, she said a quick hello, and then scooted forward. "Thank you so much for driving me, but can you step on it? I'm in kind of a rush."

"I'll do the best I can, miss. London traffic, you know."

As the car rolled, she patted her chest, as if that would get her heart to stop doing its version of the St. Vitus Dance.

"We're for your hotel first, aren't we? I'm Henry Stebbins."

"The Elgar Hotel, yes, Mr. Stebbins."

"Please, miss," he said, all smiles on his ruddy-skinned English face. "Call me Henry."

"Okay, Henry." As they rolled away from Somerset Mews, she gave him an agitated smile. At any moment, the duke could call and tell Henry to drop her where she stood. Not until she'd rushed through her packing, checked out, and was back in the car did Livvy begin to breathe a little.

"As you're in a hurry, miss, we should get on with it, shouldn't we?" he asked with a twinkle in his blue-as-a-spring-sky eyes.

"Yes, thank you." For the first time she became aware of the vehicle she found herself in. "What kind of a car is this, Henry?" She ran her palm over the baby-butt smooth seat.

"Why, it's a Tesla. An electric car. The duke would have no other. He likes to reduce his carbon footprint where he can and this lovely lady does that, doesn't she?"

"Hmm." She slipped out of her shoes and wiggled her toes in thick, lush carpeting. Red buses, black taxis, and people streamed everywhere, as if the entire population of London was crossing in front of them.

She'd gotten what she wanted, even if it wasn't the way she'd imagined it. She told herself everything was good. But she'd had to talk about her father and that had given her a sour stomach. Still, she'd cleared the air. The duke knew now what she thought of the man who was her parent.

Her heart still simmered with anxiety. Only thing, she'd let herself be too blunt with him. He could have lowered the boom on her. What had she been thinking? Maybe she was thinking about Jack, with his hot body, and his slow-to-kindle sense of humor, and that he was somewhere inside the Duke of Brompton, that stone-cold man who had, incomprehensibly, sent her on her way to Brompton Court. She shouldn't wonder why he'd done it, only that he had, and it was a gift from the gods.

At last they inched forward. Jet-lag caught up and her eyes began to close. She forced them open again. "So, Henry, do you drive for the duke a lot?"

"All the time, miss. Except on weekends. Then I nip up to my home in Moreham village. That's next to Brompton Court, you know."

"That's nice." The yawn came, unexpected. It widened her jaws and brought tears to her eyes. "Once we get on the road," she managed, "How long do you think it will take us to get to Brompton Court?"

"Well, we don't know that, do we. Because of the traffic."

Henry continued to talk as he inched his way through London's congestion zone. She told herself she should pay attention to what he was saying about the buildings and parks they passed, many of them with historic names. Except the more he talked, the heavier her eyelids grew.

"If you don't mind me saying, miss, you look a bit fagged."

It took effort to force her eyes open. "I do?"

"Why not take a nap?"

Like he'd given her permission, she drifted off. One by one, her muscles relaxed, and she got sucked into a dream.

A dream, yes. Only it felt real.

She looked out the window of the coach she'd hired and stared down at Antwerp's Scheldt River flowing beneath the bridge they were crossing. The driver—Henri was his name—was taking his time about getting to her destination. Apprehension grew as he slowed further. "Hurry, please," she called out. As if he could. Even with congestion pricing, the traffic in downtown Antwerp was ridiculous.

As the carriage slowed, she saw him. He was right where he texted that he'd wait. Her heartbeat ratcheted up. He'd propped one hand, with his coat dripping with lace at the wrist, against his hip and smiled like everything was sunshine and roses.

"Stop here," she called out. Despite the seriousness of the task she'd taken on, she couldn't stop her heart from beating out its longing for her soon-to-be passenger. He straightened, stepped up to the carriage, opened the door, and swung inside.

The carriage rocked on its axle as Charles sat on the back-facing seat. He smiled. The silly, wonderful, beautiful man.

"What are you doing standing alone on the street without your bodyguard?" she asked. "There are a lot of people who'd be thrilled to separate your head from your body, just as they did your father."

"Don't scold, my dear Jessamine." He shook his long, coal black curls off his face. "What, pray tell, are you wearing?"

She looked down. She'd left her 1659 clothes at the hotel and was wearing a white high-necked blouse, trousers, and black flats she'd gotten on sale at Nordstrom. "Don't worry about what I'm wearing. I came straight from the Count of Limousin's ball in

Paris because more than one person whispered rumors in my ear that I'm afraid might be more truth than rumor."

The carriage tipped as Charles rose from his seat and crossed to hers. She'd hoped he would. She wanted to feel the warmth of his body through his brightly-colored silks and satins. "I am sure if you think it, it's true." He took her hand in his and pressed his lips to her knuckles. "Now, tell me."

Livvy forced herself not to think about what his thumb was doing to the back of her hand. She stared, as she always did when they were together, into the dark eyes he'd inherited from his Italian grandmother, Marie de Medici, although the weirdest thing…they kept flipping to Icelandic blue. Like Jack's.

Whoever Jack was.

"Philip will continue to profess his love for you, as one king to another—"

"Though Philip has a throne, the Spanish one," he finished for her. "At the moment I have none, thanks to Oliver Cromwell, who stole it," Charles murmured.

One day, with her help, Charles would have his throne again. If only he'd stop being so careless with his safety. "His diplomats are pursuing a way to align Spain and England in a treaty. That may mean he loves Cromwell more than you, now."

"Love is not a factor when it involves a throne, Jess."

"That's why you need to leave Antwerp." Livvy had traveled through the night by TGV high-speed train to tell Charles what she'd learned. "There's not too much love here in the Lowlands for you these days. There's no guarantee you'll be safe if you stay."

Charles let go of her hand and sat back. He opened his snuff box and took a pinch.

Snuff gave Livvy a headache. She tried to remember if she'd taken her ibuprofen with her. "In the meanwhile, there are others who seek to rout you. The crowd of your enemies is growing by the day."

Charles turned the box over on its back. "Ah, yes. Friends, enemies, and the friends of enemies. It's hard to tell them apart sometimes. Have I been betrayed?"

"No. Those who love you still do. But there is a cabal of unworthy men who seek to capture you and turn you over to Cromwell. Among them is Caleb."

"Your dear brother."

"The other day, he gave me a letter and asked if, on my way out of Brompton Court, I could drop it at the post office. Weird thing, he asked that it be sent registered mail return receipt requested. I told him I would. But when I saw it was addressed to Sparafucile Malatesta, I knew I needed to see the message. I steamed it open and learned Caleb and his friends were going to pay Malatesta to assassinate you. I stopped in Paris, heard confirmation, and here I am."

He took her hand, again. "My dear Lady Jessamine, is it your opinion that I must leave

Antwerp posthaste, perhaps not even return to my lodgings for my baggage?"

She frowned. "Why are you calling me Jessamine? My name is Livvy."

He played with her fingers. "Is it? How strange."

Charles looked at her with his well-practiced cajolery, his eyes not black but blue, and his hair, not long and black, but brown, tipped with gold and worn close to his scalp. In Jack's voice, he said, "How lovely it is you think I'm a prince among men."

She gasped and shot straight up. Her messenger bag slid to the floor.

"Miss? Are you all right?"

Disoriented, Livvy pressed both hands to her temples. "No worries, Henry. I was having a crazy dream."

"I'm not surprised. It's all that flying on planes. Gives you nightmares. When the missus and I travel, we take the train."

Still trying to regain her balance, Livvy said, "That would have been fun. A train across the Atlantic."

"I'll be driving a bit slower now. For your comfort."

Bending, Livvy picked up her bag. What did it mean that her sleeping brain had put her in the 1650s with Charles Stuart, soon after to be crowned Charles II, and he thought she was Jessamine? Was it a gift from the writing gods that though her book was a biography, she should make this a part of her story?

She flipped her laptop open and began to type as fast as she could, getting everything down she could remember from the dream. Not the paranormal part about Jack being Charles. Or Charles being Jack. Or her being Jessamine. That was too woo-woo for words.

How lovely it is you think I'm a prince among men. She jerked her fingers back from the keyboard. Who said that? Charles? The duke? Jack?

She banged her head back against the seat.

"Miss, am I driving too fast?"

If he drove any slower, she could get out, walk to Brompton Court, and get there before he did. "No worries. You're fine."

"Good. I reckon it will only be another half hour."

Livvy pressed a hand against her heart, banging away at a gazillion beats a minute, but that was fine. It would drive her to keep typing. Lucky that this time her computer wasn't doing its trick—new since she'd left home—blacking out so she had to reboot. She typed fast and saved as she went, hoping she didn't forget anything. It was such a strange dream, she doubted she ever would.

When she'd recorded what she could remember, she said, "I've never found any pictures of Brompton Court. I'm excited to see what it looks like."

"We all wish we could see what it looked like."

She frowned. What an odd thing to say.

"The duke called Madelyn to ready everything for you."

"Madelyn?"

"Yes. The housekeeper. She comes in once a week."

Livvy wondered if Madelyn would be like Mrs. Danvers. It seemed like the duke had some Max de Winter in him.

Jack. She blinked. Why was she still thinking about him? She didn't need this complication. She'd made a decision and it was a good one. Jack was a distraction. She didn't need any distractions, not for the next thirty days.

Taking out her cell, she scrolled through her messages and found one of the last ones she'd written to the duke before he'd told her to come to England.

> Jessamine did keep diaries. It's all but a sure thing they're at Brompton Court. You may be a doubting Thomas—or in your case a doubting Nigel—but once I find them, be prepared to read 'em and weep! Well, maybe just read. No need to weep.

She cringed. What had made her think snark would soften him up enough to say yes to her? She scrolled through her messages again. A smile bloomed. Snark *had* gotten her to London. Maybe it could find Jack beneath the duke's forbidding exterior.

Should she do it? She had to admit it could have her making a quick return trip to Heathrow where she'd be boarding the next flight to Newark. But— and this was the big but—there'd been something there just behind the duke's cold, blue eyes that told her he was not as cold as he wanted her to think he was.

It took her a while to write her text. Her thumb hovered over SEND while she read the words she'd written. She was here. For thirty days. Her instincts told her Jack lurked somewhere inside the Duke of Brompton. Did she want to jeopardize those thirty days just to find him? Yeah, crazy girl that she was, she did.

CHAPTER FIVE

Jack felt the buzz of an incoming text. He ignored it, occupied with something much more important: sitting on the floor, playing with his niece, Lisbeth, his sister Diana's two-year-old. Within minutes of his arrival, Lisbeth had demanded his mobile. The last time he'd visited, she'd deleted some of his apps, so he tucked the phone into his pocket. When she failed to extract it, she moved onto a demand for his keys, which he'd given her.

After fingering each one, she shoved them, one by one, into the door of the playhouse he'd bought for her at one of London's posh toy stores. Then she tried to take the folded-up knife/screwdriver combination tool off the key ring, but failed to get past the safety feature. Tiring of that, she'd abandoned the keys inside the playhouse and was now, with her bottomless, blue eyes, imploring him to give her his Rolex.

He started to unlatch it from his wrist, just as her mother walked into the room. "Ah, a heist in progress," Diana said, grabbed up her thieving daughter, and glared down at Jack, still sitting on the floor. "Have you no sense? The child has dozens of toys, many of them bought for her by you, and you're about to give her a watch that cost the earth?"

"It's hard for me to say no to her." He reached into the playhouse, retrieved his keys, and got to his feet.

"That is more than obvious."

"She's my favorite niece."

"So far, she's your only niece." Diana patted her huge belly. She was set to deliver a second daughter within the next few weeks. They were going to name her Leonie. "You're making it difficult for me to teach Lisbeth that in life there are limitations."

After their father died and before Jack had made them whole again, his sisters' lives had been all limitations. Diana and Alice were well-married now, Rose was happy in her job, and his mum lived in an exclusive retirement community. But Jack was ever vigilant to any threat to them, perceived or real, including the potential threat Olivia Browne represented.

He gave his sister an apologetic look. "I'll do better next time."

Lisbeth had her eyes fixed upon Jack's wrist, not yet ready to admit she'd been thwarted. The look of pure venality, the potential of triumph over her evil mother, the absolute knowledge that with her uncle she would always prevail, shone in those brilliant blue eyes.

Perhaps that was why he'd escaped his office. As manipulative in her own darling way that Lisbeth was, there was no wondering what was going on beneath her curly blond hair. Unlike beneath the hair—dark brown shot with red fire—that covered the head of the female he'd just sent on to Brompton Court.

Diana patted Lisbeth's bottom. "And not to change the subject, but Mum called again. She's got some new ideas about how to get Marybeth writing and you aren't answering her phone calls so she can tell you about them. Would you please ring her? I can't make any more excuses for you."

"As long as Marybeth is struggling, she won't write again. Mum's ideas of encouragement are all well and good, but they won't work." He grabbed Lisbeth out of Diana's arms. Holding her high above his head, he swung her around. "Now this darling girl, everything about her works."

"That's because, dear brother, you give her back to me before it doesn't."

"That's because you are the mother and I am the uncle." He kept going round with the little girl held aloft. She shrieked with joy. "And I love seeing her laugh."

"You do know you can have a daughter or son of your own. Or even more than one."

He snorted a disbelieving laugh, but said nothing. He'd become quite cynical about women. The few he'd had more than a casual relationship with since becoming one of the richest men in the UK—on top of being a duke—had made it clear they would be happy to have that man's child. He wasn't so sure they'd be happy to have Jack's.

To make sure she didn't pursue that conversational gambit, he said, "I'll call Mum tomorrow. Will that work?"

"Brilliant. Have a care, though. She's a bit miffed since the last board meeting."

All three of Jack's sisters sat on the Anstruther Media Group Board, as did their mother. After a near catastrophe caused by his mother's dog, Monty, Jack had insisted she not bring him with her ever again, to which she'd taken exception.

As the nanny bustled into the room and took Lisbeth from Jack's arms, Diana said, "I knew you were coming for a visit."

"Oh?"

"Yes, I called to speak to you and Isabella said you were on your way, that you'd had a visitor and when she left, you did, too. Rather put out, you were, Isabella said."

"I was. My visitor was a woman who fancies herself an author. She thinks she can write a book once she completes the research on her main character who happens to be one of our ancestors. To do it she needs access to Brompton Court's library. Besides being bloody annoying, she's Robert Browne's daughter."

Diana's blue eyes hardened. "Are you actually letting her in?"

"I have done so. Henry is taking her there now."

One side of Diana's mouth pinched up. "For once, dear brother, I believe you've not thought this problem through. Though she is in far-off Lincolnshire, and not near her father or his people, haven't you heard of the internet and mobile phones?"

Diana was right. When she left the room to see why Lisbeth had begun to whinge, he called Mike Higgins, his security chief, and told him to reinstate his surveillance on the woman, something he should have done the moment she'd walked out of his office. But he hadn't because he'd not had one rational thought since Olivia Browne had fought her way into his life.

Returning, Diana said, "Is there something else about this Olivia Browne you're not telling me?"

Of course there was. "No, nothing."

"Could Browne think his daughter could initiate a plan of some kind to wrest control of Chalcott House through a back door?"

"I know what you're thinking. That he might encourage our small shareholders to give up their voting power to him, and that his daughter could help the process along."

"She might do so."

"That seems unlikely. Even if she did, think, Diana. All those we gave shares of Chalcott House to own only a tiny percentage. We own the lion's share. Which one of us, whether Mum, Alice, Rose, or you would agree that Browne would be a better steward of the company than I?"

"None of us. I've never understood why, little as you want anything to do with the rest of the company, especially *Daily Prime*, that you decided to sell it to that man." A sneer marked Diana's voice. "He's everything you despise, a bastard vulture capitalist."

Jack grimaced. "I do loathe the man."

"As well you should. His reputation of stripping the companies he purchases of their assets and leaving them with barebones staff unable to manage the work as before, preceded him. He will do it to *Daily Prime* and the small newspapers. Aren't you throwing your people to the wolves?"

"The deal we've structured does not allow him to lay off people wholesale, nor to sell assets that keep the company running at top speed."

"Are you confident you can trust him not to find a loophole somewhere?"

Jack trusted no one. Listening to Oliva Browne talk about her father, it reminded him that as much as it had become a weight around his neck, he might not want to sell *Daily Prime* to Browne after all. He'd had the odd thought that he wished he could have trusted Browne's daughter enough to ask her about her father or even to get some helpful information about the man.

"It's something I've begun to think about. And now, after this lovely interlude with my darling niece, I'm for my office. I promise. I will give it more thought."

Diana dropped the subject when Lisbeth came running back into the room with the controller for the kitchen's overhead fan in her hands. Diana snatched it from her. Over the child's cries of outrage, she said, "Perhaps you're right, Jack. You should give her your Rolex before she destroys my entire flat."

Jack laughed as Diana towed a now screaming Lisbeth from the room. As her cries faded, Jack put his keys back in his pocket. That reminded him that he'd not checked the text that had come in minutes before.

When he saw who it was from, his laughter faded.

> I need to apologize for that prince among men thing. I couldn't believe you were going to let me go ahead and look for Jessamine's diaries, so I blurted out the first dumb thing! I probably should have just said thank you!

"True," he muttered.

> Thank you, too, for letting Henry drive me all the way to Brompton Court. I wasn't sure how I was going to get to it although I'm sure I would have figured it out! I really want to thank you for giving me a whole month to find Jessamine's diaries.

Jack snorted, wondering if there wasn't an element of sarcasm in that last thank you. "A month will have to do it, my girl."

Suppose I—

> Oops! Didn't mean to SEND just then. Anyway, If you decide you need to come up to Brompton Court for any reason, please don't let my presence stop you. BTW, could you please call me Livvy? I like it better than Olivia.

She wanted him to call her Livvy, did she? She'd burst into his life like a blazing comet and now, though he knew he shouldn't, he couldn't stop thinking about her. He scrolled back through to the first of her texts that had begun two months before, when somehow she'd gotten his mobile number.

A pulse throbbed in his cheek. Few people had his mobile number. He had given it to Robert Browne's lead attorney. Had the man given it to

Browne and had Browne given it to her? It seemed so. Despite her passionate disavowals, there was little question she was—and yes, he would call it what she had— a Trojan Horse.

He'd done right, setting Higgins on her again. After a momentary lapse, he was using his head instead of that organ in his chest. It was the way, after all these years, he'd survived.

Isabella cracked open his door exactly at two o'clock. "Max is here for your meeting."

"Send him in."

There was no need. Max was already striding past Isabella, leading with his chin, his default when he thought a confrontation was ahead. He smoothed both hands down the front of his double-breasted jacket, then gave the hems a sharp tug. "Thanks for making time for me today."

Jack nodded. "I always make time for you. Why would today be any different?"

"Considering how we left things after the session at the hotel…?"

When Chalcott House was in its infancy, Max had been Jack's first employee. He was so good at his job, Jack had made him chief marketing officer for not just Chalcott House but the rest of the company, including *Daily Prime*. Though his role had expanded, Max kept tabs on Chalcott House more, in Jack's mind, than was necessary.

"It's not how we left things, it's what you had to say. Or rather shouted."

Max looked away. "For that I owe you an apology."

"No apology is necessary. An explanation, however, would not be remiss."

With a humorless twist of his lips, Max said, "It's the divorce. Cynthia is being difficult. I am not always in control of my temper."

"I'm sorry to hear it. But what has that to do with you wanting me to sell Chalcott House?"

Max took a seat, agitation more than apparent. "Trad publishers are re-grouping. For those who haven't changed their model, failure is around the corner. I fear Chalcott House is amongst those who will fail for that reason. Browne gives us the perfect opportunity to get out intact. Why don't we take his deal before we go the way of the dinosaurs? You should sell before there isn't anything left to sell."

Max was hewing to the same script he'd trumpeted at the staff meeting yesterday at Hotel Elgar. "I'm fully aware that we are on the cusp of major changes. But then, that's true of many business models these days, don't you think? Besides, the last P&L account I looked at, shows we have been and continue to be profitable. Do you know something I don't know?"

Max's gaze swerved away. "What I know is Browne's company is able to wrest double the profit from their investments in publishing in the States than we are."

"But at what cost?"

Max threw up his hands. "What does the cost matter if the profit is that extraordinary? I don't understand why you don't see it. This is not like you, Jack."

"What is not like me?"

"You've been willing to make cuts, even to staff, when it was necessary before. You've sold off parts of the company that had no possibility of ever being profitable. What's the reluctance to sell Chalcott House, given what we both know is coming in the future?"

"We? Perhaps you, Max. Not I. In my mind, book selling has a great future."

Max looked at a point above Jack's head. Not able to make eye contact with him, a sure sign Max was thinking of a way to advance his argument, and not coming up with anything that hadn't been said.

"As the company's CMO, isn't it your job to be smarter than the marketplace?" In a voice filled with the irritation he could no longer mask, Jack added, "Don't you think you're up to it anymore?"

Max went silent.

"You've been speaking to Robert Browne, haven't you?"

Max's gaze skittered away and he rubbed a hand across the back of his neck. "We spoke. Once."

Jack felt a small moment of satisfaction. He'd been fishing. And right to make his assumption.

"Browne asked my opinion about traditional publishing and what it might look like one, three, and five years on." Max lifted his chin again. "If you think I shouldn't have done, why don't you sack me?"

He folded his arms across his chest. "I might."

Max's complexion went pasty white. "Perhaps I've acted poorly of late."

"You have. Perhaps you've been a bit opinionated."

Max raised his chin again. "You pay me to be opinionated."

"No, I pay you to have opinions."

After a taut moment, Max snorted a laugh. "As usual, you're right."

"I'm also right to expect you'll refrain from speaking again with Browne."

Max looked away. "Since I work for you, that's fair."

Jack nodded once. "Good."

Max attempted a smile. "My opinion—and you pay me to have them, remember—what I think will make sense to you. Then you'll change your mind."

Max departed, leaving Jack to stare hard at the closed door. If Jack knew anything about human nature, Max would speak to Robert Browne again. If he did, and when Jack found out, then he would sack him.

Jack turned on his heel and stalked over to the sideboard. He palmed the crown of the punching bag on a stand that Rose had given him on his last birthday. 'Punch when you need to let off steam' she'd said. He had steam to let off today, but not the energy to go to war with a toy.

He picked up one of the pictures on the sideboard and ran a finger around its edges. Taken at a family dinner, it was the last one of all of them together before his father made that ill-fated trip, the one Jack would not forget, to Brompton Court alone.

There they were, with forced smiles. The story had just broken that his father had involved himself with the disreputable Freddie Camville, Duke of Lindsey in his Ponzi scheme. Every newspaper blasted how thousands of people had lost their life savings, including an eighty-year-old woman who, upon learning of the scam, took an entire bottle of sleeping pills to end her life. Jack's heart lurched, remembering how his father had been sick with guilt about that woman, and he, immature prat that he was, had dismissed his father's feelings as unimportant.

Diana had just finished telling them how she'd been rejected at her law school of choice. Alice had wept about not being able to evade the paparazzi who were hounding her no matter where she went. Rose hated the new school she'd transferred to so she could get away from the bullying atmosphere at her old one, and he'd been told not to bother applying for membership on the debate team at school. It was then he'd shouted those terrible words.

How could you put your faith in Freddie Camville who everyone else knew to stay away from? You destroyed lives. You destroyed us.

And so his father went, alone. The following evening they found him. The coroner said he'd died almost twenty-four hours previously.

Sometimes, late at night, when Jack had worked himself into a state of exhaustion, he remembered the words he'd said and shot straight up in bed with the feeling he was suffocating.

One of Jack's best memories from childhood was of sneaking out late on a school night with his dad to help him run a last-minute print job on the press which would one day become the heart of Chalcott House. It was for a lady who needed a hundred copies of a poem to be handed out at an awards ceremony the next day.

Jack's job was to work the ancient press. The press grumbled, but eventually, after coughing an indeterminate number of times, spat out a hundred copies of the winning poem, as beautiful and clean as if it had been printed on one of the multi-million-dollar electronic presses Jack housed in Prime's production facility today.

After, Jack wound string around the package as his father had taught him. He'd looked up for affirmation he'd done it right. His father grinned. "Aces, my boy. Aces."

Jack placed the picture back on the sideboard. His father had been his best friend. If he hadn't been filled with such adolescent righteousness that day, he would have gone with him to Brompton Court and perhaps, even today, his father would be alive.

The last memory Jack had of his father was the look on his face when he'd yelled his hateful words. He would never forgive himself for saying them. It was one of the reasons why he would never give up Chalcott House to Robert Browne. It was his father's legacy.

By the time Henry turned off the highway onto a two-lane road bisected with dun-colored fields, Livvy had closed up her computer, sure she'd remembered everything from the crazy dream.

She stared around her. "Where are we now?"

"We've crossed into Lincolnshire. It's lovely, isn't it?" Livvy could hear the pride in his voice.

There was a spare beauty about it, all monochrome landscape, muted colors, and pale grasses. The sky was filled with low, gray-bottomed clouds. The road curved to the left and the right, down into folds in the land and up into little hills, though it could hardly be called a road with all the potholes and dips that would have had her sick if she'd continued to work on her laptop.

Soon enough, they turned onto a lane Livvy wasn't sure was wide enough for one car, let alone two.

"Here we are." As Henry spoke, he turned again, this time beneath an arch of weathered stone and onto a road that was bumpier than the road they'd been on, the gravel worn thin in places or no gravel at all.

"This is Brompton Court. Another half mile and we'll be at the front door."

Livvy sat forward. Her destination. Finally. It wasn't a great house like some others in Lincolnshire. It wasn't open to the public, which was fine with her. Who wanted to trip over tourists while she was looking for Jessamine's diaries?

As they got closer, her excitement cooled and curiosity heated up. The house at the end of the drive didn't look anything like the drawing of it she'd seen online. It was a rangy building, framed by a stand of tall trees, their trunks scarred in places, branches leaning over the house like thick, muscled arms.

She stopped herself from flipping open her laptop to check the image she'd saved on her screen because what she was looking at wasn't it. With its faded red brick façade, gabled roof and long windows adorned with gingerbread curlicues, it looked like something out of the wrong queen's era: Victoria, not Elizabeth.

Henry brought the car to a halt and Livvy stepped out. She stared up, astounded. "Excuse me for asking, but is this Brompton Court? Because it's so…"

"You don't want to say it, do you?" Henry came around her side of the car, rolling her luggage. "Ugly is what we call it. But it wasn't always. Not before the seventh duke."

Livvy's brain ticked over the Anstruther genealogical chart, lodged in her head. "The seventh duke lived in the mid-1800s. He built this?"

Henry set her suitcase and backpack down next to the three wide steps. "He did. Ask Madelyn. She can tell you why."

Like she'd heard her name mentioned, a woman—Madelyn it had to be—opened the door. She had red-blond hair, cut short, a little messy. She wore a white, button-down shirt and khaki pants. "Miss Browne, yes?" She came down the steps and held out a hand. "Cheers."

Madelyn had a nice smile. Not Mrs. Danvers, then. "Hello," said Livvy.

"Here, Mr. Stebbins, I'll take one of those." As Madelyn did, Livvy grabbed the backpack and thanked the duke's chauffeur for the ride.

"Won't you come through, Miss Browne?"

"I'd prefer if you call me Livvy." Her last name had already gotten her in trouble with Madelyn's employer. She didn't need any more from his employee.

"All right." Madelyn's smile became a little distracted, which made Livvy wonder if there was some Brit rule about not getting too chummy with someone when you first met.

"The duke called to let me know you were coming. I will apologize for…well, you'll see. Please go through."

She had no idea why Madelyn was apologizing, but the reason became less and less important the more her confusion built. Though the light was dim, Livvy noted how the hallway marched past room after room, like so many sleeper cars on a long-haul passenger train. Each room was filled with tables covered with tasseled cloths and chairs and couches fat with upholstery. Was the library going to be like the seventh duke's addition and be more about furniture than books? That would be terrible.

Sensing Livvy was not right behind, Madelyn slowed. "This part of Brompton Court is the work of the seventh duke."

"Henry mentioned him."

"He thought it would modernize things. The way he built it, you can't get to the original part of the court without traipsing through this part. I suppose Henry mentioned that none of us care for it."

"He did."

"It was called Brompton Priory, you know," Madelyn continued. "Before Henry VIII dissolved all the religious houses. He gave this one to the Beresford barons."

Though she knew about Brompton Priory, Livvy thanked Madelyn for the mini history lesson. "Did the duke tell you why I'm here?"

"He did mention something about Jessamine Beresford, and some research you intend to pursue. But before we go on, I must apologize. Had I known you were coming, I would have prepared a room, and I would have taken care of things in the library. I would have…"

Livvy heard the rest with half an ear because they'd stepped out of the Victorian monstrosity and into the original part of Brompton Court, the part that was all the majesty that had fed her imagination.

"This is wonderful, don't you think?"

She glanced at a smiling Madelyn and then back at the open area, with its soaring height and clerestory windows. She stood still, intent on absorbing it all. Jessamine Beresford had walked on the great slabs of gray slate beneath her feet.

Stepping into the center of the room and turning in a slow circle, Livvy stared at the paintings mounted on every wall and in every possible space. There were family scenes, with children in adult dress, miniature versions of the parents they shared the canvases with. There were portraits of men and women, their hands folded prayerfully, and their eyes cast up to heaven. The largest paintings were devoted to hunt scenes. In them were deer pierced by arrows and foxes hovering in lairs with dogs and men on horseback keeping the poor things from escaping their fate.

Whatever else she might have thought about the paintings, she forgot when she spied the canvas on the wall above the entrance from the seventh duke's dark hallway. It was the biggest of the canvases. In its center was the figure of a man, clothed in ceremonial furs, tights, garters at the knees, and shoes with red heels. He wore long black curls, a mustache, and a crown on his head. He dominated the canvas. Livvy's arms broke out in goose bumps. "That's Charles."

"Yes." Madelyn came to stand next to her. "The figure kneeling at his feet is James, the first duke of Brompton. This is a re-creation of his accession."

Livvy's pulse rate kicked up. Was it a fair representation of what James had looked like at age eighteen or nineteen? She stepped back as far as she could from the painting to take it all in. It was a posed scene, with the mustachioed Charles leaning down toward the much younger, fair-haired man kneeling before him. All the other men wore broad-brimmed hats, their hair cascading, like Charles', around their shoulders. Lace dripped from the balloon-like sleeves of their jackets. The only women in the painting seemed to be servants.

"When do you think this painting was done?" Livvy continued to stare upward.

"We've been led to understand it was completed sometime in the first decade of the eighteenth century when James' son, also a James, was duke."

Eyes still on the painting, Livvy said, "I'm curious to know if James was Charles's son."

"If it's true it would mean our current duke is descended from royalty."

Livvy kept her grin to herself. Would she tell Madelyn she'd called the duke a prince among men? Hardly. She'd already revealed her smartass self to the duke.

She retraced her steps across the room to where her backpack and suitcase lay. "And it would make Charles and Jessamine way more than friends."

"Perhaps that will be one answer you find in our library." Madelyn picked up the backpack and carried it over to the grand staircase that bisected the great room.

Livvy grabbed her suitcase and followed.

Madelyn started up the steps. "How did you become interested in Jessamine's life?"

They'd reached the top of the steps. Livvy made a note to take care not to run on them. They were carved from stone, slick and dangerous. "I volunteer in my town library. One day, by accident, I found a book which mentioned Jessamine. I wanted to know more about her.

"I read everything I could find. The more I found, the more I wanted to know. I discovered she was quite the mover and shaker. That was what made me decide to write a biography about her life. Her diaries are rumored to be here. They may prove what I think they will, that Jessamine bore one of Charles' many illegitimate children. It's an essential piece that will allow me to finish my book the way it should be finished."

"Well, then, you'll not want to waste any more time. Here's the library."

Livvy turned around on the broad landing to face a pair of stately doors, dark wood with ornate, curlicued handles. Behind them could be Jessamine's diaries. Livvy's heart gave a hard thump.

Madelyn grasped both handles. "I'm surprised the duke didn't tell you."

Eyes fixed on the doors swinging open, Livvy said, "Didn't tell me what?"

"That we know about the diaries."

CHAPTER SIX

Livvy let go of her suitcase so suddenly it teetered on its wheels. She was here. In *the* library. She should be doing a hundred fist-bumps. Instead, she was busy re-calibrating her brain. "You mean you—?"

"Know about them? Of course. It's common lore. Every duke from James on has known, the current duke, as well."

Livvy was stunned. "They did? He does?"

"It's not a matter of the diaries' existence; it's more that they've never been found."

"Did anyone look?" Livvy barely felt Madelyn remove the suitcase from her hand. *He knew.*

"I would imagine some did and some didn't. I don't think Jack has looked."

But he'd *lied* about knowing. Or at least didn't say. Which was the same thing. For him, she was her father's daughter, no matter how much she didn't want to be. Still, it made her ill to think he hadn't trusted her with the truth.

"I wonder if you would satisfy my curiosity." Madelyn cocked her head to one side. "The diaries, if you find them, might give you the proper ending. But will they tell you anything else?"

Livvy pressed a hand to her middle, soothing out the knot it had twisted itself into. "Jessamine's own words will help me understand what made her tick."

Madelyn nodded. "As a new writer, wouldn't you want to write about a more notable woman?"

"Being new, it would be better to write about a woman others haven't written about, so I don't end up being compared to them and come up short." She made a face. "For a while, I thought about writing an historical fiction about Jessamine like Anya Seton's story about Katherine Swynford."

Madelyn brightened. "My mum had a copy of *Katherine*. When I was a girl, I read it from cover to cover." She sighed. "Katherine Swynford, mistress to and then married to the dishiest of men, John of Gaunt, a king's son himself."

Livvy said, "Jessamine put her life on the line to spy for Charles, who was pretty dishy himself."

Madelyn perked up. "Just think. Charles, the first duke's father…how romantic."

"The jury's out on that." Until she found the diaries—if the diaries would reveal that.

Madelyn pursed her lips. "But if you don't find the diaries and you still don't know if Charles was the first duke's father, how will you end your book?"

"Well…" The muscle above Livvy's knee began to jiggle. Livvy didn't want to think about that until she had to.

"Surely, you can come up with a satisfactory ending?" Madelyn face blanked, then cleared. "Oh, listen to me, nattering on about how you should write when I barely read anymore." She reached for their heavy, iron handles and pushed the mammoth doors open and disappeared into the darkened room. "Follow me."

Livvy stepped past her suitcase, which was next to where the backpack lay on the floor in the hallway and into the library—the very dark library. Squinting, she tried to work out what was in the room she'd come three thousand miles to see.

"Let's turn on a light," Madelyn said, her voice strangely muffled.

The sudden brightness—maybe not brightness but something more than darkness—drew Livvy's gaze upward. The light came from four ancient chandeliers quartering the ceiling, their brass arms sporting seriously low-wattage bulbs in their glass lamps. In the center, even farther above the light fixtures, was a dirt-encrusted skylight. Not dirt. Dead bugs.

Poor as the light was, when Livvy's gaze dropped down again, she understood the strange, muffled tone in Madelyn's voice. Things filled the room: sheet-covered, behemoth sized things. Furniture and lots of it. "What's all this?" Livvy blurted.

"I apologize." Madelyn inched her way back from the light switch. "While I was gone, she must have begun."

"Who?" Livvy snapped her mouth shut to keep her jaw from dropping any further. "Begun what?"

"Rose, the duke's youngest sister. Her project."

Livvy stood frozen. "Lady Rose's project is making the Brompton Court library into a storage facility?"

Madelyn flushed with embarrassment. "She told her brother the court needs what she calls a makeover." She lifted a hand and dropped it. "I didn't think she would start, not while I was on holiday. A whisky festival on Islay, you know."

That—being away on her vacation when Rose was doing her thing at Brompton Court—must have been what Madelyn had been all apologies about. Like Livvy was going to judge. "I don't suppose you brought back any samples from Islay."

"Unfortunately not." Madelyn made her way to the center of the room, flicking sheets off pieces of furniture. Which was when Livvy remembered where she was and thoughts of furniture receded from consciousness.

All her life, books had been a refuge, where she went when her world was too much to bear. She'd loved disappearing into them. Here, in this cavernous room, she truly could disappear. This was book heaven, with masses of them on shelves and shelves. She couldn't count all of them.

The books stood like soldiers, spine to spine, some more upright than others. Most showed her their dark colors, somber black or blood red. She spied an occasional rusty brown outlier. All were grimy with age.

She sighed with happiness. The next thirty days were going to be among the best of her life. Oh yes, and when she found the diaries it was going to be even better.

"Do you like our library, then?"

Livvy tore her mind away from her imagination. "That's an understatement."

She hefted up her shoulder bag and skirted around still sheet-covered Bluebeard-the-giant-size chairs and tables. Her gaze still upon the top of one particular column of shelves, she stubbed a toe. Pain shot up to her knee. "Yi," she screeched.

"Be careful." Madelyn tossed the warning as she removed more sheets from more furniture.

"Too late." Livvy hopped on one foot while she breathed over the pain. "Can you remind me again why all this stuff is in here and what the duke's sister really has in mind?" She glared down at the offending object that had been in her way. A chair she thought.

"Rose is clearing out many of the rooms on this floor. Her goal is to make Brompton Court as lovely as it once was."

So, the library *was* being used a storage facility.

"We were all surprised when her brother said he would give her free rein." She started toward the door. "I'll get some boys to move this lot out."

Livvy perked up. It was good to know her first job at Brompton Court wasn't going to involve heavy lifting. "Is there an outlet in here for me to plug in my laptop? No worries. I brought adapters."

"Of course." Madelyn trailed a hand across another dust cover before flicking it off. Beneath was a chaise longue in dark blue and green velvet.

Livvy sneezed.

"Now that you've seen the library, why don't we get you settled."

Picking up her purse and her messenger bag, Livvy followed. "I assume you're putting me in a room that Rose left furnished?"

Madelyn grimaced. "Let's hope."

As they made their way down the wide hallway to the bedroom that was to be hers, Madelyn did the tour guide thing, totting off the names of the men and women in the paintings that lined the walls, indicating which duke bought the spectacular red, green, and gold Chinese vases on the side tables they passed— duke number four it was thought—when the ninth duke had put in central heating, and how no one had bothered to replace the worn carpeting beneath their feet.

"This is the duke's suite," Madelyn said, slowing as they came to a wide double door. "Next to it, the duchess's suite, and next to it is what I hope will be your room." She threw open the door and stepped aside for Livvy to enter. "Ah, good. Rose didn't dispose of the furniture in this bedroom. It's not quite up to snuff but it will do, I think."

Livvy kept her dismay to herself. *Not quite up to snuff* described the Brompton Court she'd seen so far. Well, except for the great hall. Yes, this room had a canopied bed with curtains held back with fancy hooks on each of the posts. But the curtains had small tears in them. The carpet, like the carpet in the hallway, was threadbare. She had a fleeting thought that she should have kept her reservation at the Airbnb.

Madelyn rolled Livvy's suitcase in and propped it up next to an armoire, one of only two pieces of furniture, beside the bed, in the room, the other being a small table next to the bed. One of the armoire's doors hung off its hinge. Crossing the room, Madelyn pulled the draperies back—they were held in place by the same type of hooks fixed on the bedposts—and weak afternoon light swam in. As Madelyn fussed with the draperies, tying them back, smoothing them down, Livvy reached into her messenger bag for a pair of gloves. Shoving them in a pocket, she said, "If there's not a reason that would prevent me from doing it, I'd like to start in the library."

"Lovely. Why don't you?" On her way out, Madelyn began to close the door but then stuck her head back in. "Please be careful when you lie down on that bed. If this mattress is the one I think it is, it's a bit tricky. It dips on one side."

Livvy studied the culprit. "Is there a better mattress?"

"I don't think so. Even before Rose started her project we had to have many of them thrown out. Brompton Court remaining uninhabited for so long, they became infested with bugs. Now that I'm up here, I should check to see if there's furniture in the duke and duchess's rooms and if the beds and mattresses there are usable."

Usable was such a random word. "If one of them is better than this one, can we do a switch?"

"Let me see what I can do."

Livvy studied the canopied bed and mattress. She was lucky to be a visitor in a house rich in history— the seventh duke's addition aside. If she was sleeping in the canopied bed in this room—she eyed it with trepidation—then it was an advantage, not the other way around. "Don't bother. I'll stick with this one. It'll be fine. As long as it doesn't dump me out onto the floor."

"Oh, I rather think it won't."

A statement that didn't fill Livvy with much comfort.

After Madelyn left, she unpacked her suitcase and backpack. She looked around and snorted a laugh, imagining what her father would have had to say about this place.

He'd call it a one-star hotel. Worse, a hostel. Not a place for the daughter of a man of his stature.

"Well, you're not here to share your unwanted opinion with me," she muttered and wandered across to the windows, which faced the back lawn, if lawn it could be called, and a terrace. She laid her fingers on the cold window glass and turned her head in one direction and then the other. Below was a garden stretching the width of the house, all weeds.

Perhaps, when Jessamine lived here, the gardens had been filled with roses and lilies, or stands of purple irises. Perhaps there'd been clutches of shrubbery sculpted into centaurs, dragons, and unicorns cavorting across the then emerald green lawn. Perhaps there'd been a gazebo or two and a stream meandering along at the bottom of the slope. Perhaps Brompton Court had been what she'd imagined it was. And perhaps Jack hadn't really meant to lie. Perhaps he—

The knock on the door startled her. She turned to see Madelyn peeking in. "I've arranged for two boys to be here tomorrow morning to clear the library."

"Before they finish disposing of everything, I'll pick out the pieces I want to keep." Thinking about how dark the room was, Livvy added, "Are there lamps?"

"No worries. We'll find as many as you need."

"That's good." Livvy raised a hand to her forehead and rubbed. The onset of a mild headache reminded her she'd only had those few hours' sleep at the Hotel Elgar, and the strange nap in the duke's Tesla. Her body, grown heavy with exhaustion, wanted to make sure she knew it. "I think I'll put off starting in on the library. I should catch up on my jet lag and take a nap."

"Perhaps you should. If you come down later, I'll make something for you to eat. The kitchen is through the door to the left once you come down the staircase."

After the door closed, Livvy inched onto the mattress. It held. She let out a relieved breath. Lying back on what passed for a pillow, she stared up at the canopy, not seeing it entirely, instead seeing the man whose bed this belonged to.

She closed her eyes. As she turned onto her side, the creak of the bed became a far distant sound. She sank into the mattress, only to be disturbed by—was it seconds later—another knock at the door.

It opened, and he walked in. She sat up. "Jack?" Not speaking, he stared at her with his monk-man face, his unsmiling mouth, and his solemn blue eyes. Slowly he took off his jacket. He folded it and laid it down at the bottom of the bed. He unbuttoned his shirt, let it slide from his shoulders, and placed it on top of the jacket. Then, never taking his eyes off her, he unbuttoned and unzipped his trousers. Along with his briefs, he dropped them to the floor, and stepped out of them.

He stood still. So she could admire him. Hello. She did. His skin glowed in the dim light from the windows. He came toward the bed. He planted one hand on the mattress and bracketed her hips with his knees. Placing one hand on her thigh, he eased up her slip.

What slip? She didn't own a slip.

She ran her fingers through the thatch of light brown hair on his chest… Did he have hair on his chest?

Whatever. It narrowed down below his navel to that part of him, he'd…

Her eyes snapped open, she sat up and huffed a breath. Sharpened gaze darting around the room, she looked for him. But excuse me, how could Jack be there? He wasn't. Because it was another dream.

Misty remnants of disturbed sleep hung at the margins of her brain. She scrubbed her hands over her eyes and then held her phone up to her face. It was dark. The moon cast a sharp, blue light and stark shadows across the room. She'd slept for hours. Telling herself not to, she checked the corners of the room. He still wasn't there.

She huffed another breath, this time with a thread of laughter in it. "Awesome. Not one, but two whack-a-doodle dreams in one day." Except they'd both felt too real. Jessamine and Charles in Antwerp. Jack in her bed. Naked.

Out of the corner of her eye, she spied a note on the little table next to the bed. Switching on her phone flashlight, she picked it up and read.

Dear Olivia,

Sorry for the intrusion on your privacy. I knocked but when you didn't answer I didn't want to disturb you. I've left you a tray in the library with a bit to eat in case you wake before morning and are hungry. I've left lights on in the hall so you can find your way. I will be back at 8 a.m.

You'll want to know the lav is just opposite your room.

Livvy's bladder went from yeah, might be a nice idea, to OMG, time to take care of things right now! She barely remembered Madelyn's warning about the bed as she hopped off and dashing for the door, hoped the bathroom *was* right across the hall.

It was. Necessities taken care of, she stood on the threadbare carpet in the long, silent-as-death hallway. She was alone in this big house. She tested herself. How did it feel? Though it should have, the house didn't seem strange. It felt… She didn't know the word other than it was good.

Rather than turn any more pages looking for it in her internal thesaurus, she padded down the hallway past the duke and duchess's suites to the library. Like where else would she go when she could no longer sleep, thank you altered circadian rhythms?

She eased the two heavy doors open and stepped inside. She remembered where the light switch was, threw it, and surveyed her new realm.

No, it wasn't any brighter in the room than it had been when she'd first seen it, however many hours ago. There was still a crapload of furniture everywhere. The chandeliers, handsome as they were in their antique way, were only a couple of steps away from useless. They cast enough light, though, for her to see the long, narrow table in the middle of the room where Madelyn had left her some goodies.

Careful this time not to stub another toe, she picked her way through the maze of furniture to the tray on the table and found a roll of some kind in plastic wrap, and a thermos with coffee, packets of sugar, and a little pitcher of cream. Seeing it, she reminded herself she was starving. She unwrapped the roll, devoured it, and then poured herself some still warm coffee. Roll and coffee were enough to stave off the urge to go looking for the kitchen in a house where she didn't know where all the light switches were.

She studied the column of shelves nearest to her. The books on the bottom shelf looked to be bigger than those on the upper shelves. She stooped to lift one and carry it carefully to her table. To be safe, she'd stowed the tray with the now empty thermos and crumbs from the roll, underneath.

Laying the book on the table, she slipped the gloves out of her pocket and put them on. She held up her phone, with its flashlight, at an angle so it didn't shine directly on the book. Very slowly, she opened it and her breath caught. There on the frontispiece, the name of the book, and the date it was printed. MDCLXIV.

A shiver lit up the hairs on the back of her neck. 1664, five years after Charles Stuart got his throne back. One year after the bubonic plague swept over England, and two years before the great London fire. History in her hands.

This book was a who's who of seventeenth century England. With great care, she turned a page and then another. She recognized names: Clare, Burleigh, Lancaster. She kept turning and found more aristocratic names she recognized: Leicester, Lacy, Peverel.

Her jet lag faded away. She was here. At the source. Unlike the two crazy dreams she'd had today, this was real, and it was immediate, and she felt powerful and ready to prove herself to herself, free of any interference from people who didn't trust that she had it in her.

A breeze came from somewhere and she hugged herself in another shiver. Jack, the Duke of Brompton, thinking about him felt right, too, even if it shouldn't. She'd come here to accomplish big stuff for her life. He wasn't part of it, though she was in his house. She wouldn't let him be a distraction.

Except…

She had the hots for him. Yeah, she'd had the hots for guys before. This was different. She took her phone out of her bag and typed a text.

It was almost eight a.m. and Jack was waiting for Maisie Helfgott—who was always late—for a working breakfast. He looked down at his mobile, lying face up on his desk. It flashed to life. A text had come in at some point last night, and he hadn't seen it. He knew who it was from. He supposed he could take a moment, before Maisie joined him, to read what she'd written.

> Hi, I'm surprised you didn't say anything about knowing there were diaries.

Ah. Caught.

> I know why.

She didn't know why. He had no plans to tell her.

> But it's okay.

Good of her.

There's a lot of old furniture in the library.

Didn't furniture belong in a library?

Do you know about the skylight, the one that's become a meetup for every dead bug in Lincolnshire?

His lip twitched. No, he didn't.

I didn't wait for the boys to come to start.

Which boys?

Because you know I only have a month to search your library before the fat lady sings.

What fat lady? He picked up the phone and allowed himself a reluctant smile.

Anyway, I've already found this amazing treasure! Did you know you have an original copy of Dugdale's Baronage in your library? It was published in 1664.

No, he didn't know. And considering how little he knew about Brompton Court—and how little he wanted to know about it—he wouldn't have been surprised if she found a dead camel on the shelves.

> **Now, I don't want you to be disappointed. I peeked and there are no Anstruthers in it. Dugdale must not have thought your ancestors worthy! Sorry.**

He began to laugh and then caught himself. He didn't hesitate one second before answering her.

> **How did you get my mobile number?**

Livvy stared at her phone. She'd gone back to her room after she'd sent her text, and slept. She'd come back to the library when she woke at five before the alleged boys came on scene to take the furniture away or the alleged lamps had appeared.

She huffed a quiet laugh. After all the times she'd been texting him, it was only now that he realized she'd had his cell number almost from the beginning?

"Gee whiz, Your Grace. You haven't heard of the International Cellular Directory?"

His assistant would have known. The CEO duke? Not so much.

Livvy keyed in her answer, and included, as proof, the service's URL. As she hit SEND, she smiled. Those few, terse words he'd sent? She knew he'd expected some hemming and hawing. She grinned at her phone. "Psych!"

Ever hear of the International Cellular Directory? Jack stared at the text that came back almost immediately and the URL she'd attached. Of everything that had seemed so damning, her having his mobile number seemed the most damning. Perhaps he was wrong to have assumed she was her father's advance guard, the Trojan Horse the man had sent out to find what could be used against him. Odd that he was relieved.

Pocketing his phone, Jack pressed the top button on his intercom. Maisie was waiting for him in the anteroom. Though she was the one who was late, Jack knew, from experience, anytime she finally did arrive, it didn't pay to let Maisie Helfgott wait too long. "All right, Isabella, I'm ready for her." Although as he thought about it was anyone ever ready for Maisie?

"Jack, you bastard." Maisie marched in. "Who gave you permission to edit Hyacinth Cofield's work without my permission?" Maisie strode in, nothing slow about her and her eighty plus years. The perfume she wore, some rose-based scent she seemed to bathe in, swirled around her four-foot-nine-inch figure. This morning, she wore the kind of outfit he'd come to think of as her signature: a black hat with a wide, flat brim—red feathers dangling down over one side—and oversized gold earrings in her ears. Her suit was black, her shoes black. Her mood, as well, seemed black.

Jack had known Maisie for as long as he'd been in the business. She was lion on the outside, lamb inside. Today, the lamb seemed missing. "Maisie, what a lovely hat."

"Drop the bullshit," she growled in the New York accent she'd not relinquished, although she'd lived in London for more than forty years. "Maybe it slipped your mind that you should have first called to say you've decided to publish Hyacinth's trilogy?"

He skirted around his desk and met Maisie in the middle of his office, and kissing her on her leather-skinned cheek. "Was the sun shining for you in Ibiza?"

"Where do you think I got this goddamn tan?"

"So, a proper holiday, then, and yes, you're right. I should have told you. My sincere apologies. I couldn't help myself. Hyacinth is a wonderful writer. I thought why not start the work straight away so we can get her books on the schedule?"

"Yes, Jack. I get it. You'd made up your mind," Maisie said with a curled top lip. "No, don't say a word. The *world* knows you're a deft editor. Your notes in margins, brilliant. Tells the author just what's missing. Or is too much. Hyacinth should kiss the feet of the gods that you've taken her under your wing."

She pressed her lips together. Jack knew better than to speak.

"Let me remind you, since you seem to have forgotten." Maisie's red feather bobbed. "Contract gets signed first. After, comes the rest, including the editing. Then and only then are you allowed to channel Maxwell Fucking Perkins."

Maisie slapped an envelope on his desk. "Here's the contract. Look it over. The negotiations will go smoothly or I'll know why."

"They will." Jack indicated one of his chairs, thinking, this time, he'd gotten off easy. "Let's sit, shall we?"

She gave him a dark look. "What, you want me to sit because I'm old, and you think I need to rest before you take me to breakfast?"

Jack didn't even bother to hide his smile. "No, Maisie. If I didn't know, I would guess you were at least ten if not fifteen years younger than you are."

"What crap." She gave him a ferocious frown, but her eyes gleamed with pleasure.

"It's the truth. Besides, I like spending time with you, but if it's not on your schedule…" He let the rest drop and was rewarded with one of her rarely given smiles.

He placed a hand at the small of her back and with slight pressure, brought her over to the chair where she sat.

She lifted her coal black gaze to engage his. "What's this I hear about you selling Chalcott House?"

He paused before sitting. "Where did you hear that?"

"At Andy Baxter's last night. Is it true?"

"You know the answer to that. It's no."

"Good. One of Andy's guests was a tall, dark-haired asshole—an American I'm ashamed to say—who was the one saying he might be interested in buying Chalcott House. I didn't like his looks. He spent too much time talking about himself. You Brits hate that."

"Yes, we do. Do you happen to know his name?"

"I didn't catch it. We weren't introduced, not that he had time for too many introductions. He was busy regaling everyone with stories about the brilliant moves he'd made over the years to acquire distressed companies, and how he'd wrung major profit out of them."

"And you're sure you didn't hear his name."

"If I'd heard it don't you think I'd tell you?"

Jack knew she would.

"He made sure everyone knew he's quite the connoisseur of excellence and value and being that he is, he's in England to make a killing. Bastard." If Maisie thought spitting was an appropriate exclamation point to what she'd just said about this American, Jack would have been reaching for a tissue to clean his floor. As it was, he was cycling through who this person could be and how this unexpected piece of information connected with Browne's push to buy Chalcott House.

Maisie leaned forward and tapped him on the knee. "Maybe you're too serious, Jack. But you give your authors a chance to improve their work so it's publishable. It's a mindset that's lost on your competition. Instant return on investment and all that. You're in it for the long run."

She leaned back. "That's why I have an interest in seeing Chalcott House doesn't fall into the wrong hands. I'll do what I can to find out how serious this rumor is. Meanwhile, you need to start thinking like a fucking duke who happens to be a smart business-man. I'm not interested in helping a wimp."

Before he could respond, she was on her feet, marching to the door. "Now take me to the most expensive restaurant in London. I expect to be treated like I'm the aristocrat, not you."

CHAPTER SEVEN

Later, after breakfast, Jack was back in his office thinking about Maisie's tall, dark-haired asshole. Could it have been Kyle Bentsen, Browne's son-in-law? He was rumored to be in London. If he had to guess, it was too circumstantial for it to be otherwise.

His mobile buzzed like an electronic adder. He had another text coming in, Turning his phone's face toward him he read the short text. And yes, now he'd allow himself to think of her as Livvy.

He answered her before he could think about what he was doing.

**Now we know what was wrong
with all the kings and queens who
were his descendants.**

She sent him back a winking emoji. His smile
faded. Could he answer more of her texts? Could he
give himself permission to suspend suspicion? She'd
named herself Princess Leia. Was that a form of
proof that a rebel princess wouldn't take her father's
side?

Yes, he wanted to know her better. Who was he
kidding? He wanted to do more than know her better.
She had red highlights in her brown hair, witchy hazel
eyes, and a brain that sent odd, entertaining messages
to her mouth, a mouth he'd do a lot right now to kiss.

He spent the remainder of the week thinking
about her. The idea that he did annoyed him. On
Monday, the start of the second week that she was
tucked away at Brompton Court, Higgins rang him.

He'd dug up some information on Bentsen.
People who'd had the misfortune of doing business
with Browne—a man feared and hated even in
venture capitalist circles—spoke of Bentsen as
Browne's pit bull. He did Browne's dirty work, but
hid his killer instincts under a veneer of charm.

Higgins corroborated that Livvy hadn't had any
contact with her father since her arrival in England.

Jack found himself amused to be breathing a sigh of relief.

He wondered how her search was going. Had she found more treasures like the Dugdale? He smiled every time he thought of her not-so-gentle dig about the Anstruthers.

Each day, starting that first day, she sent him two texts: the first one came at exactly 9:05 a.m. The second wasn't so precise in its delivery time, but it came sometime between one and two o'clock in the afternoon. He'd begun to look forward to them. This morning's had been about the library and her allergies.

> The dust is crazy! I've already gone through a dozen boxes of tissue and I'm still sneezing.

He had never been bothered by allergies, though he could sympathize.

> Perhaps you need a mask to catch your sneezes as they happen.

Her afternoon had him doing more than sympathizing.

> We had to dispose of the ladders, the cool ones that hook onto runners along the shelves. All four broke. Too bad for me, I was on

one when it cracked in two. But not to worry. All I did was land on my you-know-what and there's plenty of fat on it to cushion me! Oh, and we moved one of the behemoth couches back into the library. It's a great place to rest when I want to take a break.

Worrisome, that. He was relieved she hadn't done more damage to herself beyond a sore arse, although what she meant about it being cushioned in fat, he had no idea. Remembering the feel of it in his hands, it seemed perfect.

We might want to invest in a harness we could affix by its ropes to the skylight and you could fly around from top shelf to top shelf without having to worry about visiting harm upon your lovely derriere.

By the time her text came Tuesday morning, anticipation turned to concern for her safety.

Madelyn had to move me into the duchess's room. Last night, I got into bed in the room she'd put me in and it fell apart. Not the room, the bed. I need to be careful with antecedents!

Jack didn't think there was anything funny about broken ladders. Broken beds, less so. He couldn't imagine what Madelyn was about that she hadn't thrown the thing away long ago.

After the dozenth time he pictured the scene in his head, it came to him that Madelyn hadn't done anything about any of it, because he'd told her to leave it alone. "Bastard," he muttered. He meant himself.

His mobile buzzed with an incoming message. It was from his mother. She wasn't able to have lunch with him as promised.

> I'm so sorry to cancel but Phyllida Osborne wanted me to help her with her latest needlepoint design and I couldn't say no. Sorry, dear. I'll give you more notice next time.

"Right," he muttered, looking at the latest summary of negotiations with Browne's people that had been messengered over to him this morning. Interesting that his mum's message would catch him now. She'd been telling him for years that he ought to take care of Brompton Court because it was his responsibility.

His mobile buzzed again. This time, the text was from Livvy. She didn't usually send a second before noon.

> Hi Jack, Remember the story of all the furniture that was in the library? They wanted to put some of it in the duke's rooms…your rooms. I wouldn't let them. I thought if someday you decided you wanted to visit Brompton Court, you'd hate finding all those Brobdingnagian things in your way. Don't you love that word? I do!

Of course she'd love it. *I'm a word person*, she'd said. He texted back.

> I do love that word. As Lilliputian as you are, I wonder how you manage to find your way around them.

He smiled at the message that came back right away, a gif of a very tiny mouse worming her way through a crack in a door.

He stared out his window. The trees that served to shade it in summer, now in the middle of autumn, had shed all their leaves. Perhaps he might like to go to Brompton Court, just for a day, mind, to see how she was progressing. The smile that had accompanied that thought faded to a frown. And to see what needed fixing.

Yes, that was a reason to go. He'd let Henry know they were making the trip. He'd call Madelyn and tell her to investigate any damage to any of the rooms Livvy might use whilst she was at the court, and what else might break down or fall and cause an injury. In fact, now that he thought of it, he'd have to tell his land manager, Edward Pratt, to do a detailed assessment of the entire property.

Jack might hate Brompton Court. But what kind of a person would he be if the person who was living in it—if only temporarily—got hurt because of his negligence?

Livvy found out soon enough that the furniture in the library was the least of her problems. Once it was removed—except for a few chairs and the tables she used for sorting—it was the books themselves. There were thousands upon thousands of them. The more she explored, the more it felt like they were birthing even more books.

Every time she moved one, a puff of dust billowed up. With all the sneezing she'd been doing, her nose was turning an interesting shade of red and became painful to touch. Madelyn suggested an English remedy that mimicked one of the American nasal sprays Livvy was familiar with. It was no more effective than the American versions.

She was beginning to get nervous. Ten days had passed, and she hadn't found the diaries. Was the twenty days she had left going to be enough? That first day, when she'd come across Dugdale's

Baronage, she'd thought it was going to be a slam dunk. The diaries were going to be nearby.

No such luck.

"Tea?" Madelyn came into the library, a cup of Livvy's favorite chamomile in hand.

Livvy knew she was in bad shape when she couldn't smell Madelyn's vanilla-scented perfume. "Thanks." It came out *theks*.

"What have you found today?" Madelyn set down Livvy's cup.

"A first edition of Coleridge's *The Rime of the Ancient Mariner*." Livvy pulled off the pair of gloves she'd been wearing, now caked with grime. She replaced them with a new pair. "Tell me again why no one has ever been interested enough to uncover treasures like this one?"

"The current duke's father was, but sadly he wasn't duke long enough to make a dent."

Livvy grabbed a piece of tissue and patted her poor, abused nose dry as gently as she could. "Well, he did come to the dukedom in a weird way, and then there was the financial mess."

"Yes, poor man. My understanding is that he didn't want the dukedom. He might not have accepted—although I've heard if you're in line to be a duke you must be one—except for his daughters. They begged him to say yes since they rather fancied the idea of being called Lady."

"I see," Livvy said. But she didn't. Livvy had no frame of reference for a father wanting to please a daughter.

"Jack called me this morning to find out how you were doing."

"Maybe he called to make sure I haven't sold Dugdale's Baronage on the black market."

Eyes filled with disapproval, Madelyn said, "He would never."

After the first few days, Livvy felt comfortable enough with Madelyn to tell her about her face-off with Jack in his office the morning before she arrived at Brompton Court.

"He was taken by surprise, I'm quite sure," Madelyn insisted. "I'm sure he's gotten over what set him off and you should, too. Don't let one conversation determine your opinion of him. He's really quite a good sort."

Now that he was answering her texts, Livvy hoped he might be way more than a good sort. "Well, what did he say?"

"He wanted to know about your search."

Before Livvy could answer, she sneezed and her usual headache came on. "Did he say anything else?"

Madelyn made a face. "No." She rose. "I'm for Lincoln to see a friend and do some shopping. I've added the tea you like to my list. Whilst I'm there, I'll have a look for another remedy for your nose."

"I'll be here, working."

After Madelyn left, Livvy dragged her tissue box and the garbage can over to the shelves closest to the left of the French doors. Hands on hips, she studied it. So far, all the older books she found were on the middle to upper shelves. That made sense. It was where she then began the search of each column of shelves.

Though she'd made a joke out of the old ladder smashing to smithereens, it had scared her when, as it dropped her to the floor, the breath had been knocked out of her. She felt reasonably sure her new ladder wouldn't play any kind of trick like that.

By the middle of the afternoon, Livvy had moved books off three of the middle to upper shelves. Much as she told herself to focus and keep an eagle eye out for the diaries, she kept getting distracted by the books she found. There was a thick volume of the *Aeneid* in the original Greek, one of *Augustine* in Latin, and *Beowulf* in middle English. She salivated over—but not on—the Chaucer she found. Her heart swelled with excitement over the first editions of books by Samuel Johnson and Oliver Goldsmith, and slim books of poetry by Blake, and Keats. One or more of the dukes of Brompton was a serious collector.

There was a part of her furious that these books weren't where they ought to be, in a real library, where they could be cared for properly. Another part of her was thrilled that she could run her fingers—

gloved to be sure—over their covers and, except in some cases, very carefully over their pages.

Livvy's heart beat a little faster each time she came across one of these treasures. She touched the covers with reverence. She opened a book of sermons, the pages of which were darkened with age and marked with spots.

She raised each book to her face. The pages smelled like coffee. And chocolate. With the lightest touch possible, she ran her fingers across the frontispiece and title page. The few days she had left at Brompton Court lurked at the edge of her consciousness. But this…this was so special, so once-in-a-lifetime. She wanted to adore this book and all the others with every one of her senses.

Later in the afternoon, after she'd slowed down to read a few pages here and there, Livvy finally gave in to her sensible self and went back to her search. With a spurt of energy, she climbed the ladder to the topmost shelf. Not only was the shelf barely accessible because the ladder didn't quite reach, but it appeared to be deeper than the others.

Frowning, she leaned against the highest rung and reached forward as far as she could. It still wasn't far enough. Making sure the ladder was firmly set against the shelves, she climbed to the rung just below the top, and reached in. Her fingers found a slim volume. She pulled it toward her.

Of course, it was covered in dust. She blew it off and sneezed. The ladder wiggled. She grabbed the edge of the shelf to steady it and herself. When it was rock solid still again, she leaned her whole body against the shelf she was parallel to, and studied the book's cover. It was another volume of sermons. When she got to the title page and translated the Roman letters. MDCLIX, her eyes opened wide. 1659. She was holding a book that had been printed when Jessamine was still alive and before Charles Stuart became king. Jessamine might have read one or more of these sermons. Maybe they'd given her solace. Livvy closed the book and made herself take slow steps down the ladder.

She placed the book on her sorting table next to the others she'd put there today, excited and fired up. She knew. She was close. She started up the ladder again. Once level with the top shelf, she reached in. The tips of two fingers brushed up against something bulky. Her senses told her it was leather, square, and secured with, of all things, rubber bands. There were no rubber bands in the 1600s.

She told herself to breathe deep and relax. This was a find. An important find. With deliberate movements, she grasped the case, and brought it forward.

Leaning against the ladder rungs, she touched one of the rubber bands with which the case had been secured. They promptly broke. The others followed. Pulling the case toward her by the flap, she lifted it and peeked inside to see a sheaf of papers. She squeezed her eyes shut just for a moment. Maybe, if she was living right, these papers were more than three hundred years old. Maybe it was an unbound dia— She couldn't say the word.

With fingers that trembled, she reached in to bring out a piece of lined paper, like the kind that wouldn't be three hundred years old. It said *Letters from various to Caleb Anstruther.* The note was written recently, no more than a few years ago, if she had to guess, by Jack's father.

Not a diary, bound or unbound.

Disappointment smacked her hard. But it didn't last. Whatever was inside the case, they were letters written to Jessamine's brother, which just might tell Livvy something more about Jessamine. And maybe her dairies were nearby. Livvy concentrated on regulating her breaths.

She gripped the case with one hand, and the side of the ladder with her other. The case was heavier than she thought it would be. She secured it to her chest. As old and important as these letters were, it would be a horrible thing if she dropped them. The damage would most likely be beyond repair.

She firmed a handhold on the ladder. Out of nowhere, she sneezed. It was one of the earth-shattering kind she'd wished she could cut back on. Worse, this one had the case with Caleb's letters wobbling in her arm, the ladder wobbling, too.

Letting out a little shriek, she scrabbled for a handhold on a shelf as the ladder started to slide. She missed.

Idiot! Let go of the case!

"I can't," she wheezed as her heartbeat jumped.

The weirdest thing—landing on the worn carpet, shoulder first, and then her head—it didn't hurt. It was more like a hard thump. And then nothing.

Jack looked at his watch and frowned. It was almost four o'clock in the afternoon. By this time of the day, Livvy's afternoon text should have come. He reached for his mobile and woke it up. He'd looked at it five minutes ago. There was nothing then. There was nothing now.

He paged up to her last, which had come this morning at the usual time, 9:05 on the button.

I found an albatross!

He smiled. She was a lavish user of exclamation points. Every text had at least one.

It's a first edition of the rime...OMG, couldn't nineteenth century poets spell? Why not call it the Rhyme of said Mariner instead of the rime? Just joking. I know it's about a (c)rime. Anyway, I've saved it for cataloging later. This is me telling you no diaries yet, but this afternoon I just know my luck will change!

Dogged as she was, perhaps it would.

He frowned at his phone again and sent a text to Madelyn.

> **Is everything all right?**

After a few seconds her answer came.

> **Yes it is.**

He made a sound of frustration. He hadn't asked the right question.

> **I usually get a text from Livvy apprising me of her progress each day. I haven't received one today.**

She responded.

> **I'm just coming back from Lincoln. I'll check.**

He jerked his fingers off the keys. Had he just revealed to Madelyn that he cared?

> **We want to be sure an accident hasn't befallen our intrepid researcher.**

There, a joke. Then he added:

> **I'll be there within a half hour.**

He was staring at the phone, unsettled, when his door opened a crack and Isabella peeked in.

"There's a fellow here who'd like a few minutes with you. He doesn't have an appointment. Are you free?"

"What's the chap's name? What company?"

"His name is Kyle Bentsen. He didn't give me his company's name. He told me you would know."

Jack came slowly to his feet. Why was Bentsen showing up now? "Thank you, Isabella. I'll see Mr. Bentsen."

Coming around to the front of his desk, Jack stood at the ready as Bentsen entered. He was tall. However, he wasn't as tall as himself. A lovely thing, that. He wore a navy three-piece suit and carried a brown leather briefcase with gold hardware. His smile seemed friendly enough. The light brown eyes were the giveaway. There was a flatness in them that put the lie to any friendliness in his smile.

Jack took the man's hand in a hard grip. "Bentsen."

Bentsen's smile seemed forced. "I'd address you with your title, but I'm afraid I don't know what's right."

"Pretend there's no title. Call me Jack."

"Jack it is, then." Bentsen squeezed Jack's hand incrementally harder. Jack stared.

Intense gaze flickering, Bentsen let go. "Do you mind if I sit?"

"Not at all." Jack indicated they should move to the chairs in front of his desk. "I'd heard you were in London." This had to be Maisie's tall arsehole.

"Oh" He brightened. "I'm surprised my presence was noted. And thank you for seeing me." Bentsen folded himself into the chair, setting his briefcase down on the carpet next to him. "Especially without an appointment."

"No need to worry about that," Jack said, though he felt wariness.

Bentsen looked down. "Is this a Persian rug?"

Did Bentsen feel the need to make small talk about what was under their feet? "It is, in fact."

Bentsen pursed his lips. "Hand-knotted?"

"Of course," Jack responded more than willing to go along with the man's nonsense.

"I won't ask you how much you paid. That would unacceptable."

"Quite." Jack settled back, prepared to wait as long as needed for the man to get to the point.

"I ask because my wife is redecorating my office in our new house and being such a perfectionist, she wants everything to be the highest quality. Would you be willing to give me the name of your dealer?"

Jack reached across his desk and lifted his phone's handset. "Isabella, when Mr. Bentsen leaves, please give him the number for Hagopian Fine Rugs and Tapestries." He turned, folded one leg over the other, sat back, and waited.

"Thank you, Jack. I'm sure my wife will appreciate the information."

"Your wife. Which one is it? Sylvia? Or is it Sheryl or Stephanie?"

Bentsen's eyes narrowed. "Stephanie. I suppose Olivia told you her sisters' names."

"She mentioned them."

Bentsen leaned back and mirroring Jack, crossed one of his legs over the other. "I don't think it's come up in the negotiations between our teams, but my father-in-law is a great admirer of yours."

"How very nice." Jack allowed himself a trifling smile.

"He read an article that was published years ago in the *New York Times* about your return from the dead, so to speak, how you restored your family's reputation. It explained how you bought Prime and all the local newspapers. Not many could have achieved the success you have."

"I'd forgotten that piece." He'd given the reporter permission to write it and was sorry afterward. The fellow praised his business acumen prodigiously. Yes, he'd worked hard. But as with anything else, luck had played a part. Though he'd been asked over the years, he was too private to ever give another interview.

"In part, that article is why we reached out to you to buy the part of Anstruther Media Group, your company, that you were willing to sell. Now we are at an inflection point and would like to change the scope of the AMG sale to Cenotaph."

At last. Here they were: the reason for Bentsen's foray. Jack shifted his weight so he appeared to be entirely relaxed when in truth he was as on guard as he had ever been. "From the first, I've wondered at the name Mr. Browne chose for his corporation: Cenotaph."

"I wouldn't know." Bentsen's lips tightened. "What are your thoughts on our request?"

So Bentsen didn't want to talk about why his father-in-law had chosen the Greek word that meant empty tomb. Rather smart.

"I haven't any beyond those I've shared with my negotiating team." Jack's senses were raised to the highest level. He needed to tell Higgins to find out what his disadvantages were in the attack he expected was now assuredly to come from Cenotaph.

"I see." Bentsen half-smiled. "I wonder, then, with your permission, if you and I might ask our teams to step aside and let us negotiate, just the two of us, without having to listen to all that unnecessary advice for which we pay them their exorbitant fees."

He raised an eyebrow. "Just the two of us?"

"No muddying the waters." Bentsen smiled his pit bull smile. "You and I can find a path that would lead to a better outcome for all concerned." Bentsen settled back as if he'd made a telling point and the thing had been decided.

"By all means. However, let's not waste time going over ground already covered. We can rethink the scope of the sale to include the smaller newspapers." A delaying tactic on Jack's part. Browne had never wanted them.

Bentsen cocked his head to the side. "I wonder if you would consider selling this property, as well."

"You mean this structure?"

Bentsen's laugh was offset by the way his upper lip curled in contempt. "This is a great location and can be used for many purposes. It could be converted back into a residence."

Jack was willing to play Bentsen's game as long as the man wanted. "I imagine it might be rather lovely."

Bentsen unfolded his legs and leaned forward. "You misunderstand me. The building is extra. We're interested in purchasing Chalcott House."

Here it was. "But, old man, what gave you an idea it was on offer? I believe I said from the beginning it's the one property I intend to retain."

His cold eyes hardening, Bentsen said, "I'm sure there's a way we could sweeten the deal enough to change your mind."

Jack tilted his head to the side, as if willing to listen to what came next.

Bentsen took the invitation. "Mr. Browne does not have a publishing house in his stable of properties. He wants one. We see a future for the publishing business although it will have to be re-imagined if it's to scale. Yours will fit his needs."

"It might well. But as I've said—"

"Oh?" Bentsen paused. The upper lip curled again. "If we can't buy it in a congenial manner, I am sure, we can accomplish it another way."

Jack sat back. It seemed Kyle Bentsen, for all his talk of negotiating, was at heart, a bully, and here he'd dropped his mask long enough for Jack to see. "Sorry, old man. That sounded a bit like a threat."

Bentsen smiled, his teeth showing. "Sorry. There is however one other reason Mr. Browne has for wanting Chalcott House. As you're someone who has a close relationship with your family, I think you'll understand."

Jack had perfected the ability not to blink when someone hostile shifted gears, and he couldn't know what was coming next. "Go on."

His basilisk stare on full display, Bentsen chuckled. There was no humor in the sound. "Mr. Browne wants Chalcott House for Olivia."

The quadriceps tendon over Jack's right knee tightened. "Indeed. Does he?"

Kyle Bentsen had a great variety of smiles. This one was the cat-in-the-cream variant. "He does."

"In what way?"

"You understand, I'm sure," Bentsen continued. "We do many things for family we might not otherwise do for others."

"Quite." That muscle in Jack's leg tightened more. If Bentsen didn't get to the point soon, the damn thing was going to tear.

"It's an awkward business." Bentsen paused.

Jack gave him a tight smile. Awkward, strange, and breathtakingly disturbing.

"Mr. Browne loves his daughters."

Not all of them in the same way as Jack remembered the story Livvy had told him. "How lovely. What has it to do with Chalcott House?"

"Olivia is quite smart. She has an encyclopedic knowledge of many things."

Was Bentsen one of the people in Livvy's life who damned her for having inconsequential knowledge? Bastard. Jack suddenly wanted to do something inappropriate. Throttle the man was what came to mind.

Bentsen nodded, that smug smile making a return. "Something she can focus on will do her a world of good."

"I am sure there must be another way to accomplish that other than to buy a half-billion pound publishing house for her. Perhaps an island in the Caribbean instead?"

Bentsen didn't bother to control the look of contempt that flitted across his face at that bit of asininity. "That's not what Mr. Browne had in mind."

Jack wondered how long he could continue on with this charade. "Again, your point?"

"Managing Chalcott House, she will be under her father's supervision of course. He'll guide her."

Browne's help, as described by his son-in-law, sounded vise-like to Jack. "Does she know her father wants Chalcott House for her?"

Bentsen shook his head. "Of course, she does."

Jack's quad released. He came to his feet. "It's quite an interesting concept, gifting a daughter with a publishing house. Whimsical, really. She must be quite excited."

Bentsen stood as well. "I'm surprised she hasn't mentioned it to you."

"Since she's been at my property in Lincolnshire, we've not spoken." True. Jack didn't have to mention her texts or his answers to her texts. "There are all kinds of gifts one gives one's child. Once my father gave me a porcupine quill." Jack looked at his watch. "Lovely that we were able to find the time to talk, Kyle. I should have asked…can I call you Kyle?"

"As I'm calling you Jack, why not?"

"Sorry but I do need to go. A meeting. One hates them, but they are a necessary evil."

Bentsen shifted his briefcase to his left hand and held out his right. "Let's agree to talk soon."

Rather than take the man's hand—the thought of it had him wanting to make it into a fist—Jack indicated Bentsen should start toward the door. "As to just the two of us talking, I think it would be better if we relied on our teams to go on as they have done.

They are so much more able to deal with the minutiae, don't you agree?"

Bentsen's cheeks reddened. He'd been maneuvered. Jack felt a moment of pleasure. "Now, I am sure Isabella has that phone number you wanted for Hagopian. Don't forget to get it before you leave."

Bentsen hesitated. "I'm curious. Why did your father give you a porcupine quill?"

"Ah, I wondered if you would ask. Quills are what protects the porcupine. My father wanted me to remember that we humans are animals as well. Just like the porcupine, we sometimes need to protect ourselves with our sharp-ended quills."

Bentsen's eyes narrowed. He got it. "You know there will be more discussion about Chalcott House."

"Do you think so?" Jack opened the door. "Speak to Isabella, please, for that contact information. I'm sure anything your wife purchases from Hagopian will meet her standards of perfection."

They shook hands—there was no way Jack could avoid it, this time. However, he would wash his with the strongest disinfectant available, after. Watching Bentsen approach Isabella's desk, he closed the door, leaned against it, and wondered if Browne's pit bull had any idea how many porcupine quills he was going to have to protect himself against if he truly thought he could get away with stealing Chalcott House away.

He heard the murmur of Isabella's voice, giving Bentsen Hagopian's phone number, and then allowed himself a full-out grin. Livvy had no idea what plans her father was making for her. Bentsen had lied or said differently, his body had lied. He shook his head when he should have nodded.

He paced over to the sideboard and gave Rose's punching bag a good clip. Livvy had been telling the truth. He was free to enjoy whatever this thing was that was growing between them.

His mobile buzzed. He retrieved it from his desk and stared with alarm at the message from Madelyn.

> Livvy has fallen. We've taken her to hospital. Will keep you informed.

Madelyn told me how your third
cousin, once or twice removed—
the ninth duke—put in central
heating at the court. You might
want to think about upgrading.
Text, Livvy to the duke.

CHAPTER EIGHT

Livvy opened her weighted-down eyelids to see Jack hovering over her. Her eyelids fell of their own accord. When they opened again, he was gone. So, a hallucination.

She sank back into red darkness and took inventory. Her head was sore. Her left arm was immobilized. When she moved her right arm, she felt a pinch on the back of her hand and knew what it was: an IV.

She was in a hospital. That was what happened when you fell off a ladder. She moaned.

"What hurts?"

Jack. Not a hallucination after all.

"My head."

"Do you need nurse to give you something for the pain?"

"No." It was more sore than actual hurt. What hurt more was her trying to use the rest of her brain to figure out what it meant that he was here.

"This is a very comfortable bed." Her lips were dry. So was her throat.

He pulled what must have been a chair—the sound of scraping on the floor hinted at that—closer to her bed.

She opened her eyes a crack. In the dim light cast by a lamp somewhere, she could see his narrow face and a heaviness around his eyes.

"I hope so. I paid for it to be comfortable."

Livvy couldn't put two thoughts together. "It's definitely more comfortable than the one at the Court. "Why are you here?"

"Where should I be?"

"In London, at your desk." She swallowed sudden nausea.

"No."

She tried to calm the urge to bring up what was in her stomach and failed. "You don't happen to have a barf bag handy, do you?"

She tried to turn on her side with little luck. There was a flurry of movement around her, a murmur of voices, and then nothing.

When she woke again, it was dark.

She tested herself. No nausea, which was good. She moved her toes. No paralysis. Also good. "You're a real winner, girlfriend," she murmured.

"What was that?" There was a scent of vanilla.

She opened her eyes and yes, it was Madelyn, worry clouding her face.

"What time is it? Where am I and please don't say a hospital."

"It's almost nine o'clock in the evening and you're in the Richard, Duke of Brompton Hospital. When I called to let Jack know what happened to you, and before he flew up here—"

"Flew?" Livvy managed.

"Yes, in his helicopter."

He owned a helicopter?

Madelyn went on. "The ambulance driver was on his way to the NHS hospital in Lincoln, when Jack called to make sure you were brought here where you could get the best care."

"I—" She moved her hand and halted. The pinch of the needle where the IV line fed into her body was immediate and sharp. "Is this the private hospital you were telling me about, the one Jack endowed?"

"It is. But it doesn't matter."

"What does that mean?" Livvy began to clench her fist but stopped at the IV's insistence.

"It means just what Madelyn said," said the hallucination as he came into Livvy's line of sight. He held a Starbucks cup in one hand.

In the dim light cast by the bedside lamp, she noted his hair, even cropped as it was, looked mussed. He looked rumpled, like he'd been in the clothes he was wearing—trousers and a light blue shirt, open at the collar, no jacket—for a while.

He turned to Madelyn. "I'm here now. Go home and get some rest."

Madelyn slipped into her sweater. "You'll let me know how she's doing."

Jack put his cup down on Livvy's bedside table, staring down at her with a look in his eyes she'd never seen before. "I will."

And then Madelyn was gone, taking her vanilla scent with her.

"You're too pale." He touched her IV hand. "Does something hurt?"

She pressed her lips together. "No." She forced a smile. "At least now I know what you meant when you said you paid for this bed to be comfortable."

Leaning over her, he brushed her hair back from her forehead. The nearness of him, the cedar scent of him, his quiet breaths touching her cheek…it almost stopped her from saying what she needed to.

"I don't know how expensive a private hospital is. You need to understand. I'm going to pay you back for whatever they're doing for me." If she'd been able to, she would have pointed at him for emphasis. "That means everything, including the Band-Aids." She angled her chin toward her hand. "And this really annoying IV."

"I don't think they've used any…Band-Aids you called them? We call them plasters. As for the rest? I'm responsible. It was my house in which you got hurt."

"And I bet, smart as you are, you bought a workers' comp policy. Good job. I'll file my paperwork the first moment I can."

"Please don't joke."

"I'm not joking."

Jack's eyebrows flickered. "Livvy, you can't be that concerned about the cost of your care. It's something else, isn't it?" He came closer, filling her entire vision. His eyes, so changeable, warm and blue, now slightly worried. The glint of light-brown, almost blond scruff on the cheek she wanted to cradle, but knew better than to try. His mouth so close that if he came an inch closer she could touch her mouth to his.

"I have to know if you'll—" She took a deep breath.

"If I'll what?"

"Kick me out. Tell me I've got to leave Brompton Court because I'm a liability."

Jack sat straight up. On the rushed trip from London, it wasn't liability that had his level of anxiety off the charts. It was imagining her lying on the floor in the library, with no one nearby to come to her aid. It brought to mind another time, in the same library, when he wasn't there to help. "What nonsense is this?" The words came out much sharper than he intended.

She narrowed her eyes at him. "You call it nonsense? The way I remember the last time we saw each other, I needed to convince you I wasn't my father's snitch. Since then, we've gotten friendly with the texts. But maybe you think I'm a liability of a different kind now."

He rose and placed the chair he'd been sitting in against the wall. Coming back toward her, he bent and took her face in his hands. Her eyes widened. Her mouth opened in surprise, and he did what he'd been wanting to do for longer than he'd acknowledged. He kissed her.

She blinked, once, twice. She opened her mouth and closed it again.

"Good. For once you have nothing to add. I like you that way on occasion." He leaned back, but only inches. "It's been a fair amount of time since I thought of you as a liability, if I ever did. The texts? I've begun to think of them as a bit more than friendly."

Confusion widened her eyes. "You have?"

He kissed her again. This time, he took the time to feel the sweetness of her, the sweetness he'd come to know through her daily visits on his mobile, the sweetness she hid behind her sometimes snarky, always funny words. This time he brushed his lips against hers and waited for her to open to him, and when she did, he took for himself the sweetness of her, her lips, her mouth, and her tongue.

She began to breathe faster, and he reminded himself. A hospital bed was not the bed he needed her in for him to enjoy her properly.

He forced himself to remember the thread of their conversation. They'd been talking about…proof. "Would an affidavit do?"

That little sparkle that often filled her eyes with humor flared to life. Her lip twitched upward on one side. "I suppose it depends upon what's in that affidavit."

His heart quickened with delight. He leaned close and light as air, touched the patch of gauze—the one that covered the stiches taken to close the gash she'd gotten when she fell—at her hairline. "How about this? Our agreement is null and void."

Her eyes widened again. "Just to make sure I understand the agreement you're referring to is…?"

"The one where you only have a month to find the diaries," he said, finishing her sentence. "You can stay at Brompton Court for whatever time it takes."

Her beautiful, hazel eyes closed and then opened. She searched his face. "That's the new deal?"

"It is."

"You know when you make a deal, it's the same as a promise. It's not something you can unpromise."

He leaned in so his lips were a breath from hers. "Will you give me permission to add unpromise to my personal lexicon? It's a lovely, expressive word."

A pulse jumped at the base of her throat. "You can use it any which way you want."

"Thank you. There is one thing, though."

She narrowed her eyes at him again. "Is this a but?"

He shook his head. "It's that from this moment on, as you go about your search for Jessamine's diaries, you're to do it safely. You'll have help to keep you from falling off ladders."

Taking a deep breath, she smiled. "I'm good with that." And she fell asleep.

He watched her for a long time before stepping away. She'd just come from having a CAT scan when he'd bolted into the hospital. There was definitely a bleed, according to the radiologist. It showed up on the film but it wasn't extensive and she felt it would heal itself in a week or two at the most. The patient was in good health. There was no reason to think she wouldn't be back on her feet and able to resume her regular activities within that timeframe. As for her shoulder, it had been a simple dislocation. Having it in a sling was a precaution.

She looked young and sweet with her eyes closed. It was a mistake to think that. Livvy Browne was a formidable woman unlike any he'd ever known and she was a match for him. He intimidated people with his silences. She shredded silence with words, lots of them. His silences made people nervous. They felt the need to fill them up. Sometimes, unwittingly, they gave away their secrets to him. She shut people up by overwhelming them with speech. They had no idea how to respond. He included himself in that group.

He held the door open and looked back over his shoulder at her tiny figure looking even tinier nestled in the depth of the wide hospital bed. He wasn't willing to let her go just yet. Perhaps he never would.

Jack was up at five o'clock the next morning. This time it wasn't one of his usual dreams—of paparazzi chasing his sisters, or the look on his mother's face when finding out his father was dead. Or not being there to save him. This dream was filled with falling ladders and collapsing beds.

He could do something about collapsing beds. He would start things in motion after the world around him woke up, and after his trip to the hospital.

In the meantime, he could call his British team— it was not unusual for someone to be in the office this early—and discuss Bentsen's threat.

After, and as the gray light of dawn lightened to day, he made himself a breakfast of cheese and bread and a cup of tea. In the middle of reading one of his online news sources, he heard steps.

"Cheers, Jack," Madelyn said rushing in, a little breathless. "Did you get some sleep?"

"I managed a few hours." He stood and slid his mobile into the back pocket of his jeans.

"I didn't. The ladder…I dreamt about it all night."

Had Jack known he and Madelyn were having similar dreams, he would have rung her and they could have had their much-needed conversation then rather than now. "Madelyn—"

"No, Jack, wait. I must confess. I—"

He held up a hand. "If this is about that ladder, there's no need to confess. I have responsibility here." He was beginning to think that was a gross understatement.

She made a face. "Will you at least let me say I'm sorry I didn't tell you about the beds, the rooms, and the furniture?"

"No apology is necessary. Rose asked me if she could do a simple redecoration. It seems the simple decoration became something rather more complicated."

The look of distress on Madelyn's face told Jack she didn't think his words absolved her. "I'm curious. Is there a reason why the furniture was put in the library rather than in storage on the upper floors?"

"The floors are beginning to fall in."

"Ah." That was something to add to the ever increasing list of problems at Brompton Court.

Madelyn began to twist the ring she wore on her finger. "Jack. Your Grace."

Madelyn never called him Your Grace. He prepared himself. "Out with it, please."

"Mr. Pratt came by yesterday afternoon. He looked over the building, as you requested. He wants to talk to you about the leak we have in the roof."

Jack ran a hand across the top of his head.

"It's quite extensive, Mr. Pratt says."

Madelyn headed into the room nearest the kitchen, a pantry of sorts, used now for bits and bobs no longer of use. Although the more Jack thought about it, almost everything at Brompton Court was no longer of use.

"Mr. Pratt had someone from Littlefold Engineering come by to investigate. His man went up on the roof and saw many places where water has seeped in. Worse than the leaks, he found dry rot."

Jack looked around at shelves piled high with silver platters, so blackened he couldn't imagine when last they'd been polished. There were teapots of various sizes, mammoth pots and bowls filled with utensils that hadn't been used since the time of his father's predecessor. "What does Mr. Pratt suggest?"

"He didn't tell me, but I think he wants to give you an earful."

Guilt chasing him, he strode toward the front door. The broken ladders, useless furniture, floors falling in, leaks, and dry rot, even the blackened silver, the place was letting him know it didn't appreciate his attitude. Apparently Pratt didn't, either. "I'm on my way to see Livvy and, one hopes, to bring her back with me. Tell Mr. Pratt to be here at noon."

Madelyn hurried after him. "Mr. Pratt says the roof is only part of what needs to be fixed. For years we've done nothing but patch."

Jack uttered the most foul curse he could think of. "Let's not pass the bloody mess on to another generation." He stepped outside where Henry waited, back door of the Tesla open.

Henry touched a finger to his cap. Jack paused and wheeled around. "What about the library? Any leaks or rot there?"

Madelyn stood on the top step, wind blowing through her short hair. "There's the skylight."

He looked at his watch. Just after eight. "Get Mr. Pratt here, now. Whatever is wrong with it, I want that skylight fixed before I return from the hospital."

Henry said, "Good morning, Your Grace."

Jack slipped into the car. "Let's go."

As Henry moved behind the wheel Jack thought better of his irritable tone while thinking of the skylight and whether it entailed any immediate danger to the woman who spent her days beneath it. "How is Mrs. Stebbins these days? Better, I hope."

"She's as good as could be expected, after what the doctors have been saying about the infection in her lungs. Thanks for asking."

Stebbins drove slowly. He had to. The road insisted. "I appreciate how you got her transferred to our hospital."

For a moment Jack wasn't sure which *her* Stebbins was referring to. "So, Mrs. Stebbins has improved?"

"She's doing quite well." And then Henry proceeded to fill him in on what Jack thought must be all the local gossip in every village, town, and city in Lincolnshire.

"—The Lincolnshire Egg Throwing Championship."

Jack frowned. "Beg pardon?" He'd been thinking about leaks and rot. And the skylight in the library.

"In Sleaford this weekend. I think I'll take Mrs. Stebbins to watch the fun."

"Quite." Jack shifted. He couldn't get comfortable. He wondered if he were coming down with something. He knew better. His conscience was poking at him and his failure to address his responsibilities.

Henry slowed. "We're here, Your Grace." He eased into the circle in front of the hospital and brought the car to a stop by the entrance. "I think I'll walk down to the Lone Man for a pickle sandwich."

"Do that." Jack was out of the car before Henry could come 'round to open the door.

Livvy woke often during the night. She couldn't blame it on the nurse—who seemed to have taps on her shoes—coming in to take her blood pressure or look at her chart, or just to turn on the light. It was Jack who appeared in her dreams that had her coming awake. Every time her eyes popped open, it was to see if it were true. If truly he was leaning over her, cupping her face, and pressing his lips to hers.

How his mouth on hers had felt. How his breath had felt mingling with hers. How she hadn't wanted him to stop.

Something had changed last night with that kiss.

There was the sound of steps outside her room

and she knew this time, it wasn't a nurse coming her way. Breath held, she stared hard at the closed door until the moment it opened and there, the man of her dreams.

She'd stood next to him at Club Chaos. She'd gazed at his back when she entered his office. She'd never seen him enter a room. It stopped up her breath.

He'd combed his hair. All the gold-tipped curls lay flat in gleaming submission. He wore jeans this morning and a light blue, starched, button-down shirt. If she couldn't see anything but the severity of his angular face or his serious, unsmiling lips, she would have been chilled through. But his Tahiti-warm eyes told another story. They were fixed upon her as if she were a destination. It made her heart jump inside her chest.

"You should always wear blue. It makes your eyes look dreamier," she blurted, her words way ahead of her brain. If she could, she'd have clapped a hand to her mouth to shut it up…if she had a hand to do it with.

His dreamy eyes crinkled. "Thank you, I think." Smile fading, he came farther into the room to stop next to her bed. His gaze roamed her face. His mouth tightened and then released. "How do you feel?"

She tried to swallow and failed. He was looking at her with an intensity that made everything inside her seize up. "I'm good."

Pulling the chair next to her bed around, he sat,

elbows on his knees and leaned forward. His slow-blinking, duke-ish, blue eyes bore into her. "Yes?"

He closed one hand over her wrist, and held her in a light grasp. His strong, lithe fingers gently encircled her wrist. She lost sense of any other part of her body but that band of skin.

She managed to swallow her nerves. "Are you checking my pulse to see if I'm alive?"

His hand tightened and then let go. He sat back, lips once again in that straight, disapproving line that seemed to be his default. "You're alive, by the grace of God only."

Livvy didn't care about anyone's grace. She wanted his hand back. "That's a little overstating it, don't you think? I hit a couple of shelves on my way down."

The slight frown became more pronounced. "Must you joke about everything? Do you know how foolish a thing it was for you to climb to the top of that damn ladder?"

"What was I supposed to do? Beam myself up? I thought I was close to finding the diaries. I got excited."

His frown intensified. "I wish you'd told Madelyn you needed a better ladder."

"Are you saying it's my fault after all?" There was no more hiding behind snark, not with her anxiety exposed. "Last night... You meant it, right? You're not going to kick me out because I was careless?"

The frown eased. "No. And why would you

make that assumption?" His eyes had softened again.

"Why? Maybe because you just implied it was me who caused the problem?"

"I."

"That's what I said."

"I, not me. Wrong pronoun."

She wouldn't let him see her smile. In a soft voice, she said, "You're giving me a lesson in grammar? Maybe it could wait until I'm on my feet?"

His eyes glimmered with quiet humor. "I believe in proper pronouns."

Whatever she might have thought about the proper use of pronouns flew from her head. She was with a man who worried because she'd fallen. He wasn't blaming her for it. And he wasn't criticizing her for using the wrong pronoun.

Her ability to form a sentence that would win approval from the people at the Chicago Manual of Style faded away. All those weeks ago, she'd told herself it would be okay. It would be fun to text him daily and find the hot guy she might have been interested in for a moment, a guy who was inside a stiff-upper-lip type she could never be interested in.

Except with each text and each day she saw glimmers of the man he truly was. With each text and each day, it felt like she was peeling away layers of protection he'd sheltered behind. She wanted to keep on peeling until she found all of him.

She ran her tongue over her lips to moisten them. They'd gone bone dry. She tried to speak and failed. Tried again, failed again. Until she came up with, "I'm ready to…"

At the same time, he began, "Are you ready…?"

An odd suspension of time hung between them. She took a breath and said, "Yes, in answer to your question. I'm ready to blow this popsicle stand."

In no more than a beat, the contours of his face changed. Softened. The quality of his smile grew luminous. "That wasn't quite how I would have phrased it, but okay. I've arranged an ambulance to take you back to Brompton Court."

"Once, when I fell and bit through my tongue, I rode in an ambulance with my sister, Sheryl. If Brit ambulances are similar, no shock absorbers, driving on roads around here, then maybe not. Is there an alternative?"

"My car is just outside. Will that do?"

"More than do. So, you really flew up here in a helicopter?"

His smile became a tease. "I did. I have one at my disposal."

"Okay." She paused. "But…"

His eyebrows met in the middle. "But what?"

"Why did you?

He stood. She let her gaze wander up his long, spare body, to his long fingers and capable hands, to his shoulders and arms that could carry a grown woman a gazillion city blocks, to his face with its look of determination.

"It's simple, really. I had an epiphany."

Brompton Court's grand staircase
is grand, but a carpet runner down
the center would not be a bad idea.
Text, Livvy to the duke

CHAPTER NINE

Of all the things Livvy thought Jack might have said, this wasn't it. "You mean epiphany as in a religious experience?"

"A revelation. Do you want me to tell you about it?" His warm, blue eyes crackled with playfulness.

Not just determination, then. Drollery. Whimsy. She very much liked discovering this part of him. "I believe in instant gratification."

Both of his eyebrows went up. "So you'd rather not wait until we get back to the comfort of Brompton Court?"

"Did you really put the word, comfort, and Brompton Court in the same sentence?"

His mouth relaxed into a wry smile. "I meant where we can talk without interruption. Just the two of us."

Just the two…. Livvy didn't let herself be distracted by those three words. "I'm up for it now," she said to keep it cool. "If I have a relapse because the epiphany is about something not so good, what better place for me to be than in a hospital where they can revive me?"

"Why hadn't I thought of that?" He pulled the chair closer to the bed. "I had a visitor yesterday. An unanticipated one."

"Oh? How unanticipated? Not my father, I hope." Her belly did a little back flip.

"No, not your father. Worse or better, depending upon how you look at it. Your brother-in-law."

Sometimes, answers were so startling that a gap opened inside your brain equivalent to the distance between Montauk Lighthouse and Land's End. She waited a tick for her verbal skills to return and then said, "Kyle came to see you?"

"He wanted to know where I'd bought the rug in my office."

"Oh, great. Non-sequitur time." Livvy wanted to jump out of bed and pace around the room. Except she was on a tether. "You want to tell me why you were talking about rugs?"

"He said it was for your sister. He's—"

"—An interior decorator, now?" She didn't try to tamp down the sarcasm because her nerves were shrieking with alarm. She'd done everything she knew to get away from her hyper-critical family and they were still butting into her life. "Is there anything Kyle

Bentsen can't do? The talent of the man takes my breath away."

"Livvy." Said with chiding. "It was a diversionary tactic. He didn't want to get to the burning question."

Her lungs ached with the effort she was making not to breathe so hard she'd hyperventilate. "Which was?"

"Talking about adding Chalcott House to the mix of properties your father would like to purchase from me."

"Why?"

"He wants Chalcott House for you."

"Me?" She had to be falling down a rabbit hole. "What does he think? Oh wait. I know. He'd be the puppet-master and I'd be the puppet, although he'd probably give me a title. President Puppet. Yup. There's your reason. He hasn't been able to manage me the last ten years and each year it kills him more, so this is his over-the-top way of doing it. You believed what Kyle said, right?"

"Do you think I did?"

"Why wouldn't you? When I gave you my reason for wanting into Brompton Court, you thought I was lying."

"Livvy. If that were so, why would I have told you not twenty-four hours ago that you can stay as long as you like?"

Her heart gave an almost painful jump. She slipped her hand out of its sling and flattened it against her chest to keep the thing from breaking through. She stared deep into his eyes looking for the lie. She saw deep blue honesty.

Jack inched closer, so close she could see a tiny mole on one side of his nose. His woodsy scent filled her head and the smile in his eyes held warmth. "I didn't believe him. His body language gave him away. Your brother-in-law shook his head."

Her heart, the stupid organ, happy-danced because maybe, just maybe, this story was going to have a good ending. "What's the big deal about that?"

"It's a tell. When I asked him if you knew about your father's intentions, his words lied. He said you knew, but his body told the truth."

"Okay." But what he was saying didn't feel okay.

His face grew solemn. "That text you sent me about how you got my mobile number; that was the start. And then these last few weeks, I felt better and better."

"Better and better about what?" A rock formed in her chest.

"Better about knowing I could trust you. What Bentsen said was corroboration."

Livvy pressed her lips together while he went on talking about his fascination with body language, a new thing he'd been reading about to see if it would help him in dealings he had with those he didn't trust, like her father. She wasn't listening. Instead she thought about how—was it just moments ago—she'd wanted to loop her arm around his neck, draw him down to press her mouth to his, and kiss him. How she'd wanted more than kisses. How she'd wanted his body.

Not so much now.

"As you've been given the go-ahead to be released, I think it's time to leave." The way his features cleared it was obvious he felt good about things. And had no idea she didn't.

"I have a surprise for you."

"What is it?" Livvy didn't know how many more surprises she could take.

"I've gotten rid of that ancient bed you've been sleeping in and have ordered a new one to replace it. Actually, I've ordered two: one for the duchess's room and one for the duke's room. They should have been delivered by now." He glanced at his watch and stood. "I'll be back with nurse in tow. I assume you want her to take out that IV."

"Good thought. I wanted to rip it out, but while that would be oh so dramatic, I'm sure I wouldn't like the result." She made herself laugh.

He was out the door then, and she complimented herself on what a great actor she was. She smiled when the nurse appeared and insisted she be taken in a wheelchair to where Henry waited at the front of the hospital. Still, she wondered. How she was going to deal with the fact that the man who, against all reason she wanted, only trusted she was telling the truth when he could affirm it based on Kyle's body language?

***

The lane curved through the countryside and past the land belonging to his neighbors, whom Jack didn't know. It was bumpy enough that it couldn't be any fun for Livvy. She'd formed a fist against her knee, so tight, her knuckles showed white.

Jack reached for her hand. She loosened her fist, but didn't turn her hand over to hold his. He frowned. "Should we go back to the hospital?"

"No, it's just my arm." She spoke in a flat voice. "The nurse wanted to give me something for the pain and I told her no because I was feeling better."

Was she? It didn't seem so. "Would it help if you leaned against me?"

"No, that's okay."

Who, he wondered, was this subdued, rather distant woman sitting next to him, her hand limp in his? She was not the Livvy whose eyes had grown big when he kissed her last night, kissed her because he knew. The kiss was a statement, not just for her, but for him. He searched for something to say to bridge the uneasiness and came up with, "You've done me a favor."

One side of her mouth ticked upward in sarcasm. "I'm always happy to help."

"Had you not fallen, I wouldn't have known there was so much that needed fixing at Brompton Court."

"When the roof fell in, you would have."

"True."

Henry drove on, slow as an aged snail. Into the silence, fragile with something that Jack didn't understand, he said, "There's some thought that the roof in the section of Brompton Court built by the seventh duke can't be fixed at all."

As the Tesla dropped into a particularly big dip in the road, Livvy canted toward him. He caught her before she could go over. Her scent—hospital antiseptic with an overlay of her light, floral scent—sent a stab of anxiety through him. "I don't need to be told anything about this road, though. I'm experiencing its deficiencies."

"Sorry, Your Grace, Miss Browne," Henry called out.

Trying again, Jack said, "My land manager, Edward Pratt will get someone here to take care of this road." It would be one of many things he would discuss with Pratt when he saw him later today.

"Nice, even if bossy. But then you're the boss." She spoke in short, colorless spurts, never looking at him, instead staring at the back of the seat in front of her.

He exhaled a quiet breath. "Henry will drive me back to London this afternoon."

"That's good."

It had all changed, a beginning. But then this coolness. Had he been wrong? "I'll ask Madelyn to find someone to help you today, though it may be a few days before you can start looking for the diaries again."

He spoke to her pale cheek.

"Don't worry about me." Her words fell like so much ice into a frigid, far north ocean.

"How's the cat?"

That drew her attention. "What cat?"

"The one that got your tongue."

Her lips tightened.

"The Livvy I know—though not a long time, mind—wants to blister me over something I've done. Why not let me know what it is? Why not get it over with?"

At last, she looked at him, hazel gaze direct. "Did you believe me?"

As Henry slowed in his approach to the court's entrance, Jack shifted to face her. "I told you I did."

The blank look in her eyes since they'd left the hospital—no, that was wrong, since they'd left her hospital *room*—was replaced by a hard slice of temper. "Yes, after Kyle blinked his eyes and his head fell off and he did some magic body language thing."

He froze. So this was it? This...nonsense? "Livvy. I believed you. What your brother-in-law did and said was merely confirmation."

She raised both eyebrows almost to the gauze bandage at her hairline. Jack felt a stab of shame. As Henry brought the car to a stop, he hopped out and came 'round the boot to open her door. "I suppose you saw that as a no-confidence vote."

Livvy slid out of the car and looked up at him.

"Bingo."

"I should not have been so thick-headed."

Her eyes softened. "Self-awareness is a beautiful thing."

Jack was rarely called on to recognize it in himself. This woman, whose head didn't come to his shoulder, apparently saw through him to his core. He was hard pressed to decide which emotion he felt for her more: admiration or desire. He decided he'd have both.

Touching her sling, she said, "This is going to be better within days. My head will be fine, too. You should go. London misses you."

He didn't miss London. "There are repairs that need to be made. I should be here to supervise." There was a minimal element of truth. Pratt would have all in hand, once Jack gave orders to proceed. Then he could leave.

"Oh, so it was for how Brompton Court is falling apart that you flew up here in your snazzy helicopter, not for me?"

She was back to teasing him. He ought to tell her now that it was hardly for Brompton Court. Except he didn't have the words yet.

"Too bad. Just think of the story I could have told my children one day. Drat."

A picture came into his mind of her making children with a man she'd meet after she left Brompton Court. He didn't like it. "I'm sure it will be charming. Don't say a word. I'm helping you inside."

She gave him her arm and he took it, satisfied that he had her now rather than that bastard, the future father of her children.

He didn't let her go, not even as he opened the heavy front door. Silently, they made their way through the long hallway to the great hall. He brought them to a halt. Staring across the gray slate floor monks had walked on centuries ago, staring up at the steps, worn, uneven, and slippery, he said, "I'll walk you up to the library. I'm assuming you'd like to check on things there before you lie down."

She gave him a tight smile. Her skin had paled. This long walk wasn't so easy for her. "Good idea. I don't want to take a header and end up back in the hospital, comfortable as it may be."

That had him holding onto her all the way up.

"Thank you," she said as he threw open the doors to the library. She headed toward the frightfully ugly sofa she'd said she'd saved from the bin man. "I think I'll rest for a second." She eased down, lay her head against the couch's back, and closed her eyes.

As always when she was still—and silent—he marveled at how small she was, though there was nothing tiny about the reality of her, not when her eyes sparked with amusement and devilry, or when her smile tilted up with mischief.

She sighed and he knew no matter her saying she was ready to get back to her work, she was not. He bent to touch the bandage at her hairline. She opened her eyes.

"I need to spend a few minutes with Mr. Pratt. Before I do, though, there's one thing I'd like you to do."

"Yes?"

There. That spark in her eyes. This time it didn't foretell a tease, but rather a little wariness.

"Promise me again. You won't climb on any ladders for at least a week, perhaps more. You'll leave the climbing to the person I'm hiring to help you. I'm firm on this, Livvy." Before she could tell him to naff off, he added, "Of course, whoever I hire will take direction from you."

She gave him one of her tiny grins. "No problem. I promise to remain earthbound until I feel better. But there's going to have to be a quid for your quo."

He stiffened. "And what would that be?"

"You have to tell me why you hate this house."

All that texting over the last weeks had revealed some of the Jack inside the duke. It hadn't revealed everything. Livvy wasn't surprised when she got that blank look he was so good at. If there were going to be more between them—including kisses—she needed to unmask the duke further. "Why would a rational man like you have a hate-on for stone, wood, and a lot of useless furniture?"

He turned on his heel and paced away from her. She savored the look of him, all lean, lithe elegance, perfect in every part of him, physical and cerebral. He ran a hand across his scalp. Livvy's fingers twitched.

"It's complicated."

"What isn't?" she muttered.

He drifted on, stopping here and there, around the perimeter of the library. He glanced out the windows. "What have you done to this room? It's different."

Narrowing her eyes at him, she said, "If you call applying a little furniture polish and vacuuming different. Answer the question, please."

He ran his fingers across a shelf. "I was a boy when I first saw this place. It was right after my father became duke. I remember thinking it dark and forbidding. It felt…" He turned to face her. "Wrong."

"How can a place be wrong?" The blank look was gone, leaving in its place an odd vulnerability.

He stopped next to the long, ugly table with its scratched and nicked surface on which she placed the books she took down from each shelf for sorting.

Putting a hand on the back of the chair pushed up against it, he smoothed down the sweater she'd hung there, the one she put on when it got colder than she could stand in this already cold room.

"Everything changed when my father became duke. We moved from the rather cramped—for two adults and four children—house in Camden where we'd lived as long as I could remember to the grandiose town house in Kensington belonging to the

Dukes of Brompton. At first, my mates were happy to visit me in the posh part of London. But then came the jealousy, little things said, and then not such little things, the bits about the rich boy. I knew soon enough I could no longer count them as friends." He gave her a self-mocking glance. "Poor kid, right?"

She wanted to take his hand and squeeze it, tell him with her touch that she felt his pain because that's what it was beneath the words. "How old were you?"

"Thirteen. Neither fish nor fowl."

Livvy remembered thirteen. She'd grown a hard shell by then, past trying to change her father's mind about her worth. Instead, she'd made it a point to do everything she could to annoy him. "So you changed schools, I guess."

"My mother insisted I go to a school more fitting my new, elevated state as a ducal heir and so I was enrolled at Eton. It didn't suit me. All the boys thought I was an upstart. Where before my old mates thought I'd become too posh, at Eton they thought me a social climber. Who knew I could be both?"

She ignored that bit of acidic humor meant to mask remembered pain. "But all this isn't why you hate Brompton Court."

"No, it's not."

She waited.

"Between my old life and my new, my father became my best mate. Even that was short-term. He spent less time with me as the call of the dukedom grew louder. No more trips to the print shop. He did, however, make a number of trips here. Sometimes he asked me to go along, and I did. Then I went away to uni and became something of a stranger to my family."

"That's natural." Although, as Livvy thought about it, she'd always been a stranger to her family. She gave herself a shake. This was about him, not her. She needed to listen.

He'd propped his forearms on his thighs and stared downward, rubbing his hands together. "Then came Freddie Camville and his Ponzi scheme, my family's nightmare. Inside my nineteen-year old self was the little boy that wanted to blame my father for once more mucking up my life."

Again, the silence. Then, "My father asked me to join him the weekend he decided to come up to Lincolnshire to get away from the reporters for a bit—they'd been chasing him, all of us, really. But I didn't go, because I was sulking."

Jack came to his feet and paced over to the window. Hands on his hips, he stared out. "Later that evening, or perhaps it was morning—we're not sure and the coroner couldn't say—my father died here in the library. They only found him so soon because my mother rang up the police when he failed to answer her calls."

He lifted his head to stare upward. "I've always wondered if I could have saved him if I'd said yes."

She'd asked a question. She'd found out more than she'd expected.

"I despised the dukedom from the first. As a boy, I decided it took both my happy life and my father. And then it truly did. Yes, the court is only brick and mortar." He made a scoffing sound. "Falling down brick and mortar. I shouldn't hate it, my sensible self says. Perhaps, one day, I won't."

He swung around and gave her a self-mocking look. "Sorry for being so unforgivably Byronic, but does that answer your question?"

"Yes, it does. It *is* about furniture polish."

A baffled look crossed his face. She wasn't stopping there. He'd allowed her to peer beneath the layers of his *noli-me-tangere* self, and she'd seen the pain locked up inside. It burned away at him. She needed to do something about that.

"You know, Jack. If I were you, I'd cut myself some slack. Show me a nineteen- year-old male with all the typical hormonal crap you guys seem to go through, and then tell me. You really would have understood what your father was coping with?" She gave him her most extravagant eye roll. "Give me a break."

A slew of emotional reactions passed across his face until he smiled, a crooked smile, but a smile. "So you're rejecting my Byronic angst out of hand?"

"None of this has anything to do with Byron. As for the furniture polish, what I'm saying is it's just a house—or do I call it a mansion or a castle?

Whatever, maybe it helps to think of what it was for your father. A treasure. If he'd lived and you'd had more time to travel up here with him, you might have seen it through his eyes. I'm going to bet from what little I've heard about your dad that he saw this place as beautiful and family history. Most people don't have stories about their ancestors going back three hundred years. Look how lucky you are."

She stood and walked around the way he had. "I have different feelings for this place than you do. When I'm in this room, I feel the pull of it. Weird…sometimes it feels like I'm back in the womb."

He'd decided to follow her on her circuit around the library. "What an odd thing to say."

Livvy reversed her direction and walked up to the table where someone—likely Jack—had put the folder that held Caleb's letters. She huffed a self-deprecating laugh. "It's odd, a little strange even for me who believes in this kind of thing." She touched a finger to the folder's worn surface.

"It's like in another life I lived here. The way the floor is uneven and creaks when you step on the boards right in front of that bookcase…" She pointed to the ones in question. "I knew they would creak. The circulation of the air, how it carries the scent of old leather into every part of the room, I knew how it would smell."

"You believe in reincarnation, then, do you?"

She'd caught his attention. "I do. Is that so bad?

Maybe I want to find Jessamine's diaries because it will help me remember a life I lived here."

One eyebrow went up. "That is a bit—"

She winked. "Weird, right?"

He laughed as she'd meant him to. She'd spoken of furniture polish in that wise-ass way because he'd shown her his realest self. A man with an amazing sense of humor, a man she was hot for. To find that he had a deep self-awareness so rare in highly successful men… This was going to complicate things for her more.

She wouldn't risk telling him how. She turned the portfolio over and slid the note out. "To the point I was trying to make. He wanted to explore your family history."

"That's my dad's handwriting." A sad smile flickered across Jack's face. He took the note from her. As Livvy slid the sheaf of papers out, he said, "What do you think these letters will tell us about Jessamine?"

"I'm not sure. I do know Caleb and Jessamine were half brother and sister. His father married Jessamine's mother, who was a Beresford. Brompton Court became Caleb's father's when they married. Though Caleb was a staunch Catholic, after Charles I was beheaded, he pledged loyalty to the Protestant, Cromwell."

"A hypocrite, in other words," Jack noted.

"Major hypocrite. When Charles was back on the throne, he suddenly become all friend-of-the-Stuarts again."

"A seventeenth century toady." Jack placed the note down on Livvy's work table.

"Jessamine died here sometime in the spring of 1660, after giving birth to James, just as Charles was about to be back on the throne. Then, when James was six or seven, Caleb put himself forward to foster him."

"I marvel at how much you know about my family, which is considerably more than I do. Did he foster James?"

"He did."

"Why do you suppose Caleb wanted James in his household? He was a bastard, father unknown."

"I'm surprised, Jack. You didn't guess?"

"Why don't you tell me?" he said, features deadpan and Livvy knew he knew, but was going to let her tell him.

"He never claimed James as one of his, which was odd. Charles owned up to so many of his bastards. The question is why didn't he own up to fathering James because it's a pretty good bet James was Charles' son."

CHAPTER TEN

Jack was not looking forward to what would happen when she found the proof. He would have to tell her everything then. "Lascivious as Charles was?" The laugh he gave her was careful, not mocking. "Half of England could be descended from him."

"I think you're in that half. Did you ever think of that?"

"I have not," he lied.

Later that day, as Henry drove him back to London, he sat, as always, on the right side, any papers he'd carried with him in a neat pile on the left. Henry's monologue, which usually provided him with white noise if he were working, or anesthesia if he weren't, didn't work this time.

For all the years since his father died, alone, Jack's nightmares had a theme that didn't vary. In them, Jack saw himself reaching out. *I'm sorry, Dad.*

Please forgive me. But his father only smiled, shook his head, said *I can't hear you.* And then he fell to the floor. Jack woke up each time just as his father fell. He didn't need a therapist—not that he would ever visit one—to tell him what that meant. He lived with the guilt, though he wished he didn't have to live with the nightmare.

Jack had shocked himself, telling Livvy what he dreamt about. He'd never told his mother or his sisters. The way Livvy looked at him after she asked her question... *You have to tell me why you hate this house...* there was no challenge in it, or pity. There was only a request for understanding. It was all he needed, it seemed, to unburden himself. Afterward, while she was describing her connection to the house—*his* house—realized he felt better that he had.

He supposed he could learn to tolerate Brompton Court while Livvy inhabited it. Not that he would tell her any such thing. It was enough that she had edged her way into his life on a level no one else had.

His mobile dinged. Grateful for the interruption, he reached for it.

> Jack, I forgot to tell you. Madelyn bought a space heater for my bedroom, which is a good thing. Otherwise I'd be freezing my...well, you call it an arse. I call it an ass!

He laid his head back, closed his eyes and smiled. She did that. Made him forget the problems he was dealing with. No, it wasn't that he forgot them. It was that he could manage them better.

All during the following week, each time he read Livvy's texts—and they came all the time now—electronic conversations, really—he could put Max and Robert Browne and MaryBeth's failure to meet deadlines in a place where he could manage them.

> Jack, I'm not climbing on things. Yes, Archie Henderson is really nice. I do appreciate you hiring him to help me, though you didn't have to. Did you know Archie retired from the postal service? Anyway, he must have been born a Sherpa! He's been up and down the new ladder, bringing me everything I want to look at. This morning, he brought me a first edition of *A Tale of Two Cities*.

Jack smiled into the silence of his office. I can feel your excitement.

> One or more of your ancestors must have been great collectors, but didn't do much reading. Well, at least the ancestor who bought this book didn't. I think I'm the first one to crack it open! And no, I don't mean crack. I mean peek!

He could picture her, curled up on that ugly chaise longue, legs pulled up under her, with one of Dicken's best in her hands. He keyed rapidly.

> Are you casting aspersions on my forebears? On second thought, please do. From what you've been telling me, they deserve every aspersion cast upon them.

It didn't take her long to answer.

> When it comes to your forebears, you are quick to asperse. Have I made that word up? I like it! Anyway, I decided to take a break from searching for the diaries and am re-reading the Tale. Before you have a heart attack, not the one I found. I ordered it on my e-reader. I'm up to the part where Lucie realizes her father is alive. Oh, and in case you were wondering, I haven't found the diaries.

Though the tone of her texts was unfailingly lighthearted, he could feel her frustration. She'd find them, eventually. He was not looking forward to that.

His door opened a crack. Isabella peeked in. "Your mother called to ask if you would give her a raincheck. She has to take Monty to the vet."

She was standing him up again. "Of course I will."

As the door closed behind Isabella, Jack sighed. At some point his mother would forgive him for banning Monty from Board meetings. He'd had no choice but to do it. Doing doggy business in a corner of the room whilst business was being conducted? Not a lovely thing.

Looking down at his mobile, he scrolled back through Livvy's messages. She wanted him. Her eyes, her smiles, her body told him that, even the words she wrote, told him. What would it take for her to show him? And when? If she didn't, he would. And soon.

He jumped up. As he strode into the anteroom, Isabella looked up. "I'm going up to Lincolnshire tomorrow morning, first thing. Change the meetings I have for the next few days to video calls. Adjust my calendar and I'll look it over in the morning."

The next morning, Henry got him to Brompton Court in enough time to make a scheduled nine a.m. meeting with Pratt at his offices in Moreham. Going over what needed to be fixed, thinking of what not fixing them meant, Jack knew Livvy was right. No matter his memories, Brompton Court was a building that needed renovating.

During their discussion, Pratt surprised him by admitting to a broad knowledge of Anstruther family history.

Once Jack was satisfied that all was in hand for the repairs to begin, he made his way to Brompton Court. By that time, it was late enough in the morning that he knew he would find Livvy in the library. Since she wasn't doing any climbing, he was sure she'd be at work on her book.

He detoured first to the kitchen for a cup of coffee and something to eat. In the kitchen was a surprise. Livvy at the table. She looked up from her mobile phone, propped up against a pair of salt and pepper shakers. She gave him one of her cheeky smiles.

"Hi again," she said. "Tell me I'm wrong, but in the last few weeks, you've made the trip from London to Lincolnshire more times than you have in the last ten years. Could it be that you're learning to like this place?"

He didn't think she was fishing for a compliment that he'd made all his trips because of her, which of course, he had. "Feeling better are you?" He felt better, seeing her. He took a scone out of a basket set in the center of the table.

She'd dispensed with the sling, which lay on the table, folded up, next to her. "I'm good. I'm ready to climb ladders, and would, if I could convince my Sherpa that the library isn't Mount Everest."

He held up a hand. "I hired Archie to protect you against yourself. It sounds as if he's doing a brilliant job."

"Naturally, you would think so, Mr. I-Am-In-Charge. But if you're so worried about me I think you should know my temperature's spiking with cabin fever."

He snorted a laugh and set the scone on a plate. "We cannot have that, can we? Why not let's do something."

Her eyebrows flickered. "Is that a plural pronoun?"

He'd surprised her? Well, good. It was nice to be ahead of her, for once. "Clever woman."

She half-stood to reach for the coffee pot on the counter. "What did you have in mind?"

He set a hand on her shoulder and nudged her back down. He poured her a cup and took one for himself. "How about an excursion to see something besides these walls?"

She leaned forward. "Wonderful as these walls are—minus the ones that need fixing—getting away from them sounds like an awesome idea."

He put the pot back on its caddy and sat. "I have a particular place in mind. It's nearby."

She put her good elbow on the table. "Ooh, the mystery."

Since he'd met Livvy, Jack had discovered a heretofore hidden trait: he liked to tease. Although, so far, she was the only one he teased. "No mystery. I told Pratt why you're here."

"Pratt? Your land manager? Why?"

"He knows a thing or two about my family history and thinks Jessamine is a worthwhile subject for your book." He pulled out his mobile and drew his chair next to hers. "He sent me a link to a magazine he reads about oddities of English history."

She leaned forward and he breathed in the scent of her light, flowery perfume. "Can I see?" She held out a hand for his phone.

Perfume was something a woman dabbed on herself. The most common reaction Jack had to perfume was a desire to step out of range. Breathing Livvy's in, he wanted to get closer, bury his nose in her hair, the more to surround himself with her essence.

She took the mobile from him and squinted at the screen. "This looks like a gravestone."

"It is. It's supposed to be Jessamine's."

Her eyes widened and she tapped to open the rest of the story.

While she paged up, he leaned closer to breathe in more of her. On what part of her body had she sprayed it besides her hair?

She handed the phone back to him. "Where is this graveyard?"

Imagining how he would discover all the parts of her body where she'd dabbed scent, it took him a moment to answer. "In an out of the way place a mile from a village that is itself out of the way."

"And that village is called…?"

"It's called Bisby."

***

Jack was standing in the great room below the painting of Charles II, his forebear, making James the first of the Brompton Dukes, when he heard Livvy's steps. He took a breath and turned and see her come down the stairs.

All rational thought flew from his mind.

She was a vision, all smiles, and dressed for an outing. He enjoyed it for seconds only before frowning. Yes, she held onto the balustrade, a damn good thing. The steps had been trod on by centuries of Anstruthers. Steps that were hard like the rock they'd been carved from were especially dangerous for a woman still recovering from a concussion. When she got to the bottom and set foot on the slate floor, he let go of the breath he'd been holding. "Are you ready, then?"

"So ready." She gave him a grin. "I feel like I'm about to be released from prison."

She'd pulled her hair back into a pony tail. The bandage at her hairline was gone, as were the stiches, taken out yesterday. All that remained was a scar. He hated that scar.

He held out a hand to her. "Let me help you escape."

She took his hand. "Jack, who knew you had accomplice-ment in you?"

It was a simple touch. It should have meant nothing. Except for the jolt of energy that passed through the capillaries in the tips of his fingers to heat the blood in his palm and wrist, and then every part of him. He kept her hand in his. "Another one of your made-up words. It's odd how they always work."

She cocked her head to one side. In her hazel eyes was a wicked glint. Today she'd chosen to wear a red, high-necked, hip-length jumper and black skin-tight trousers. On her feet she wore a pair of flat-heeled shoes. But her feet were not what knocked him back, nor the jumper, though the way her trousers fit her hips and bum did hold his gaze captive. It was that, with her hand in his, everything felt right.

"There's more where that came from." She squeezed his hand.

He felt that tightening of her hand in his groin. He took a steadying breath. "I expect so."

"When you told me the name of that village near where Jessamine is supposed to be buried, it rang a bell, but I couldn't think why."

As he led her through the long, narrow hallway to the Court's front door, a frisson raised the hair on the back of his neck. "But you have remembered now, correct?"

"I have. Bisby is where The Ocular is located. It's run by Annie Lukin, brilliant American chef. Have you got an objection to having dinner there?"

Annie Lukin happened to be Charlie Camville's wife. And the Duchess of Lindsey. "It's almost impossible to get a reservation there on short notice."

Jack didn't want his complicated thoughts about the Duke of Lindsey to interrupt the pleasure of this day.

"We can try. And if you're worried about the expense, we can go Dutch, which means—"

"I know what it means." He took her hand from his and pulled it into the crook of his elbow. "No matter what we do today there will be no going Dutch."

Livvy waited while Jack went to get his car. She supposed she was excited about finding Jessamine's grave, but why? It wouldn't be like there'd be an arrow on the headstone and carved below, THIS WAY TO THE DIARIES. Being with Jack? Now *that* she could get excited about: remembering the feel of his lips on her hand, the warmth in his eyes, the way he held her face in his hands so tenderly as he pressed his lips gently against her skin, against her lips.

He'd talked to Pratt about her. Why? If not for those kisses at the hospital, she would have thought it was just him making conversation. One good thing, though. At least he no longer thought she was a shill for her father.

As the Tesla snuck up on her—the only warning, the sound of its tires on the gravel—she blinked away her navel gazing.

He brought the car to a halt and hopped out. "Please don't think you're going to open that door."

"Oh, yeah. I forgot." She made a face. "When I fell, my hand stopped working." But she let him take the handle because she wanted to feel the heat of him on her back and shoulders. She wanted to think about stepping back one little step, so she would be in his arms.

But she didn't do any of that. And then it was too late; they were driving away over Brompton Court's potholes and she'd missed the opportunity to say, listen Jack, inquiring minds and stuff, are we just taking day trips in your fancy car? Or eating at Michelin starred restaurants, she hoped? Or maybe you're interested in sharing that bed you bought for me, maybe even tonight?

Despite the kisses, Lord Enigmatic could still give her the side eye, no smile on his severe but so hot mouth and say something depressingly Brit like, I beg your pardon. What was she supposed to make of that?

"I've been all over Google Earth," she noted. Yup, she could talk about that. "I've taken virtual rides down lanes and paths in the county, even to Lincoln where I climbed that amazingly steep street to the castle and the cathedral, but I never found anything else about Jessamine."

He grunted.

"That's why it's going to be awesome to see Jessamine's grave." Not really.

"Quite."

They were back to that word again.

"How long has Henry driven for you?"

Lord Monk Man gave her that side eye he was so good at. "Why do you think that interesting?"

"Because I can't get you to talk about anything else."

He grinned, and didn't that bring the sunshine out on a gray day?

"Point made. It was when I needed to visit my various properties around the country."

"Smart. You could work while he's driving. Henry told me London traffic is a bitch."

"Quite."

"Yes quite."

He pressed his lips together against another smile because he knew she was teasing him. She touched his shoulder, because she could and because she wanted to. "Don't try so hard not to laugh. You'll give yourself a hernia."

He grinned. "That would be painful. How's this?" He glanced at her and he was Jack unadulterated. Smiling eyes, smiling mouth. She wanted to kiss that mouth. Have his body. She wanted his mind, too, which he worked really hard not to give up. But she'd do none of it when he was driving. She didn't want to be a patient in a hospital again.

She made it up to herself by staring at his hands and fingers where they rested on the steering wheel. She'd read somewhere that sex hormones determined the length of a person's fingers. His were well-shaped at the tips. And long. Could it really be that—

"I've had to be hard-nosed for quite some time."

She blinked. "Sorry, did we start a conversation about something else and I was sleeping?"

"No. I want to tell you about Chalcott House because we've never discussed it." And suddenly he was all seriousness.

"Okay. I'm all ears." And all antennae, too. She was about to be on the receiving end of not just the story of Chalcott House but more on the life of Jack, the Duke of Brompton.

"When my father died, I knew it was going to be up to me to sort out what Freddie Camville had done."

"What was that like?"

He gave her a quick glance before focusing again on the road. "To what do you refer?"

Even when making conversation he was still wary. "Getting Chalcott House back."

"I didn't have to get it back. We'd lost much of everything else and I did have to work to get that back. But Chalcott House had been too insignificant to be included as collateral. Building it up? That was difficult. In the end, Chalcott House was what saved me."

"You were fortunate."

"I didn't know what I was. Glad, angry, confused. All three, I suppose. I knew I needed to get work for the press, which was the only way I was going to make enough money to support my family. That happened when Marybeth came to me with the first book in her Red Dragon Saga. No one else would touch it, it seemed. More fools they."

As they drove on, Jack told her about how he was salesman, office manager, and press operator and how he kept his mother, three sisters, and himself housed and fed.

As he spoke, Livvy wondered whether that was when Jack got the lean and hungry look.

"It took me five years and publishing Marybeth's books before I had enough capital to buy back the local newspapers my father lost in the debacle. From then to purchasing the *Daily Prime*, it was a fairly steep climb. But that was my goal. No, that's wrong. It was my obsession."

"Why ever did you buy the *Daily Prime*? Wasn't it one of their reporters who wrote those articles that destroyed your dad's reputation?"

"So you knew that." He shrugged. "I knew a good investment when I saw one." He paused. "It gave me the opportunity to sack that reporter."

"Ow."

"I gave him time to find other work."

"Did he?"

"Yes."

"Not everyone would be so nice to someone who screwed them over."

"One should never burn bridges."

Livvy chewed on that. Her father burned bridges, people, whole communities, and while doing it, enjoyed every moment.

"In fact," Jack continued, "the reporter, Tom Quigley. I speak to him on occasion."

"You are a complicated man."

He slowed into a curve. "Is complicated a synonym for bad?"

"I'll let you know."

They drove on, silent again. For once, he'd talked, been chatty even. He'd stunned her because he told her more than about Chalcott House. He'd given her another glimpse inside himself. Yes he was a calculating Cassius, monk-man, whose ice-sharp eyes could destroy with a cutting glance. That he would help someone who had hurt him, destroyed his father even?

She brooded. Maybe the Jack who flew up from London to be with her was the same one who gave that reporter time to look for a job. Maybe he'd taken her on a ride because he felt sorry that she'd been cooped up. Maybe he was making sure she was being cared for because it was the right thing to do. Maybe he was just being nice when nice was the last thing she wanted him to be.

She sagged into her seat. Maybe she was the only one thinking it would be way, way more than nice for them to be lovers. Maybe she needed to get over herself.

She didn't turn her head to look at him. Instead she stared ahead, a lot more than a little depressed.

He slowed into a decline and a cluster of buildings ahead. She sat up. They'd arrived in Bisby.

How fortunate, were the people of Bisby, Jack thought. Until the now Duchess of Lindsey had opened her renowned restaurant, it had been a place time had forgotten. As Jack drove down the High Street, they had to slow for construction. Lumber stood in piles in the street, a cement mixer churned out cement for new pavement. He'd heard the project was being driven by the duchess, reputed to be a serial do-gooder.

They passed the last of Bisby's stores and came upon a largish manor house. There was a car parked in front, a Jag. If he were to guess, Jack would say it was Lindsey's. Interesting, that. If he and Livvy were to stop at The Ocular for lunch, would he be there? And what would it be like to see him?

For years, Jack had kept a distance from the duke. Charlie—he'd become Duke of Lindsey less than a year previous—was well-respected in London's business community. And he'd been not much more than a boy, just as Jack had been, when the debacle had occurred.

He stepped on the gas and they cruised by. Their destination was not much farther, down a narrower lane. As Livvy sat straight up and leaned forward, he slowed and came to a stop in front of a white stone church with a modest bell tower.

Almost before Jack brought the car to a halt, she threw open her door and flung herself out. Without looking to see if he followed, she set out on the path to the graveyard off to the right.

"Wait, Livvy. Not there."

She slowed and looked over her shoulder. "Why? We're looking for a grave."

"Jessamine will be interred inside the church."

"That's how they do it in England?" She retraced her steps back to him.

"If they were gentry, yes. They were buried beneath memorial brasses."

She wrinkled her nose. "I'm adding that bit to my treasure trove of inconsequential knowledge," she said, making for the church's entrance, the hem of her red jumper flapping in her wake. Jack stood for a second to appreciate the way joy seemed embedded, even in her clothing. To her retreating back, he murmured, "Sweet Princess Leia, your enthusiasm has caught me."

It had flagged there, in the car as they'd approached Bisby. He didn't know why. Most shocking, though, was him coming to realize how her enthusiasm, or lack of it, impacted his.

He followed her inside the church and almost ran into her where she'd come to a halt at the entrance. A typical parish church, the space was all white-plastered walls and rounded vaulting. The pews were well-worn, darkened wood. At the front under the chancel stood a pulpit.

Placing one hand at the small of her back, he pointed with the other. "There. At the front. If there are any brasses, they'll be there."

She hurried forward. He followed.

There were quite a number of brasses, but none for Jessamine Beresford.

Livvy frowned. "Maybe Jessamine is in the graveyard after all."

The graveyard was dank and dark. Tree branches dipped low in places, leaves piled up against gravestones. The dirt around each was hard-packed. Some of the death dates, though hard to make out, read in the 1700s and 1800s.

They looked everywhere. Jack concluded, "If Jessamine is buried here, she's buried in a grave with someone else's name on it."

Livvy blew out a hard breath "Maybe Pratt was wrong."

"Perhaps he was. It was a good try, though." Jack started back toward the car. He stopped when he realized there wasn't a crunching of leaves behind him that said Livvy was following. He turned back. "Aren't you coming?"

"I'm going to take a walk around the back of the church. You know, just in case."

He allowed himself a little smile. When she had the bit in her teeth, she was impossible to stop. He strolled after her along the uneven path.

"Jack, you have to see this."

He picked up his pace to the back of the church where he found her standing by a small fenced-in plot. She looked up and grinned at him. "Here she is. Your grandmother."

For an odd moment, Jack thought she meant his mother's mother, but then he remembered Livvy's piquant sense of humor and stared down at the headstone inside the fenced-in area. And there it was: the final resting place of Jessamine Beresford, his many times great-grandmother.

Unlike the other graves, this one was well-cared for. The iron enclosure was painted black, not a spot of rust anywhere. A clipped frieze of shrubbery surrounded the enclosure. Though it was almost three-and-a-half-centuries old, the legend on the stone was easy to read. Someone over the years had made sure the name and death date did not fade into history.

"I didn't think this would be exciting, but it is." Livvy flipped up the gate's latch. It swung open soundlessly and she stepped into the enclosure. "There's a difference between reading about someone in a book and seeing that she really existed, even if she's now dead."

A strange zing coursed through him. He knew what she meant. He'd never given more than a passing thought to the life of Jessamine Beresford. By sheer force of will, Livvy had pulled him into her search for his ancestress and she'd become more real to him the more time Livvy spent at Brompton Court.

Livvy crouched down. "You have to wonder. Why is this grave so well kept? And why wasn't she buried closer to Brompton Court? Other than the name and death date, some of the inscription is a little hard to read." She ran one hand across the front of the stone. "In Youthful Years…Devine Power…in Grave…"

He crouched down next to her, squinted at the incised text, and read, "The Sound of Trump Do Summon Me to Rise."

A ray of sunshine cut through the clouds and illuminated the headstone. Livvy cocked her head. "Do you believe in spirits?" She held a hand up to the sunlight and wiggled her fingers in the dust motes. "They're telling us they're glad we're here." She palmed the feathery plantings that marched around the bottom of the headstone. "There's another word, here."

Smiling at her whimsy, he helped her flatten more shrubbery. He turned his head to look at her. "It's rather a lovely word to be found on a gravestone. Or anywhere. Dearling."

In the stark relief of daylight, he saw her every feature. Her eyes, hazel with tinges of true green in their irises. Freckles he'd not noticed before that crossed her nose and the crest of her cheeks. She hadn't bothered to color her lips this morning. They were moist and plump.

"It's such an anachronistic word." He shifted closer.

"I'm willing to bet this gravestone was ordered by someone who loved Jessamine." She turned her head and gazed avidly at his mouth.

Their lips were only inches apart. "Yes. Someone who loved her."

"And maybe," she said, her voice lowered to a whisper, "it explains why someone at this church is taking care of this grave when none of the others seem to be cared for."

He skated a finger across one cheek. "Perhaps."

Her eyes closed and her lips parted on a soft exhale.

As if the gods needed to remind Jack that they were on dangerous ground, the church bells rang.

Her eyes opened wide. She took in a quick breath.

He held out a hand to help her up. She took it and stood, never taking her eyes off him.

There was an awareness now between them that was new.

"Maybe I shouldn't have bent down that way," she said, her voice breathy. "You know, my head. Recovery."

"Let's go see if anyone is inside the church now," he said. Her breathlessness had nothing to do with recovery.

CHAPTER ELEVEN

Livvy knew. The moment he crouched down next to her, the moment they touched at shoulder, hip, and knee, the way he turned to stare at her lips, the way she'd begun to hear his breaths, Jack was thinking of her, not Jessamine.

She wasn't thinking of Jessamine, either. She'd been wrong about why he was with her today, and didn't that make her feel like doing cartwheels?

She didn't let go of his hand as he led her around to the front of the church and inside. The day was cool and his hand was a center of warmth and steadiness and safety.

This time, the church was occupied. Standing at the front was a slender man in dark slacks, and a light blue sweater. He looked up as they entered. Smiling, he crossed the church's stone floor toward them.

"Hello. I'm Peter Harcourt. Welcome to St. Columba's. How can I help?"

Livvy reached out to shake his hand. "We were wondering about a grave you have that's separate from the rest in the churchyard."

The man brightened. "You mean Jessamine Beresford's grave. What would you like to know?"

Livvy looked at Jack. He, naturally, didn't react, which was okay. She could react enough for both of them. "How is it her grave is so well taken care of? And why is the grave separated from the rest?"

"I believe I can answer both those questions." He turned and motioned for them to follow. "There's an agreement." The man stepped into a spare room to the side. The room held a table, a chair, and a gray metal four-drawer cabinet. Unlocking the cabinet, he bent to slide open the bottom drawer. Flipping through a series of folders, he stopped at one near the back and pulled it out. "Here we are."

Opening the folder, he laid it on the table. "This is not the original. That one lies in the Cathedral Museum, although I doubt anyone has looked for it in decades, if ever." He turned the book so they could see the entry in question. "There was a sum of money donated to pay for the upkeep of the grave. It tells us there can be no grave placed near hers. It's to stand alone, in perpetuity."

Livvy stared hard at the cramped print and wondered how the man assumed anyone else could read it, other than a doctoral student, whose specialty was the Restoration.

He tapped the page. "I'll summarize it for you. It says the Dukes of Brompton are to make sure the funds left for the maintenance of the grave are well invested so as to ensure there will be no lapse in care."

"I have another question," Livvy said. "There's a word carved in the stone at the bottom of the grave: Dearling. Do you know who might have had it engraved there?"

"Whoever it was, we must assume the fellow was very much in love with the lady." He stroked his chin. "I would go a step further. Assuming it was he who made the endowment, he wanted to be sure the love he felt for her would be remembered forever."

The entire time in that little room in St. Columba's, Livvy remained aware of Jack's hand at the small of her back. It messed with her ability to concentrate on what the vicar was saying. Even as they said their goodbyes, she felt that hand like a piece of clothing she never wanted to take off.

Jack only let go when he opened the passenger side door for her. As he started the car, she said, "For sure, whoever it was who loved Jessamine enough to pay for the upkeep of her grave forever, I'm going to guess it wasn't Caleb. I doubt he would call his sister, Dearling."

"I agree, and if it were, he wouldn't have had her buried so far from Brompton Court. I—" He held up one finger and said, "Hold, please. My mobile is reminding me that someone's left me a message." He pulled his phone from his pocket, looked at it, and then activated the message. He frowned. "Didn't you say you wanted to visit The Ocular?"

"I did."

"That message was from the Duke of Lindsey, Charlie Camville. He heard I was visiting Brompton Court and asked if I would like to stop by the restaurant."

"What do you suppose brought that on?"

Silent so long, Livvy didn't think he would answer. But then, "He suggests since we are both major landholders in the county and here at the same time, we might want to take advantage of the opportunity— since it has been so rare in the past— to discuss business."

"Don't you think it's strange that he should call you just like that?"

Jack stared at the road, silent, before answering. "I think we should make your wish come true and stop at The Ocular."

So, he wasn't going to tell her he thought it was strange. She felt a pang of disappointment but then rejected it. They were making progress. She could hope. "What a great idea." She rubbed her hands together, pretending anticipation. "The Ocular, I can't wait. Dinner at a Best of Britain restaurant with two dukes. How exciting to be me."

Jack continued toward Bisby. "Don't assume a meal will be in the offing."

"I'm channeling positivity, Mr. Caution." Her positivity wasn't only about the meal.

Minutes later, they were driving onto Bisby's High Street. Livvy pointed. "There. Behind that pile of stones on the sidewalk. That's The Ocular."

Jack parked the car away from all the construction site rubble. He cautioned Livvy to be careful where she stepped.

Reaching their destination, Livvy studied the restaurant's front. "Wow. The door is not exactly what you would call Best of Britain worthy."

Holding the knob, Jack said, "It's not worthy because of the door."

Livvy wrinkled her nose at him. "True."

He kept his hand where it was.

She shifted from one foot to the other. "Are we going to stand here or go in?"

He tightened his lips and pushed the door open.

As they stepped into a cool interior, a strange sight greeted them. Two people, a short, very pregnant woman in a white apron that barely covered her belly, black hair in a braid down her back, and a tall, dark-haired man in worn jeans and black sweater fought for control of a mammoth pot. They didn't know they had company.

Jack closed the door with a snap.

The combatants stopped mid-tug and looked up. With a deft maneuver, control of the cookware went to the male, who smiled and said, "Brompton, is it?" He came forward. "Lindsey here. Welcome."

The man Jack had avoided his entire adult life had embraced the pot with one arm and held out his opposite hand to him. "How do you do, Lindsey," Jack said, and took his fellow duke's hand. It felt less strange than he'd thought it would.

"I hope you'll call me Charlie and I hope I can call you Jack."

"I'd like that." Jack realized it was true.

Eyes on her husband, the diminutive woman grabbed the pot from his arm, and transferred it to the stove, where if Jack had to guess, she'd wanted it to begin with. Then, she trundled back to them. "Good to meet you at last. I'm Annie."

She turned to Livvy. "As you may have noticed, I'm expecting. My husband doesn't listen when I tell him just because I'm pregnant doesn't mean I should stop picking up pots—"

"But not pots that weigh more than you do," he interrupted.

"As I was saying, picking up pots, which I've done my entire adult life."

"Annie doesn't seem to understand that because she has, doesn't mean she should now," Charlie said, gazing at his wife, love and frustration shining in his eyes.

Jack felt like they'd intruded on a private moment. Looking away, he scrutinized the room. It was a surprisingly small space for such a famous restaurant. But, with its dark wooden floor, lighter paneling, round tables spaced out, and in the tables' centers, lovely pots of herbs, it radiated warmth.

"Enough of this chit-chat." Annie waved a hand. "It's lunchtime and I'm making pumpkin gnocchi. You're invited to join us if you like."

"We'll say yes, as long as it's not an imposition." Livvy cast a triumphant glance at Jack. "And I'm Livvy."

"It's not an imposition." Annie took Livvy's arm and urged her farther into the charming room.

"Jack?" Charlie indicated they should follow the women toward a table that stood squarely in the pathway to the kitchen. Annie had Livvy's hand in hers and skirted around it. "We'll do a quick tour of the kitchen. Then we can eat."

"It's rather a good thing that the kitchen is small." Charlie gave Annie a mock frowning look. "Otherwise my wife would be walking longer distances than she should at this time of her life."

Annie grabbed a handful of Charlie's shirt. "Come here." She pulled until he'd bent far enough down for her to plant a kiss on his lips. Then she grinned at Jack. "Isn't it cute the way he worries about me?"

Natural English reticence had Jack looking away again, in this case toward Livvy. "Worry can impact all of us."

Annie's gaze made a quick foray from one of them to the other. "Curiosity shouldn't kill the cat, but what are you talking about?"

It fell to Jack to tell the story of the ladder. Frowns of concern from Charlie and Annie traveled Livvy's way.

Charlie guided Livvy to the table. "I think you should sit and forego the tour of the kitchen."

"I agree," added Annie. "It's small and only interesting to me."

Giving Jack an I-told-you-so grin, Livvy said, "Since I'm about to be treated like a VIP in a starred Michelin restaurant, I'll sit wherever."

If he hadn't known it before, the meal that followed told Jack The Ocular's reputation was well-deserved. The pumpkin gnocchi were complemented by a salad of delicate greens with a dressing Jack was hard-pressed to describe, other than to say it was delicious.

"That is so fascinating," Annie enthused, when Livvy described the search for Jessamine's diaries and their trip to St. Columba's. "Your Jessamine is buried there? Who knew? I've passed that church so many times and never thought there was anything about it that was mysterious."

"I hope the diaries, when I find them, will reveal who fathered James, Jack's ancestor. That's a big mystery."

Jack leaned forward. "It doesn't matter to me who fathered my ancestor. I care only in a purely academic sense."

"It's not academic for me." Livvy eyed him a moment before glancing back to Annie. "I'm writing a biography of Jessamine's life. So while the diaries are my goal—and my writing the book, too—I've been distracted by Jack's library. It has so many treasures in it. To make matters worse, I'm dealing with a baby-sitter Jack hired to climb up ladders to get to the top shelves where Jessamine's diaries might be. He's very slow. I'd be much faster."

Annie's eyes brightened. "That's so exciting, writing a book. I'd like to write down some of my recipes and compile them into a book that we can sell here in Bisby, once our medieval village concept is complete."

Some good-natured discussion about Bisby's redevelopment followed. When it was exhausted, Charlie said, "Let's leave the women for a bit and take a walk."

"All right." Jack came to his feet.

As they began their stroll down Bisby's one street, Charlie said, "Annie and I began this project to combat the rampant unemployment in Bisby. We felt it our duty to do something. We're in the process of making Bisby a destination location, a medieval village of sorts, which will bring many jobs to this part of the county."

Jack's discussions with Pratt included a review of not just what needed fixing at Brompton Court, but what needed fixing in Moreham. Seeing what the Camvilles were doing in Bisby, his interest sharpened.

Charlie pointed out what kind of business would be housed in each of the buildings being repaired. On an empty lot where there'd been a building too far gone to save, a group of men were learning how to fight with swords, while a smaller group of women were taking instructions in how to churn butter.

Jack raised one eyebrow. "If Livvy saw this, she'd wonder why it wasn't the men who were churning butter and the women learning to fight with swords."

Charlie exhaled a short laugh. "Annie has insisted on including my ancestress, Nichola de la Haye, among the characters who will be part of the medieval village. Whoever plays her will be as fierce as Boadicea."

They continued on like that with Jack admiring how though Annie was the one who wanted it, husband and wife had taken on the renewal of Bisby as equal partners.

"We're moving a bit slower, now. Annie is feeling the strain of her pregnancy. Among other things, it's why I try to keep her from lifting pots."

Jack doubted, having observed the duchess this afternoon, that she'd let Charlie keep her from doing what she thought needed to be done whether in her restaurant or the village reconstruction.

They passed by the manor house, which was being renovated like everything else in Bisby. "We've moved in," said Charlie. Interested as he was in Charlie's tour guiding, Jack was ready to learn the reason Camville had called.

"I wanted us to meet at last." Charlie shoved his hands into his pockets. "Our fathers had an unfortunate history. Getting to know each other might get us past that."

Jack said, "That would be a positive outcome."

"Anything that was between them should never have involved us." Charlie stopped in front of a building at the far end of the block from The Ocular. The entire thing seemed to have been gutted, with only the inside columns remaining. "There were times I wanted to approach you. Not at the beginning, mind. Feelings were too raw, yours and mine both. I was furious at my father and I think even a little at your father for believing mine."

Jack made a face. "I would be less than honest if I didn't tell you that I was angry at my father for allowing himself to be fleeced by your father." He waved an apologetic hand at Charlie. "Sorry."

"No offense taken."

"Even when I mourned him, I wondered why he didn't ask someone who might know about the investment your father wanted him to make."

"Didn't your dad teach philosophy at uni?"

"Yes."

"One would expect such a fellow to be rather unworldly."

Jack could hear the sound their shoes made in the gravel as they continued back toward The Ocular. "After my dad died I became obsessed with getting everything back he'd lost."

Charlie nodded. "I understand that bit."

"I didn't much care for the dukedom."

"We differ there. I cared." Charlie folded his hands behind his back as they walked on.

"Our situations were different."

"Different and yet the same." Charlie stopped. Jack did, as well. "I took a chance before leaving you that message."

Jack straightened.

"There was another reason I had for wanting to meet."

"Oh?"

Charlie cleared his throat. "One of my people came across something odd in a search we're doing for a client. It concerned neither my client nor the person he's asked us to investigate. So, he showed it to me."

The skin prickled on the back of Jack's neck. "I assume it's something you think I want to know about."

"Quite right. It seems you're in for a battle over control of your publishing house."

Jack made himself walk on. "Who did you say your client was?"

"His name doesn't matter." He raised an eyebrow. "What matters is there are some less than savory tactics being employed. Your purported purchaser, Robert Browne, has already set them in motion. I'd like to help you protect yourself against this if you'll let me."

Jack shoved his hands in his pockets. "Why?"

Charlie gave him a wry smile. "Perhaps this is my way of making up for what my father did to yours."

With those words, whatever animosity Jack felt for anyone whose last name was Camville was gone. "All right. What do you know?"

"Browne has let it be known that he won't buy Prime unless you include Chalcott House in the sale."

Here was confirmation. "May I ask…does my marketing director, Max Honeywell, fit somewhere in the picture?"

"He does, indeed. He's spreading it about that you're taking Chalcott House in the wrong direction, that under your misguided stewardship it will fail within the next few years. Worse, you've kept the board in the dark and you should be replaced."

Jack exhaled a sharp breath. "The board consists of my mother and sisters. Some years ago, after Chalcott House reaped massive profits, I gave a small percentage of shares to some of my directors, who sit at the table. I don't see how Browne thinks he can wrest control of Chalcott House from us." He thought for a moment. "Is there something else that I haven't taken into consideration?"

"That I don't know. What about Honeywell? Is he one of those who holds shares?"

"He does, yes." Jack sighed.

"I suppose you're going to sack the man."

"I will. But only when the time is right."

"Wise. My offer to help stands."

"Thank you, Charlie." Jack was amazed at how much better he felt, knowing.

Conversation done, they started back toward The Ocular. Jack's mind was alive with what had happened on this short walk around a village coming alive, again. Here he and Charlie were, on the same side of a fault line ripped open so many years ago. Jack didn't want it to open again.

"You know I almost didn't reach out."

Jack hesitated and glanced at Charlie, who had an apologetic smile on his face. "But you did."

"Yes I did, though you might have thought it rude on my part to suggest we talk about your business when we've had nothing to do with each other all these years."

That was what Jack might have thought, but not now, not at all.

"I want this reconciliation, Jack." This time, looking apprehensive, Charlie held out a hand. "Shall we move forward without the foolish enmity that has held us back?"

Jack took his hands from his pockets. Here he was, in company with a man who he couldn't imagine he would ever think of as a confidante. Yet, it was what he had become. "I would like that, if you think it's possible."

"Do *you* think it's possible?"

Jack reached out, taking Charlie's hand in a firm grip. "I do." Something that had been closed off inside him for too many years bloomed in the mid-afternoon light.

By the time they got back to The Ocular, they were friends. Swinging the door open, Jack saw the women deep in discussion. Heads close together, their body language told Jack they had become friends, as well.

Annie looked up as Charlie walked toward her, and bending, laid one hand on her belly. She lifted her face to his, and he kissed her softly. "Duchess, how do you feel?"

It was obvious to Jack, though he and Livvy were in the room, neither Charlie nor Annie cared. The elation he'd felt thinking a new chapter had opened in his life, faded. A strange feeling of loneliness washed over him. He'd never been in a relationship like Charlie and Annie's. His always managed to peter out. The most important relationship, if that was what it could be called, was with his work.

He turned toward Livvy, whose attention and smile was centered on the couple in their intimacy and Jack knew. What he'd felt before was not embarrassment or discomfort. It was jealousy. He wanted what Charlie and Annie had for himself.

Later, as they made their way back to Brompton Court, it was hard for Jack to concentrate on Livvy's recital of the tales she'd told Annie about everything falling apart at Brompton Court. Because Livvy was a natural born storyteller, they'd sat together, laughing, all four of them.

Livvy kept chatting away about the restaurant and the renovations, and how she'd invited Annie to take a tour of Brompton Court. She hadn't bothered to ask him if it was all right. But then, why should she? She'd said the library seemed like home to her.

"It seems you've made a friend," Jack said.

"I think I have. They almost didn't make it, you know."

He blinked. "What?"

"Charlie and Annie. Some secret of hers came up that she hadn't told him, and it almost broke them apart."

"Mmm." He didn't elaborate on his non-verbal answer.

After a second or two, she asked, "Are you okay?"

He gave her a quick glance. "Perfectly okay."

"So, you didn't mind spending time with Charlie? Not that you should feel like you have to tell me."

He flexed his hands on the wheel because he could tell she knew he was holding back. He wanted to tell her, but something stopped him. "It was…interesting."

"The Chinese curse."

He didn't know how she would take what Charlie had said. He didn't want to spoil this wonderful day with talk of her father's machinations to strip him of Chalcott House. "Beg your pardon?"

"Relax, it's nothing. I'm just being nosy." She leaned forward. "Thank you for today. I loved meeting Annie and Charlie. And I loved seeing Jessamine's grave." She laid one hand on his thigh.

"No thanks necessary," he heard himself say because suddenly he wasn't so distracted. His focus narrowed to that one place where her hand lay.

"Now all I have to do is find those diaries."

"I'm actually quite tired of this discussion about diaries." Jack blinked as the words flew without thought, from his mouth.

She withdrew her hand into her lap and went silent. The only sound was that of the tires on the road. He wanted to reach across the console and take her hand and kiss it into an apology. He couldn't tell her why he'd spoken the words, though he knew. When she found the diaries, she would have no reason to stay at Brompton Court. She would leave England. And him.

***

For the remainder of the time it took to return to Brompton Court, though Jack wanted to bridge the silence that grew more uncomfortable with each mile, he could not. By the time they'd entered the grounds, he knew he had no choice but to explain.

When he brought the car to a halt, Livvy didn't wait for him but slipped out of the car. By the time he'd pulled around to the garage and come back, she'd gone up, either to the library or to her room.

He could have followed her. Said the words, though what words he still didn't know.

On that frustrated thought, he decided to take care of some business. He made calls to his British and American teams to tell them about his conversation with Charlie. He checked messages and dealt with them. When, at last, he went upstairs, it was dark. After preparing for bed, he turned off his light and dropped off into sleep.

On some level he heard the water come on in the lav. In its way it helped him slide into a deeper sleep. But then he heard the thump and close on its heels the high-pitched, very loud scream.

He shot straight up, threw off the covers, and stood.

Bolting across the worn carpet into his dressing room, he threw open the door to the bath. The sight that greeted him—the shower curtain off the rods, down in the bathtub, water coming from the shower head like a summer deluge—told him what had happened. She was flailing away at the curtain which somehow had wound itself around her. He stepped through the puddles of water on the tile floor and reached into the bathtub to yank the shower curtain away.

Her glorious hair was plastered to her head, neck, shoulders, and across her face. He threw the shower curtain behind him, and turned off the water. Heart pounding, he grabbed her upper arms and lifted her upright. "You fell? How did you fall?" He pulled her over the lip of the bathtub and stood her on the now soaking wet bath mat.

His head pounded along with his heart. "Livvy, talk to me."

She slapped her hands onto his hips, pressed her face against his chest, and moaned. "I was reaching for the shampoo."

He wound one arm around her back and shoulders and pressed her wet body to his. "Did you hit your head?" He palmed a hand to her scalp, feeling for a knot. "What about your shoulder?"

"I landed on my back and my butt, not my head or my shoulder." She lifted away from his chest and raised a hand to push at the strands of hair still curling across her cheeks. Drops of water broke, streaming in rivulets down her forehead and nose and chin. She blinked her eyes.

"Livvy…" He was almost sure she'd sustained no lasting harm. Still, he needed to know if he should pick her up. Or call an ambulance.

He exhaled a sharp breath. She did the same. Until she stiffened in his arms and he stiffened likewise. He dropped his hands from her shoulders. She dropped her hands from his hips.

They both stepped back.

He stared at her. She stared at him.

They were both naked.

CHAPTER TWELVE

It was an idiot move to take a shower so late at night. But Livvy couldn't sleep so she got up to pace. She thought about going to the library. Like that was a brainy idea. She'd have to pass by the duke's suite and if she knew anything about Monk Man, he probably slept with his eyes open and he'd be up and out the door asking her what's up.

What was keeping her awake wasn't that she'd fallen in love with his library. It was that other way more dangerous thing. She was falling for its owner. Only every time she thought it would be okay, he did or said something that had her doubting her mental sharpness. Like making a cutting remark about the diaries.

And now here they were, naked. Whatever she might have been thinking flew out of her head. Naturally, she began to babble. "I wanted to wash my hair and don't say I shouldn't have." She raised her fingers to her forehead and hoped they weren't trembling. "The stitches are out, and I don't care if I get the scar wet, and anyway you didn't have stitches in your head, and have no idea how stitches, even after they're out, can be so itchy."

In the poor light from the fixture above the sink, she could see how pale his skin was. Not so pale were his eyes. They blazed hot, incandescent blue.

She licked her lips. "I had to close my eyes because my hands were soapy and my eyes stung and I should have opened them so I didn't get dizzy, which I didn't and I—" She licked her lips again. "Sorry for the scream."

But she wasn't sorry for looking because without his clothes, the Duke of Brompton was the finest specimen of man she'd ever seen.

There was a patch of soft, springy hair in the center of his chest, so yeah, that dream of what decorated his chest back weeks ago was right on the money. It narrowed down to his waist and below where his really impressive—what should she call it…cock, dick, penis, member…whatever…it was demonstrating interest…in her. This was testament to the truth that lay between them, that from the beginning, this was, and had been, inevitable.

He pushed her hair away from her eyes and forehead. "Can you stand?" His brilliant eyes bore into hers.

"I am standing."

"I'm going to let go but only for a second. Will you be all right if I do." Words clipped, he wasn't asking her a question.

"I won't move a fraction of an inch."

But she hadn't finished her sentence when he let her go, grabbed the towel she'd hung on the hook on the back of the door and wrapped her tight, folding the towel around her from shoulder to knee. With one hand, he made a fist, holding the edges together. He pulled her against his body. She laid her sopping wet head against his chest and felt the frantic beat of his heart. "I'm sorry I scared you."

"You did." He stepped away, bent, slid one arm beneath her knees and the other beneath her shoulders and lifted her into his arms. He pushed open the door that led through the duchess's dressing room, padded across, and deposited her on the bed he'd just bought for her.

She sat up straight and shimmied to the floor. "You want me to get my sheets and this brand new mattress wet? I don't think so."

He put his hands on his hips and now she really had to stare. The man was endowed, rampant, and it was a very good look.

"I wrapped you in your towel for that very reason."

She looked at an interesting crack in the ceiling, snuck a hand out from the towel, and squeezed a coil of her hair. "You didn't wrap my head."

He turned on a heel and without saying a word, disappeared into the dressing room. Just as she hadn't been able to take her eyes off his front, she was unable to take her eyes off his ass. His shoulders were wider than they appeared under his made-just-for-him suits. The width of those shoulders, so masked by his clothing, told her why he'd been able to carry her. Muscles in all the right places. His torso, trim waist, narrow hips, and perfect, tight ass. Awesome.

He returned with another towel in hand, which he wrapped around her head. Not too tight that it would hurt, but tight enough that it would wick up the wet. "Now you can lie down."

She did, not that it changed any of the turmoil she felt inside. His eyes darkened. And once more he disappeared.

She felt loss. And confusion. Before she could tease any of it out, he was back with boxers on and easing himself down on the mattress next to her.

"Scoot over." He pulled the covers up over both of them and slipped his arm beneath her shoulders. "Livvy, I must apologize."

Talk about being confused. Was this foreplay or not? "For what?"

He reached out to switch off the bedside light. Then, he rolled her toward him. "I weigh everything I say before I speak. Sometimes, I'm too careful, too cautious. But sometimes I—"

She did not want to discuss apologies or any of his Monk Man cautiousness. She wanted what they both wanted and she wasn't willing to wait another moment longer. She ran her fingers across his stubbled cheek. "Let's talk about it later."

It was dark in the room, but not so dark that she couldn't see him. He gave her his typical slow smile. Snaking his fingers underneath the turban he'd fashioned around her head, he said, "Do you think your hair is dry, now?"

He didn't wait for her reply, but slipped it off her head. He dropped it over the side of the bed and then, turning her on her back, he kissed her on the pulse that was beating madly just beneath her ear, and then placed a string of kisses around her collarbone.

She ran a hand down his body to his ass. There. The offending boxers. She grabbed a handful of the elastic waistband. "You're an idiot, a nicely, noble idiot. But you're still an idiot. Why did you put these on?"

He ghosted a laugh against her skin and kissed the side of her neck, the edge of her jawbone, her ear, the jut of her cheekbone. "I wanted to give you a choice." But then he eased the boxers off.

She expelled a shaky breath and snaked one arm over his shoulders to caress the hot, taut, silk-like skin of his upper back. She eased the other hand from her side and placed one palm on his chest. She splayed her fingers through the soft hair between his nipples.

The air was still. The moon, peeking through the clouds, threw shadows across the bed and cast a bright band of light across her forearm.

His kisses grew heated, purposeful. He kissed one side of her mouth and then the other. He eased a thigh between hers and pressed it against her core. She almost went up in flames.

"Not now, Livvy. Wait." His mouth demanded that hers open beneath his. And she gave back what he gave her, challenging him with her mouth as he challenged her, their tongues and lips and teeth invading, retreating, joining again.

He smoothed one hand over her damp hair and pushed it back across her forehead. "Beautiful," he whispered.

She reached up to run her fingers over his tight curls. "Beautiful."

He shuddered and buried his head at the juncture between her neck and shoulder. His hands were everywhere. Cupping one breast, thumbing its nipple to a crest and then doing the same for the other. He ran a hand down her body to her navel and rimmed it with one finger, dipping in and out.

She arched upward, urging him on, but he seemed intent on continuing to tease her. "Oh, no, that's not flying," she whispered on a sibilant breath. She grabbed his wrist and placed his hand where she wanted it most. At her cleft. He didn't resist. He cupped her, he stroked her, he dipped his fingers into her. She moaned. "Jack…"

She ran the sole of her foot up and down the back of his hair-roughened calf. She kept one hand on his scalp, in the cropped, gold-tipped brown curls she'd wanted to touch for so long. She ran the other hand up and down his arm to the wrist and then to the hand that was performing magic things on her body, and tangled her fingers with his. Their bodies were slick with sweat.

After that, she stopped thinking about what he was doing and let herself be in the moment except for that one sliver of her brain still functioning, the part that stood apart to be grateful that as he slid into her, he'd remembered protection.

Gone deep, he stopped. "All right?"

He sounded winded.

She curved her arms around his broad shoulders. "I was worried."

"About what?" He managed the words, though he gasped as he said them.

"That we would fit. I'm so short and you're so tall."

He breathed a laugh. "The parts that match, match." Then he began to move. Slow thrusts. And then faster and she urged him on and reached down between their bodies and wound her fingers around the root of him. He groaned and moved faster until all she could do was be caught in his frenzy.

The bed frame creaked. The headboard banged against the wall. She pressed her head into the pillow and made the long climb to completion, chanting his name over and over again. She tightened her legs around his waist, and canted her hips into him. Until everything broke and she rode the crest to the end.

After, he braced himself on his elbows so he wasn't flattening her into the brand new mattress. She stroked his back, still sweaty. "That was a long time coming." She snickered. "Oh, wait. I better be more careful with my words."

He shifted to the side and pulled her to him. "Why bother?"

She nestled into him, burying her face against the notch where his neck joined his shoulder. Despite wanting to enjoy the moment for as long as she could, despite him getting out of bed—she supposed to dispose of the condom—before slipping back in, she fell asleep. And somehow, didn't wake until dawn. She knew he kept his arm around her, shifting now and then, groaning something about how it had fallen asleep.

By the time she woke fully at dawn, she was alone. She ran a hand over the sheets where he'd been lying. Still a little warm. Which meant he was nearby.

This time when she took her shower, she made sure to put a towel down in the bathtub. She dressed and went looking for him because she wanted to kiss him good morning. She wouldn't let herself think too much about it, but she let her mind drift to the possibility of giving him a kiss not just this morning but every morning.

Jack had known he would have to tell Livvy what Charlie had told him. He hated the thought of disturbing their brand new intimacy. But there was no way to avoid the truth. Her father was inserting himself in her life in a way Jack knew Livvy didn't want.

He'd risen, careful not to disturb her, made his way through the library, and out onto the terrace. There was a chill in the air despite the bright October early morning sunshine.

He roamed from one side of the terrace to the other, avoiding the places where the stones were coming loose and weeds inched their way up between them. It would be a lovely place to sit on a warm afternoon. He'd tell Pratt to add shoring up the pavers and getting rid of the weeds to the list of things to be done.

The sun was up over the tree line when he heard the door from the library open and her steps come across to where he stood. He turned. Her skin was rosy and flushed, her eyes bright, but ever so slightly wary. So intuitive she was…looking at him, wondering what his face told her.

"Good morning," she said, breathless.

"Good morning."

She frowned. "Is it?"

"Yes. It is." He gave her a smile then.

She stepped into him and reached up to lay one finger against his mouth. "Are you sure? I like this smile, but it's not one of your really good ones."

Taking her face in his hands he bent. With his mouth inches from hers, he whispered, "How about a kiss? Would that make up for a smile that's not quite up to snuff?" He was gentle, at first, grazing his lips across hers, but that was all it took for last night's passion to come roaring back. He lifted her in his arms and opened his mouth over hers. She lashed her arms around his neck and her legs around his waist, and their mouths dueled, their tongues thrusting and parrying with wanton fury.

On a breath taken, he remembered. Carrying her back to her bed to strip her and himself of their clothing and then do what he wanted, would put off the inevitable. Somehow, he was able to step back from the edge. "Livvy." Just her name, voice winded. "It's morning and we have all day. Let's have something to eat."

"Why don't we eat each other?" She licked the hollow beneath his ear.

"A meal delayed is a meal appreciated." He placed a light kiss on her lips and untangling himself from the legs she'd wound around his waist, said, "We need the calories to make up for the thousands we used just a few hours ago."

She stuck out her tongue at him, the tongue he'd been dueling with just seconds ago. He started to question his reasoning powers. But, no. He wanted this done as soon as possible so they could have each other. Free and open.

"Well, okay then." She took his hand and together they stepped into the library and made their way down the stairs to the kitchen.

She kept up her teasing chatter as he set out cups, along with the rolls they'd brought back from The Ocular that Annie had baked and were waiting to be re-heated in the oven. He put a pot of coffee on to brew the multiple cups he knew Livvy would want later.

When everything was in place, he took her hand and brought her to the table, making sure his fingers grazed the back of her neck. Pulling out her chair, he said. "Sit, please."

She tilted her head back, wound, pulled his face down to hers, and gave him a soft, open-mouthed kiss. "Who knew a duke could make breakfast all by himself, even setting a table and brewing coffee for his American guest?"

"If I'm not mistaken, there's a compliment in there somewhere."

"You know there is." She reached for a roll. "Yum. I'm starving."

Jack felt a silly grin stretch his lips. "All that exercise you've been doing. Of course you're starving."

She laughed and threw her napkin at him.

He poured her coffee and took some for himself. The rolls were perfectly heated and the butter, with its high fat content, was mouth-wateringly lush, and the greengage plum jam Annie had made this past spring was both sweet and tart.

When they had eaten all but two of the rolls and drunk enough coffee, Jack decided he couldn't put it off any longer.

"I didn't tell you everything Charlie and I talked about on our walk about Bisby yesterday."

"I didn't tell you everything Annie and I talked about while you were gone on that walk around Bisby yesterday," came her cheeky reply.

"You know Charlie's business is cyber-security, right?"

She dipped a spoon in the jam jar and then stuck the spoon into her mouth. "Mmm, yes. I knew."

"Whilst doing some work for a client, one of his people came across information about your father that speaks to how he intends to wrest control of Chalcott House from me. The fellow brought it to Charlie's attention. That was one of the reasons why Charlie called."

She started to dab at her mouth with her napkin and stopped. Then, folding it in quarters, she placed it back on the table. "That thing this person discovered would be…?"

"Your father's first step is to take over my board and oust me as chairman. Once done, he can fill the board with his people and then, he thinks it will be simple for him to wrest control of Chalcott House from my hands."

Slowly, she straightened. In her eyes, where the light or lack of it always told him what she was thinking, nothing. On her mouth, a slight press of her lips. Then, slowly, she came to her feet and leaned her hands on the table. "You believe I knew, right?"

He started. "What? No! Why would you think something like that?"

She stood back from the table. "Because you once did."

Her eyes heated with blistering wrath. She slammed her hands on the table. The silverware jumped. "That shark, that swindler, that—!" Her nostrils flared. "Tell me now, and don't lie. Do you believe I know what he's doing?"

He came to his feet. Reaching across the table for her hand, he took it, and gave her a reassuring squeeze. "I know you didn't know. Absolutely."

Her hand lay limp in his. His alarm grew. He'd thought she would be upset thinking her father was meddling in her life. He hadn't given a thought to how upset.

Never letting her hand go, he came to his feet and took quick steps around the table to pull her into his arms. She went, but made no attempt to put her arms around him. "Livvy. You needed to hear it. I wanted it to be from me."

She canted back against his arms to look up at him. Her eyes, grown large, a tempestuous green, not their normal warm hazel, glistened with emotion.

His heart leapt with anxiety. "I'll say it as many times as you need me to. I believe you."

She took a deep inhale. "He has no faith in me. If I thought you didn't have faith in me…" She never took her eyes off his, as if she was trying to catch sight of truth in them.

"Darling, Livvy…" He drew her closer into his embrace. After long seconds of hesitation, she finally wound her arms around his waist. He exhaled in relief.

Face pressed against his chest, voice muffled, she said, "Okay. But you need to know you scared me there. It was the look on your face."

"What look?"

She raised her face, and the fierce green was gone, replaced by the hazel warmth he loved. "I have names for your looks."

"Do you? What are they?"

She half-smiled and shook her head.

He wasn't going to learn what they were, not today. If she told him what they were some other time, so be it. Now, what was important was that he assure her of his certainty in her. "This is about that stupid business with your brother-in-law, my idiotic fascination with body language and what his told me, right?"

"Yes, exactly."

"I hope I am forgiven for that rank stupidity. Good Lord, I am not your brother-in-law, or worse, your father, not in any way. You will never have to prove anything to me, ever. Is that good enough?"

He separated them and placed his hands on her shoulders. She took a shivery breath. Raising her hand to his lips, he turned it over and placed a kiss in the center of her palm. "Though we thought it, now it seems it's much more than a possibility. This is your father's goal: taking Chalcott House from me. For you."

"I don't understand. He's let me know in so many different ways that he thinks I'm a failure because I go about doing things the wrong way. What I don't understand is why he doesn't abandon me to muddle through on my own?"

Jack wouldn't say what he thought. Not now. It would have to be for a time when she would be receptive to his words.

A self-mocking smile ticked up one corner of her mouth. "Can I tell you the story about when I broke with my father for good?"

He played with her hair, winding strand after strand through his fingers. "Why not? You're a storyteller. Witness the brilliant texts you send me twice a day."

She gave him a hard nudge in his side and he flinched. "Hold the compliment until you hear this particular story."

Jack stood back.

"Ten years ago I met a guy at a bar. His name was Doug. He wasn't exactly handsome and after a few minutes, I knew he wasn't the sharpest pencil in the box. But he looked at me like I was the most awesome person, and I needed that at the time."

Jack had known about Doug, her husband of a day. Higgins had discovered it, once they knew her name was Browne, not Sterling.

"In case you think Doug knew about my family and he was in it for the money, he didn't. Anyway, I was still in possession of my virginity, and hot to lose it. He seemed like the type I wanted to lose it to.

"Then, on an impulse I said, 'Let's get married.' I'm not sure what I thought. But he was as foolish as I was and it was easy to convince him to fly to Las Vegas and do it. We used my money because Doug didn't have any. We found someone to marry us and after getting drunk at a nearby bar, somehow we made it to the hotel and fell into a drunken sleep.

"We were awakened just after eight a.m. by a call from my father. He'd found out where we were and threatened Doug with all kinds of trouble if we didn't come home immediately. I was annoyed, but more I felt guilty. Kind of like when I ruined that briefcase. Because yeah, once more a screw-up.

"He was there at Newark Airport, waiting for us at the gate, with his phalanx of men, when we got off the plane."

She put phalanx in air quotes.

"He was in full hedge-fund-master mode. He told Doug he would take care of him and sent him off with one of the men. I begged Doug not to go, but I could see he was petrified of my father, and no way was he going to stick around."

She patted her chest. "I, on the other hand? My father let me have it right there, outside the gate as people poured off the plane and slowed to watch me get called names, like screw-up, selfish child, idiot. It was quite the show."

Jack caught his breath. Bad enough to call one's child names in private. To do it in public? He wanted to hold her in his arms against the humiliation, though it was ten years in the past.

She folded her arms across her chest and shivered. "I wanted the floor to open up. But that's not how it worked. No, I had to stand there and take it. The next thing I knew, my marriage was annulled and Doug wouldn't take my calls."

She rolled her eyes. "He weighed it all out. Wife, on one hand. Payoff money to buy a new BMW and computer equipment he'd been jonesing for on the other. No brainer."

Gone silent, she looked away but only for a moment. "That was the day I decided. I was never going to let my father disrespect me ever again. So, I stopped talking to him, and for the most part I haven't. Except when I'm forced—birthday parties, for example. But hey, that trip to Las Vegas? It did accomplish something."

"And that was…?"

Her laugh was forced. "I did lose my virginity."

She dove back into his arms. He kept her there, knowing how much it had hurt to tell her story.

After long minutes when all Jack could offer was body heat against the occasional shiver, she stepped back. Eyes and mouth set, her jaw hardening, she said, "I need to do something. Come with me." She hurried out of the kitchen and up the steps to the library. She made a beeline for her computer and woke it up. "What time is it in New York?"

"It's just before six o'clock in the morning."

"He gets up before dawn. Probably is already at the office." She opened up her video conferencing app. Only what seemed like a moment later, her father was on the screen.

"Olivia. What a pleasant surprise."

As Livvy leaned forward on folded arms, Jack stood off to the side so Browne wouldn't see him.

"So, the word out there is you want to buy Chalcott House for me. You want to tell me why?"

Browne was broader at the forehead and narrower at his chin than the few pictures Jack had seen of him suggested. His eyebrows were heavy and his eyes black. His nose seemed small for his face and his mouth was, of all strange things, prissy. How often, Jack marveled, that truly evil men often looked harmless.

Browne's prissy mouth widened in what some might have called a smile. "How did you find out?"

"No thanks to you, I know." Livvy began to rhythmically tap one hand on the opposite forearm. "Were you going to bother to tell me?"

As the man leaned back in his chair, Jack got more of a look at Browne's office space. Or at least what was behind him: a wide expanse of window, showing stands of skyscrapers, their windows lit in the almost gray of dawn that was six o'clock in the morning in New York.

Browne stroked his chin. "When I thought it was time."

"And you think it's something I want, huh?" The tapping continued.

"There's no reason why you wouldn't."

"In your mind."

Browne's hand continued its rhythmic stroking. "Naturally, you don't see how it would be beneficial for you."

Livvy half came out of her seat. "Then I don't understand why you bother."

"Your sisters understand. Why is that you don't understand I bother because you're my daughter."

"That's just an accident of nature."

Browne's deep set eyes burned through the connection. "That's an outrageous statement, Olivia."

"Hardly."

Jack wanted to reach out to soothe her, but he didn't think she would know his hand was there for support. And he didn't want Browne to see him.

"I hope this misplaced anger of yours isn't more of that nonsense about your name." Browne pressed his lips together. "It's old and it's unacceptable."

Jack's anger ticked up. What Browne couldn't put up with was that unlike her sisters, Livvy wouldn't fall in line and let him manage her. That was what was unacceptable.

Browne's features tightened in disdain. "You need to be smarter about your life than you've been. What possible return on investment do you think you can achieve, writing a book?"

A pulse beat rhythmically at Livvy's temple.

"None. Leave that to others," he continued. "Let *their* books make you money. And that's the reason I will buy Chalcott House."

Livvy shot up from her chair. She swayed a bit. Jack lifted a hand to brace her. She held him off.

"Listen carefully old man. I'm writing a book, not looking for a return on my investment."

"Olivia, Olivia, it never ceases to amaze me." He shook his head. A sneer lifted one side of his mouth. "You a writer? No. As usual, you've fixated on something foolish. And as usual I need to save you from yourself."

Livvy's face became blotchy with fury. "You mean like when you saved me from Doug?"

Browne's face darkened.

"If you don't back off I am going to do something to back you off. And if you think I don't mean it, just keep on with what you're doing." She disconnected.

She turned back to Jack. "Did that do it? Do you have any more doubts?"

He pulled her into his arms. She was trembling all over. "What did you mean, you'll do something to back him off?"

"I don't know. I haven't figured it out yet."

"Livvy, I've got to get back to London to deal with what your father has started." He put her away from him. "But before I go, I need to say something."

"What?" She leaned her forehead against his chest.

"We both know what that last bit was, him saying you're not a writer."

She banged her head against his chest. "He's gaslighting me."

He cupped her face with both hands and placed a gentle kiss on her lips. "Yes, he is. Don't let him make you doubt yourself. Don't give him that power."

The look on Livvy's face, awash with pain, brought out a fury in him he didn't know existed. He wanted to wipe away the words Browne had spoken to her, but they'd been said and he couldn't. And so, he did the one thing he knew he could. "Would you say I know the difference between someone who thinks they can write and someone who can't?"

Hazel eyes wary, she nodded.

"I haven't seen your book. You haven't shown it to me, yet." He placed a finger across her lips. "No, don't say a word." He pulled her back into his arms and continued. "You've been writing to me for months and I have loved—" She began to object. He gave her a little shake. "Quiet until I finish. I have loved all of it. You have an enchanting way of looking at things and it shines in your word choices and your observations. You make me laugh, not an easy thing to do. Your daily texts have been the highlight of my days these last weeks. There is no doubt in my mind. You are a writer."

"But Jack…" She tried to pull away but he wouldn't let her. "Just because I can send a wicked text or two doesn't mean I can write a book."

That was true, though he wouldn't say it. Once he saw her work, he hoped he wouldn't have to say it. "Do you know who the people are who are most likely to doubt they're writers?"

She wrinkled her nose at him .

He tightened his embrace and gave her a smile. "Writers."

CHAPTER THIRTEEN

It took Livvy a couple of days after Jack left for her to write again. True, she hadn't done as much writing as she would have wanted since being in England. She blamed the library and its treasures for that. Blamed in a good way.

It was that thing her father had said to her.

You a writer? No.

She cringed every time she thought of it and she thought of it a lot. She remembered the day in Edgewater's library when it came to her what she should be doing with her life. Telling stories. She hadn't allowed herself to think writing a book was the best place to start, that starting with something smaller might be better. She just jumped in.

She was already writing something smaller. Her blog posts. They were followed by thousands. Surely, that meant something?

Her father didn't think it meant anything and on those few occasions when they were together at family parties, he let her know. Unlike every other time in all the years she looked for something to do with her life and didn't find it, this time she knew she'd started something good. This time, his scorn washed right over her. The decision she'd made to use skills she'd been perfecting—writing that blog and the reviews for that literary magazine—was the right one for her. For the first time in her life, she'd felt like she had a direction.

So if she didn't care what her father thought, why couldn't she stop thinking about the video call? It wasn't as if he hadn't said belittling things to her before. Why this? Why now?

She wandered out onto the terrace to see if the clear air would shake her gloom loose.

You a writer? No.

She pressed both hands to her temples and moaned. Suppose he was right? Suppose she was too blind to see it and she was just spinning her wheels? She began to pace. She knew where all that self-doubt led. Nowhere. The more she wound herself up thinking about whether she was as no good as her father had always told her she was, the less she was able to function.

She came to a halt. Was she really going to do what she knew not to do? Let the man into her head? Truth was it didn't pay to think about why he treated her the way he did, and she wasn't going to waste another moment thinking about it. She turned on her heel and marched into the library, and the pile of books stacked on the corner of her desk.

She moved Caleb's letters from her book pile and placed them in front of her. She was right to continue her research. It was going to lead to the best book she could write. Her father could take a leap for all she cared. She'd continue to do what she knew she was meant to do.

Forcing her melancholy away, she slipped on a pair of gloves and carefully pulled out the topmost letter from the folder she'd put them in. It was a request for Caleb to pay up. He was being sued by the Crown for failure to remit his taxes on tin mined at an Anstruther property in Wales. The seventeenth century equivalent of the IRS was after him.

The next letter she picked up came from Charles. She couldn't help the little squeak of excitement that escaped her. In the letter, he asked Caleb about James' progress. How was the boy? How were his studies?

The next one was also from Charles. In it, Charles asked whether the boy had received the fine wool cloak he'd sent for his birthday. She put it aside for another, this one dated 19 July, 1667. In it, Charles directed Caleb to take James up into the mountains should the plague that was decimating London that summer reach Lincolnshire.

The more she read Charles's letters to Caleb, the more she realized the King of England was exceedingly interested in the life of Jessamine's son, more proof he was who she thought.

The buzz of her cell phone startled her. She looked up to see the sun low in the sky. She'd been so immersed in Caleb's letters, the hours had flown and she hadn't known it. The cell buzzed again. She smiled.

I'm on my way back to Brompton Court.

She picked up her phone to key in an answer to Jack.

In the helicopter?

He replied.

Use it or lose it, I always say.

"No, you don't." She snorted a laugh. "But you *are* learning how to be my kind of smartass."

Shall I get myself ready for anything in particular? She wondered if she should ditch her black tee, jeans, and sneakers for something provocative.

Her smile faded when there was no answer. She put the phone down and sat back. He was busy. Or he got a phone call. Or… Whatever. It could be that he was trying to figure out the answer to the mess with her father. She made a face.

She took a bite of the sandwich she'd made for herself earlier. The bread was stale. She pushed the plate aside. She pushed Caleb's letters aside, too. She'd gleaned what she could from them today. Besides, she'd been sitting too long.

She stretched and looked around the room. The last shelves Archie had cleared for her were to the left of the doors leading out to the terrace. She'd thought them good candidates for the location of the diaries. The yield? Nothing.

Tapping her lip, she took a slow turn around the room. Gazing at each shelf, she made a full circle until she was once more staring at the doors. Madelyn pulled open the drapes that covered them every day to let light in. Livvy stepped across the room and pushed aside the drapes on the right. She blinked. There, beneath them, was a narrow section of shelves. The drapes, whether they were pulled closed or not, had hidden them. She went out into the hallway and called. "Archie!"

There was no answer. She began to call again and caught herself. There'd be no answer no matter how many times she called his name. She'd given Archie the day off.

She paced slowly back to the just-discovered section of shelves. The more she looked, the more they called out to her to investigate what was on each. Looking down at the ladder Archie had set on its side, there at her feet, Livvy wondered if she—

"No, Livvy," she muttered. She'd promised.

Something on one of the middle shelves caught her eye, something that did not look like a book. It looked like a case. Her heart jumped. The only other case she'd found was the one that held Caleb's letters. Jack's father had put them in that case. Now, here was another. Was he responsible for this one, too? What was in it? Would it be something of historic value, maybe even—No. She wouldn't give it a jinx.

She fidgeted. She bit her lip. She had to see inside that case.

Reaching up, she stood on tiptoes, her fingers just touching the edge of the shelf where it lay. She heaved a frustrated breath. Taking a step back, she looked down at the ladder. If she were to set the ladder up, there'd be hardly any climbing involved. If she fell, she wouldn't fall far. She'd hurt herself more if she tripped over the edge of the rug.

Before she could think about it, she'd hoisted the ladder into place. Two steps. That was all it took and her shoulders were parallel with her goal. It was nothing to reach in and grab the case.

It was sturdy, heavy, and covered with dust. She refused to sneeze. Easing the case forward, she closed her right hand around its edges. It was tied up in string, frayed a little at the knot on the top. If there truly were any diaries in this library, and if the gods of research were kind today, the diaries would be here. She squeezed her eyes shut and sent a message to her brain to calm itself.

She'd begun her retreat down one of the two rungs she'd climbed when she heard quick steps. Archie was here? Guilt washed over her. The ladder was supposed to have stayed put. Without turning, she said, "It's not what it looks like. I didn't really climb. Only a little."

"That's not what I see," came the snappish reply. "What the hell are you thinking?"

Jack was here. She laid her forehead against a ladder rung. It was cool against her skin in contrast to how, in the instant she heard his voice, her blood heated up every other part of her. "Jack, This thing…I think it's really old."

"I'll tell you what's old. Telling you to be careful and you not listening."

"Sorry, sorry." Much as she was, it was hard to speak with her heart doing cartwheels around her lungs. "Is this it? What your father found and stashed away? The diaries?"

He didn't answer but planted a hand on the small of her back.

"It's okay." She put one foot on the floor. "I'm good. I've got this."

When her second foot hit solid ground, he swung her around and gripped her upper arms so hard she knew she'd find marks later. "You've got this? Is that your flippant response?" The blue in his eyes steamed like water in a hot spring. "Do you like scaring me half to death?"

It had been a rationalization, the climbing on the ladder, because though it had been a mere nothing, she had done what she'd promised him she wouldn't do. In a small voice, she said, "Maybe that was a dumb thing to say?"

A vein stood out in the middle of his forehead. "The last ladder you stood on put you in the hospital. I told you not to get up on another one."

That was a little high-handed. But then she probably deserved a little high-handedness. "You did. And I haven't climbed this one before today. Not until just now. The thing is, I'm not much for following orders…" She swallowed whatever else she was going to say at the look of fear rippling across Jack's face.

She put the case down on one of her nearby worktables, looped her arms around his waist, and laid her chin against his chest. Angling her head back, she stared up at him and in a contrite voice said, "That's not true. I follow orders when there's danger involved. I truly didn't think there was any danger. I'm sorry I scared you."

For a moment it seemed he wasn't going to react, but then he swooped down and placed a hard, punishing kiss on her mouth. Only for a second did she think pain, until the thinking part of her stopped thinking.

He pedaled her backward to the shelves she'd just been investigating, lifted her up so the difference in their height wouldn't matter. He dipped his mouth to feast and lick and bite her throat. She laid her head back to make it easier for him. Bracing one hand against the shelf beside her head, he shoved his thigh between her legs.

"Jack," she whispered, panting. "Madelyn may be in the house."

"I don't care," he said, words muffled, his thigh rubbing back and forth against where she ached.

"The door is open," she gasped, her breath coming short.

"I don't care."

After that, everything happened fast. He put her down, stepped back, unsnapped her jeans, and along with her underwear, yanked it all down over her hips to her ankles. She watched, wide-eyed, as he fumbled with his zipper and slipped a condom from his pocket. Within seconds he was suited up and inside her. It should have hurt. It didn't. She should have minded. She didn't.

"Fuck." He spit the word out with controlled ferocity. One tiny part of Livvy's fevered brain was shocked. His language. She'd never heard him say *that*. Most of her concentrated on the feel of him pumping into her body, driving himself home, all domination.

She levered her arms around his neck and held on, bringing her pelvic bone flush with his. It was enough to bring her to climax, an atoll explosion of atomic proportions.

He settled, heavy against her, heat pouring off his body. She felt the edges of the shelf dig into her back. Her thighs trembled. She wasn't positive, once he set her down, if her legs would hold her up.

She shifted and he, perhaps becoming aware that he might have been crushing her, braced his hands against the shelf and separated them. He stared down at her, his serious monk's face suffused with passion.

"That was an awesome way to say hello." She began to ease her clothing up over her hips and waist and snapped her jeans shut.

His expression softened. "I'd say I was sorry, but I'm not. Sometimes Livvy you bring out the animal in me."

She liked the animal in him, but knew better than to say so. Not while the remnants of fear remained on his face.

With jerky movements, he adjusted his clothing and glancing at her once, walked away toward where her tissue sat on her worktable. Depositing the now discretely wrapped condom in the wastebasket, he looked down at the case, which sat where she'd put it before… Which she couldn't regret.

"When I walked in, I saw you on the ladder and irrationality took over. I had visions of you lying in that bed in the hospital, that IV in your arm." His gaze sharpened, though humor lurked faintly in his eyes. "I suppose you could say you got what you deserved."

What humor there was faded from his eyes. "And then to see you with that thing in your hand…" His face set in determination. "You'll want to know why I didn't tell you I knew about it and that it contains the diaries."

The anticipation Livvy had felt finding the case dimmed. "Well, that's getting right to it. You suppose right." Her stomach had begun to jump in time with the beat of her heart. "I can wait for whatever it is you have to say. I've waited long enough to see what's inside here."

He stepped out of the way, as she moved to the desk, reached for the case, and fumbled with the string.

"Do you need some help?" He indicated the knot.

She didn't bother to look up. "I can do it myself, thank you."

"I ask because I remember my father tying it quite securely," Jack went on, though she was hardly paying him any attention. "I remember him saying we couldn't dispose of something of such historical importance even if what's inside is not something we want known."

As the knot gave way and she unwound the last of the string, she glanced up at him. "Of course you couldn't dispose of this. This is your family history."

With deliberation, she lifted the flap. And there they were. Two little books, one smaller than the other, separated by a piece of cloth. She caught her breath. As long as she'd thought about Jessamine's diaries, they'd been alive in her imagination. Seeing them, touching them? This was surreal.

She reached for a pair of gloves. As she slipped them on, she said, "I wonder if I should take them out."

"Why not? My father did."

Her breath caught. This…this was permission.

She lifted first one and then the other out of their resting place. An odor rose from them, an earthy smell, almost smoky.

"There were six," Jack said, as she stared down at them, now side by side on the table in front of her. "Four were beyond saving. They were dust, really. The conservationist my father hired told us they were lost when whoever put the diaries on a shelf piled them on top of each other rather than upright, spine to spine. One by one, they were eaten away by the acid in the wood."

She felt a momentary pang of sadness, thinking two-thirds of Jessamine's diaries had gone beyond redemption. But the realist in her recognized that she had these two and that had to be enough.

The first one was covered in a reddish-brown, mottled leather, edges ragged. The top of its spine was torn back exposing the way the cover boards had been sewn together. At one time there'd been a clasp, now missing except for a remnant of hard leather stitched to the bottom board. The smaller of the two books was a true brown with a gold-tooled design on its front cover. There was no clasp.

With fingers that trembled, she reached down to pick up the larger of the two, the one covered in red. Opening it with great care, there, on the very first page, Jessamine Beresford's writing. Livvy had to blink away the emotion that threatened. She held her hand over the page, fingers extended, a pretend tracing of each letter, each rounded at the top, each ending with a flourish.

Jessamine had written in a slanted hand. She'd wasted no space, covering each page with her words, top to bottom and side to side. Even for those who were well-off, paper—in this case—paper made from linen rags—was expensive. In some places whole words faded away. But there were more than enough that were entirely legible, Jessamine's most private thoughts, never meant to be seen by anyone but her.

Livvy hesitated. Then sending a mute apology to wherever in the universe Jessamine's spirit might still exist, Livvy began to read.

At first it was all every day-ish. But then, Jessamine wrote about the inconvenience of travel. There were whole paragraphs devoted to the different kinds of wind that blew across the Channel and how on some crossings she feared death lay in the next wave. She wrote of Calais, the French port that was often her destination and of the stench of the streets, so bad she had to hold two handkerchiefs over her nose. She commented on how difficult it was to step around the waste in the streets just to get to her waiting coach.

Two whole pages were devoted to the details that came out of a meeting she sat in on with Charles and representatives from Parliament. They'd come to the Hague, where Charles was then living, to ask him to come back to England as king. They wanted to get his assurance that he would not punish the men who ordered his father, Charles I, to be beheaded. Jessamine counseled him to make such assurances. If he wanted to, once the crown was back on his head, he could find a way to send each and every one to the scaffold.

At some point as she read, Livvy knew a light had come on. So engrossed was she in Jessamine's words that only on a subconscious level did she recognize that it was Jack who had turned it on once the room had grown dark.

When her eyes began to burn, Livvy knew it was time to stop. She looked up and blinked. Jack was sitting in the chair not two feet from her. "Have you been here this whole time?"

He smiled. "That would have been an idiot thing for me to do. No, I was on the phone, doing some business because otherwise I would have been alone. You'd left for the 1600s."

"This is amazing stuff, Jack." She stood. "Did you know Jessamine advised Charles?"

Jack stood, too. "A woman who didn't hide behind her beauty and wit. Smart, my many times over grandmother."

"Yes, and at this point your grandmother is frustrating me. This diary is from late 1659 and according to when James was born—in late April or early May of 1660—she was already pregnant."

Livvy walked around the room, throwing her hands up and dropping them and then doing it again. "She starts off in this diary, writing about her spinsterhood—she's all of twenty-five—and how the way things look, she's never going to marry. That's a little sly, don't you think? She talks about Charles so much in these pages, it's hard for me to understand why she doesn't admit to sleeping with him."

Jack looked at her with an odd intensity. It was a look that reminded Livvy of being in his office that day he accused her of being a spy for her father and feeling rocked off her center.

After everything they'd shared—sex, texts, confidences, sex—this was not a feeling she liked. "What does that look on your face mean? Are you dancing around something you don't know how to tell me? It would be nice if you just came out with it. Like why did you let me come to Brompton Court if you had secrets here you didn't want anyone to know about? Why didn't you write to me all those months ago and just say the answer is no, Olivia? You're not coming to Brompton Court. Ever."

He ran a hand across his scalp. "There's quite a good reason why I didn't."

But she wasn't finished because now that she thought about it, she wasn't willing to restrain her long-held frustration. "Good reason? You mean when you talk about lies, or at least not telling the whole truth, why is it when I told you my last name was Sterling—a lie as you pointed out—it was way worse than you not telling me you knew the diaries were here?"

His skin reddened. "There's some truth to that accusation."

"I'd say there's more than *some*."

He turned away from her, inhaled deeply and began. "I told you about how the press hounded my father after Tom wrote the exposé about the Ponzi scheme. Tom called my dad the 'Deceitful Duke', by the way. His opinion was Freddie wasn't smart enough to come up with the scheme so he attributed it to my father. It stuck. The tumult that resulted affected my sisters."

At the mention of his sisters Livvy kept what she might have said next bottled up.

He came back to stand next to the table. Looking down at the diary, safe in its nest, he said, "Diana was twenty-two, a poised twenty-two, when it happened. While the tabloids were writing about my father, it was nothing for her to be followed down the street from front door to the store where she worked in

West London and have cameras stuck in her face. She became quite good telling the paps to sod off."

He touched the case. "Alice became a master at sneaking out the back. She thwarted almost every one of the bastards' attempts to catch her. It was Rose who bore the brunt. It changed her life."

"Rose, the sister who is redecorating Brompton Court?"

He gave her a quick smile. "Yes, that one. It started when one particular fellow set up shop at the entrance to her school. She was fourteen, but already tall. There was thought that she might one day become a model."

"She must be pretty."

A soft smile curved Jack's mouth upward. "She's lovely, inside and out." The smile was replaced by a hardness she'd not seen on Jack's face before. "After, she no longer wanted to be a model. The thought of another camera pointed at her was too much for her to bear."

A pulse beat at his temple. "The one particular fellow, an unsavory character, who made it his life's work to make hers miserable, tried every kind of game to get her to react so he could shoot a provocative picture he could sell to the tabloids. When he couldn't get her to react otherwise, he crowded up against her in an overtly sexual way. She was terrified. She told our mother she wanted to go to another school where that man couldn't find her, but

Mum insisted she stay where she was, that she should never run away from a bully."

Jack ran a hand across his face. "That was a mistake. She should have allowed it. One day, as Rose was walking home, the bastard cornered her against the side of a building. He pressed his lower body against her and took shot after shot. She was crying but that was what he wanted. Somehow, she evaded him and ran right into the street. A lorry came barreling along and would have hit her had a car not pulled out into traffic and the lorry swerved away.

Livvy clapped a hand to her mouth. "Oh my God."

"For years, she had nightmares. In them there's no car. She wakes just as the lorry throws her up in the air and down onto the pavement and she dies instantly."

"Jack," Livvy whispered and took his hand. "Next time I'm in a supermarket checkout line, I promise I won't look at any of the pictures in those terrible newspapers they sell to keep you from being bored while waiting to put your broccoli on the conveyer."

He gave her a ghost of a laugh as she meant him to.

"What happened to Rose is terrible. But I don't understand. What is there in these diaries that has anything to do with today?"

He lifted up the second of the two diaries and handed it to her.

"Are you saying whatever the big deal is about them, it's in this one?"

"I'm saying what you find in this diary is dangerous."

She barked a disbelieving laugh. "Dangerous? That's a little extreme, don't you think? It's not like when I open this thing up, bubonic plague germs from the 1660s are going to fly up off the pages and strike me dead."

"That's nonsense." His eyes were a clear, concentrated, sapphire blue. "The diaries aren't dangerous for you, either in fantasy or reality. They're dangerous for me. They are especially dangerous for my sisters."

CHAPTER FOURTEEN

There was a reason why Jack hadn't told her. He pointed to the diary, the one she hadn't looked into yet. "Open it at the back."

After a brief hesitation, she did.

There, where there should have been an endpaper like the one in the first diary, was a roughly fashioned pocket, torn on one side, and in it a paper, folded in two. Slowly she opened it. One finger hovering above the paper, she traced from left to right. "Whoever wrote this didn't have such good penmanship." She bent over the page, turning her head one way and the other. "Okay, I can read a name. Jessamine Elizabeth Maria Beresford. I can read, the date, too. 22 January, 1660."

Livvy's beautiful brown hair hung down on each side of her face. Jack flexed his fingers, thinking about sifting his fingers through it as he had last night in bed.

"According to what I read in Caleb's letters, James was born in April 1660." She paused. "This means Jessamine was pregnant when she signed this piece of paper, whatever it is."

She was silent until she sat back and her head came around to stare at him, eyes wide. "There's another name here. Or at least part of a name. Charles. Is this Charles Stuart?"

He nodded.

She stared, wide-eyed. "This can't be what I think it is."

"But it is. It's a marriage certificate."

She slapped both hands across her mouth. "So if Charles and Jessamine were married, this means James was Charles' legitimate son. It means that…" Her voice trailed off.

"Exactly. And now you know the danger."

Tho' I am united in love with my love I know what must be done will cause us pain if not now in future time. 12 May, 1660.

As if they had some power to hold her, Livvy read these words, the last ones in the diary, over and then over again. Did she imagine she would have to declare her baby fatherless?

Without taking her eyes from the page, Livvy slipped on a new pair of gloves and with great care, turned back one page. There, in flowing sentence after sentence, Jessamine's grief poured out. She would never have a life with the man she loved to desperation, her husband. She berated herself for not realizing that this was the one thing she'd wanted of Charles that he couldn't give her. The political reality was, in his fledgling status as King of England, Charles would need to form an alliance with one of Europe's royal houses. The best way was through a marriage to a French, Spanish, or German princess. And so her marriage, so recently celebrated in such love, would remain a secret. Forever.

Livvy had to push away from the diary. It was one thing to have tears fall on her cheeks, but to have them fall on this particular piece of paper? Not such an awesome thing. She rose and backed away from the table and the bleak words Jessamine had written. Perhaps they'd consoled her in some small way to write them. They were no consolation for Livvy.

It was only then she realized she was alone. Jack had left her with the diary and was out on the terrace.

She wiped the tears from her face, opened the door, and stepped outside.

Under the bright, autumn moon, he stared off into the woods. It was a strange feeling to look at him and think he was descended in a direct male line from Charles II.

She came up behind him and placed a hand on his back. He took his hands out of his pockets and turned to take her in his arms. She put hers around his waist and laid her forehead against his heart.

They stood in silence until she sighed. "You don't intend to do anything about this, do you?"

"What would be the point?"

"A righting of English history?"

"That's ridiculous. There are centuries' worth of men and women who should have sat on the throne but were passed over or disappeared or were murdered. Think of the princes in the Tower. Or Bonnie Prince Charlie, who some still say had more right to the throne than George I, who couldn't speak a word of English. Or think of that farmer in Australia who might be the true king. And what would have happened if Stephen won rather than Matilda?"

Livvy smiled against his shirt, took in the steady beat of his heart, and the clean cedar scent of him. "Is it that you're worried the queen is going to send her beefeaters to club you to death with their ceremonial staffs?"

"Livvy…" He shook her a little.

"Seriously." She gazed upward to his face, in shadow in the dark. In a voice without humor in it, she said, "Don't you think what we have in the diaries deserves to be a footnote to the history of the British throne?"

"Did you think I used the word, danger, lightly? What do you suppose would happen if this story got out? What I endured, more importantly what my sisters endured in the aftermath of my father's disgrace is bound to be repeated, made worse now because of my high profile in the business world. It's not hyperbole to say our peace of mind, perhaps our lives would be cut up. In the end it would change nothing."

They stood in the dark, arms around each other, swaying in silence.

After a while, she stood back. "I still don't understand why you removed the diaries from the shelf where I found them and then put them back. Even less, I don't get why you put the marriage paper back if it was dangerous for me to find it. That *totally* makes no sense."

"It doesn't? But I haven't been sensible about you from the beginning. I just didn't know it." He was smiling but there was a quality to his smile that suggested a hesitancy Livvy wasn't used to seeing on hyper-confident Jack Anstruther's face.

She bit her lip. "Jack, do you know what all those texts I keep sending you have been about?"

"You punching holes in my ego," he answered promptly.

"Well, yes, that." She rubbed a hand up and down her arm. "But it was me looking for the real you."

A frown knotted his eyebrows. "I had no idea I was lost. I rather think I've been right here."

She stepped into him and slipped her hand under his where he'd placed it over his heart. Making small circles against the nubby texture of his sweater and feeling the heat of him beneath, she said, "You weren't, but you are now."

Keeping her hand in his, he wrapped his fingers around hers. "Talk about not making sense, you aren't."

She took a step back and gazed up at him. "It started out because I'd been hot for you that night at the club, for your fabulous, amazing body and your fascinating monk-man face. And then you disappeared into the cold, almost scary duke who thought I was my father's hellish handmaiden. I didn't like the duke very much. I wanted him gone and to have you back. I wanted to know if there could have been something between us that was more than sex, although sex between us is a good thing."

He drew her into his arms. She went, winding her arms around his waist.

"Livvy, darling. The sex isn't just a good thing. It's an extraordinary thing." She felt his voice reverberate inside the ear she'd pressed to his chest. "I think I know what you mean about having back the part of me that's not the duke. Although I must know. What's a monk-man face?"

She snorted a laugh. "It's the face you show the world when you're acting your too serious, austere self."

"Oh, that person. I've worked hard to make him who he is."

She tightened her arms. "Well, make him go away, if you don't mind."

"You, on the other hand, don't hide behind any mask, do you? What you see is what you get."

She felt his chuckle.

"In the short time that we've been together, you've taught me things about myself. That I am suspicious by nature when I don't have reason to be, that I'm too serious. That I hold onto notions about who I am and who I ought to be."

"That's me." She rolled her eyes. "Teacher extraordinaire."

He tightened his arms around her. "Yes, it is you. A woman who will say something self-deprecating so she doesn't have to show she's touched by a compliment."

She angled her head back and looked up at him. "Maybe because I've been conditioned not to recognize them."

"That's done with."

Mute, she squeezed her eyes shut. This incredible man, he knew. He'd seen how she'd protected herself against barbs and insults her whole life. "It is?"

He sifted his fingers through her hair. "You can count on it. From now on, you will have to put up with so many compliments you'll accept them because they're what you deserve."

He cupped his hands around her cheeks. "Sweet girl, if anybody dares say one thing that's less than glowing about you, they'll have to answer to me."

Her eyes stung with tears. As one and then two and then more trickled down her cheeks, she said in a shaky voice, "What happened to you? So talky. Where's the Jack-of-few-words I thought I knew?"

He ran a finger over her eyebrows. "I felt it from the first, this thing between us, though I put it aside."

"How could you not, once you found out my last name was Browne?"

"Hush. You know what I mean." He took her hand. "Let's go inside. You're cold." He slipped an arm around her shoulders to lead her into the library. Dropping back into one corner of the ugly couch she'd brought back into the library after it was removed, he pulled her against his side.

He began to play with her fingers. "It was when my thoughts turned from the wholly physical need I had for you to something deeper. Yes, it had to do with your texts." He raised her right hand to his lips and kissed her fingers. "But it was more about the way I looked forward to reading them, and darling, so clever, sending one every, single day at 9:05 a.m. I began to salivate at 9:02, like one of those sodding dogs."

Livvy turned her hand to cup his cheek, and she shivered. He was looking at her in a way she had never seen him look at her before. Her heartbeat began a slow thud.

"Back to that moment. As I rushed to my helicopter, I was entirely focused on being here with you. I was frightened. All I could do was send prayers heavenward that it wouldn't be bad, but if it were, I would do everything you needed me to do for you. Everything."

He sighed. And then he pulled her into his lap. Winding his arms around her, he buried his face in her hair. "I didn't put words to it then, but I must have known."

He lifted his head and oh God. His eyes were so soft, so warm and sweet, and more tears flowed down her face to trickle beneath her chin.

"So, dearest Livvy. Perhaps my heart knew it was you I wanted and finally, it let my head in on the secret. I love you because you make me laugh. I love you because you challenge me. And I love you because though your family tries to mold you into something they want you to be, you don't let them. You remain your sunny, funny self. When I am with you I become the better me. I've never said that to anyone. I doubt I will ever say it to anyone else. And now I don't believe it but I am about to say something entirely disgusting it's such a cliché. You are the missing piece of me."

"Oh, Jack," she sobbed.

"Why the tears?" He smiled and blotted each with his thumb.

"Because I was afraid to tell you I've loved you since the first time you answered one of my texts. I thought you would laugh. Or worse."

He raised her face to his and kissed her. It was a kiss with promise and heat. "Now you know."

They held each other, then, for time they didn't quantify. Until he said, "I need you to understand something."

He took her hands in his. "Take whatever else you can find in the diaries and make them part of the book you're writing. But you must keep the secret of the marriage to yourself."

Livvy understood. How could she not, after hearing that harrowing story?" Poor Rose," she murmured and stroked her thumbs across Jack's knuckles. His skin was cold. "She must really hate paparazzi."

"If she does, she doesn't show it. In fact, she writes for *The Edition*, an excellent online news magazine. On occasion, she finds herself in places where paps are present. She tells me it doesn't bother her. I'm not sure I believe her."

"Maybe she's faced her demons."

"Perhaps. But I don't want her nightmares to once more become reality."

"Jack." Livvy wrapped her hands around his. "I can make you a promise. No matter what, I won't write about Jessamine's marriage to Charles. Ever. Because you asked me to, I will keep your secret."

***

That night, in the dark, in her bed, they talked. Jack felt the need to tell her more about what drove him. "I spend every day focused on business. Even when I take a day or two away—I've taken a few weeklong holidays—I can never quite unwind. There's always something on my mind, something I think I've left undone, something coming up. I find myself preparing for what dreadful thing might happen unless I prepare, and meet one self-imposed deadline or another."

Her legs entwined with his, all of her meshed with all of him.

She reached down between them. "Can I help you relax and forget at least one self-imposed deadline?"

"If it's not too much trouble. I won't object."

"Anything you want, darling duke." Her fingers danced across his body and his mind followed. When he reached for the condom he'd tucked beneath his pillow, he took control, flipped her on her back, and joined to her. They were alone then, the two of them, revolving about, together, in their own solar system.

Later, Livvy slipped out of Jack's arms and slid off the bed. She couldn't sleep for worrying about what her father was planning.

She headed down the hall to the library, where her laptop sat charging. She dithered for a moment, deciding whether she should call Sheryl, but the urge to know something—anything—was strong.

Sheryl was awake. "Hey sweetie. How's it going? Have you got an English accent yet?"

"Not yet. I'm deciding between whether to adopt a posh accent or Cockney, or maybe even Scouse."

"Scouse? What's that? No, don't explain. It's just you being you and saying something odd to get a response." Sheryl mussed her already mussed hair. "I was sure you'd call before this and when you didn't, I figured you must be crazy busy. Is England everything you wanted it to be? How's Brompton Court and the Duke of Brompton? Is he as withholding in real life as he was electronically?"

"Um… He's not withholding."

Sheryl's eyebrows shot up. "Really?"

"I'll tell you all about him some other time. I called because something hinky is going on with Dad and I need to know if you know what it could be."

"Why are you asking?"

"He wants to make a change to a deal with Jack about buying his company. I was curious if he or Kyle discussed the change with Elliot. You know, to get Elliot's advice."

"Funny that you should ask. Kyle came to the house a couple of weeks ago to speak to Elliot."

Livvy sat forward, engaged. There was no love lost between Elliot and the Browne family. "Now, that's interesting."

"Strange is more like what I thought. Anyway, they walked out to the backyard and Kyle started to talk. Elliot listened. His face got darker and darker. Then, he thrust a hand in Kyle's face and Kyle stopped in what looked like the middle of a sentence."

Livvy's eyebrows went up. "Elliot lost his cool?"

"I know, right? When does that happen? He started yelling at Kyle and Kyle backed up. And then, just as I cracked a window open so I could hear, Elliot stormed back into the house, and Kyle left."

"Did you ask what it was about?"

Sheryl nodded. "I did. But he wouldn't tell me. Not that I was surprised. In the world of forensic accountancy where Elliot lives, discretion is golden."

"Even when it concerns a brother-in-law you can't stand?"

"Even then. Do you want me to ask Elliot? If I tell him it's about the sale of your duke's company to Dad, he might tell me something because we both know he hasn't much more love for Dad than he does for Kyle."

"If you can, great. If not, well…" She hedged. "You won't say anything to Dad about me calling, right?"

"Of course not. Isn't it weird, though? Somehow or another, you know he always finds out."

That was a thing Livvy feared.

Not many minutes later, still troubled—and with nothing to show for her effort—Livvy cracked open the door to the bedroom, tiptoed across the threadbare rug and slipped into bed. Jack's quiet, rhythmic breathing told Livvy he was sound asleep, faced away from her. The blankets had slipped, and she could see the outline of his shoulders in shadow.

She inched across the mattress to snuggle up to him. The moment she slid her feet next to his calves, he yelped.

Right. Walking around in frigid, cold Brompton Court without socks on would do that. She pulled her feet away from him. "Sorry."

"You're freezing." He turned over to face her.

"I know." She wanted to make nice to him, but she knew her hands were probably as cold as her feet.

Getting used to the dark again, she could just make out his smile. "Was my lovemaking so lacking that you had to leave the bed in the middle of the night? Or were you working?"

Working would have been way better than what she had been doing. "You are ridiculous."

"I am. And ridiculously attuned to everything about you." He eased an arm around her, pulling her onto her side and flush against him. "What's wrong?"

On a deep exhale, she said, "I'm worried."

He began to play with the ends of her hair. She loved when he did that.

"What worries you?" He cupped her head and began a gentle massage.

She wanted to give in to the feel of his fingers against all her pressure points. She couldn't. He needed to know, and she had to say. "My father worries me. This thing with Chalcott House worries me."

Shifting closer, he bent his head and brushed his lips against hers. She closed her eyes so she could savor and talk at the same time.

He kissed her again, this time thoroughly. "Stop worrying." He slipped his other arm around her shoulder, his fingers a breath against her skin, skimming down her back, settling at her hip.

Gradually, she began to relax. "Easy for you to say."

"It is. And I will be the one who does the worrying if there is any to do."

"Jack." She shifted around in his arms. "You don't know him. He will do whatever he must to get what he wants. He has no moral compass when it comes to business."

"Is there a moral compass in business?" He smoothed her hair back from where it had fallen across her forehead.

"Yes, there is. Look in the mirror, Mr. Duke. I remember that story you told me about how kind you were to that guy, Tom, who wrote those terrible things about your father."

He stopped stroking her hair for a beat. "I did it because I needed to live with myself. No matter what, I won't destroy lives."

Placing both hands on his shoulders, she squeezed gently for emphasis. "My father is different. It's not just that he's an ends over means guy. It's that he goes for the jugular and then tells himself whoever or whatever had it coming." She shook him, this time not gently. "There is nothing he won't do to get what he wants."

He sighed and brought her even closer. "You are so principled," he whispered, his lips against her cheek. "And not a Trojan Horse."

She laughed. "Trojan Horse. Leave it to me to be ridiculous when all I needed to say was no way would I ever help that man out."

He shifted. "Yes, but calling yourself a Trojan Horse was so colorful."

She punched him. "You're such a monk man." She smoothed her fingers over the place where her fist had landed between his shoulder and his collarbone. She couldn't help the grin. "Cassius."

"Ah, Cassius. You've called me that before. Monk man, too. Why? I've been wondering why the pet names?

"It started the night we met at Club Chaos." Then she proceeded to explain.

After he stopped snickering, he said, "Seriously, darling, don't worry. I've got this. I promise."

She cupped his cheek. "Be careful. Keep your eyes and ears open."

He took her hand in his. Drawing it toward his lips he turned it over and pressed his lips against her palm. "Thank you for the warning,. But truly, this time your father has met his match."

As he drew her beneath him, she forgot whatever else was on her mind.

The next day, after Jack left, Livvy headed for the library where, leaning her elbows on her desk she cupped her chin in one hand, and let herself daydream. He'd kissed her so long and so deeply she thought he might decide not to return to London. That would have been nice for her, but a bad thing for him. He needed to do everything he could to head off her father before he did something irreversible.

She straightened and frowned. She'd forgotten to tell Jack about the conversation she'd had with Sheryl. She should have. Even though Sheryl hadn't heard what Elliot said, maybe it would help?

Picking up her phone, she called Jack. It rang and rang. While she waited for his voicemail to pick up, she scanned the desk where the diaries lay. She was staring down at the smaller of the two, when Jack's voicemail message kicked in. She spoke at the beep. "Hey, call me." And hung up.

No harm. She'd wait for him to call back. It would be time enough to tell him about whatever it might have been that Elliot said to Kyle and Kyle said to Elliot that day in the backyard.

In the meantime, she'd immerse herself in Jessamine Beresford's life, and what she had to say those last days.

> *4 June, 1660*
> *The pain began this morning when I woke. But that pain is of no matter. My milk will not come and my little James cries and cries. My poor babe hungers and I am shattered. It pains me deeply but I must hire a wet nurse.*

> *5 June, 1660*
> *All is well with James, tho' it is a knife in my heart that I cannot feed him. When I am better I will dismiss the wet nurse and feed my little one myself. I have written to Charles. I have reminded him that he has made me a promise, to honor my wishes, tho he is surrounded now by men who see me as a danger to the throne. They wish me and my son nothing good.*

> *6 June, 1660*
> *Today, I am fevered. I have called for the midwives. They present faces filled with worry. So many die in childbirth. I have always been robust in health and my pregnancy was easy. My tiny son thrives,*

which is all that is of importance. He must live. I must win my dear husband's promise—and yes I will call him husband— that he will care for James, his firstborn, and give him what is due a son of the king of England. I grieve that he cannot be Charles' heir, but perhaps, considering these times, it is better that way and that our marriage must remain a secret, for I am Catholic.

7 June, 1660

I am weak. The fever came on of a sudden and now it will not break. The doctor Charles sent to me has tried all manner of things but none help. Charles has now come. He was with me in my bedchamber last eve and remained so 'til morning when he was called away. He has prayed for my health. I cannot write more today.

11 June, 1660

I have not written in my diary for many days. Today I am stronger. I will be sure to write my thoughts so no one will mistake my wishes or the promises Charles has made to me. I have fashioned a pocket in the back of this book where I have hidden my marriage lines. If Charles foreswears his oath to me, I have asked dear Father DePaul who married us in secret only six months ago, to make our marriage public. But I am foolish. Charles will not forget the promise he made to me. He will take care that no evil will befall our son, James. Charles does not accept my death is coming soon tho I assure him it will. I was most undone by the tremble of his lips. I kissed the tears away that flowed upon his dear face.

14 June, 1660
My womb has swollen as if I am to deliver another babe tho the midwives say there is no other. I write only what I must, today. I have asked Charles not to give James to my brother, Caleb, to foster for he will raise him a Puritan.

15 June, 1660
Surely my soul will reside in hell. So thinks my family. I lay with a man not my husband and bore his child out of wedlock. For them my disgrace is assured. But my dear Lord in Heaven will take me into His arms, for He knows the truth.

16 June, 1660
They bring James to me. I will hold him.

Livvy read the last words Jessamine Beresford wrote, covered her face, and wept. The sadness of it. To be so important to history, Jessamine still had been victim of that great killer of women over the centuries.

Removing the gloves she'd been wearing, she threw them away. Jack was confident he could keep her father from doing his worst when it came to

Chalcott House. Her spidey sense was telling her he was too confident. Jack didn't know her father as she did. All the logic in the world couldn't be offset by the vague, unformed fear she couldn't define.

In the meantime, her book could no longer be a biography. Maybe she could turn it into some kind of historical thriller. Maybe in some record somewhere there was proof that Jessamine truly did save Charles' life when she rushed to Antwerp to caution him about the anti-Royalists who planned to capture and kill him. That made sense.

Excited to think maybe, just maybe, she had her answer, she opened up her laptop. Her screen went black. Again.

She made a sound of frustration and went through the process she'd determined worked—force quitting and then booting up again. She immediately saved her work. She hadn't been able to find someone in Moreham to repair this thing. She'd ask Henry to take her to Lincoln, where surely there was someone who could.

She scrolled through the last chapter she'd written. It led to the marriage she would never write about. That was okay. Because she knew what she was going to do.

Jack spent the entire trip back to London on the phone with his solicitors. By the time Stebbins had them approaching the Elgar, he was convinced he knew what needed to be done to scuttle Browne's scheme. Fifteen minutes later, Jack entered the Hotel Elgar's lobby and headed down to the conference room for his scheduled staff meeting, a grim smile on his face. There was a low sound of people chatting in the conference room. As he opened the door, the chatting stopped. He took his usual position in the middle on one side of the long, rectangular table.

"Let's begin. This won't take long. I intend to bring everyone in the room up-to-date on a rather serious concern I have, and let you know what comes next."

He looked around the table. "There's been some rumor lately about Robert Browne—I assume you all know negotiations for the sale of Prime are going forward?"

Almost everyone nodded except Max. Who looked down.

After a beat, Jack continued. "Browne's standard operating procedure is to eviscerate the properties he buys for maximum short-term profit. One of the sticking points in my discussions with him has been about how he pursues profit by sacking people wholesale. I've received agreement from Browne that there will be none of that at Prime for a minimum of five years, except for those sacked for cause." He looked around. "For those of you who work at Prime in addition to Chalcott House, there's nothing to worry about on that front, is there? You lot would never be sacked for cause."

The burst of laughter that followed was spontaneous.

"Browne's reason for purchasing Prime is we've forged a strategy that will ultimately realize profit both online and off. He wants what we've developed. But now he wants more. He's decided he wants to get into traditional publishing."

Max's assistant, Ardis said, "As I remember that first discussion we had about Browne, six or seven months ago, you said you would never sell Chalcott House."

"That was true and still is." Jack eyed Max. "To do it, Browne's decided to bull through the purchase of the company's shares—and your votes—to control the board."

A clamor rose. Ardis half-stood, as if that news had her levitating out of her seat, until she thought better of it and sat. "But you're not letting that happen, are you, sir?"

"No. Chalcott House is controlled by my family. Though all of you at this table have shares, even if you were to sell them to Browne, it wouldn't make a difference. He could make noise at board meetings, I suppose. But that would be the extent."

Silence.

"Browne may have approached some of you already."

The silence that followed was as sharp as the laughter before. Then Quentin, Jack's sales manager, cleared his throat and said, "How would we have been approached?"

So Quentin had not been. Good. Jack turned to Max. "Can you give us some idea, Max?"

His head snapped up. "Sorry, Jack. My mind was elsewhere."

"Any thoughts on how Browne would have approached staff?"

Max's face reddened and he looked back down at his mobile in front of him.

Ardis stood again. Placing her palms on the table in front of her, she stared at Max. "Is this why you've been asking me to meet you after work for a pint?"

Eyes wide, Max looked up at her and then looked away.

Ardis resumed her seat. Without relinquishing her daggers-filled stare at Max, she said, "I wouldn't have said yes. I hope you know that, sir."

"Well done." Jack stood. "I won't ask if any of you thought of selling your shares or your vote to Browne. But you need to know the only way he could ever gain control of Chalcott House's board is if he were to convince my family to throw in with him. What do you suppose the chances are that he would succeed?"

Jack was silent for a moment. Then, he said, "All right. Meeting's over."

As chairs were pushed back and everyone shuffled to their feet, he added, "Those of you who are solely with Prime, you need not worry about your jobs. For those who work for Chalcott House as well, please trust that it will go on as strong as ever. I see nothing but wonderful growth ahead. Under my management."

He paused. "Max, I need a word. Please remain."

With nods and curious looks at Max, and a couple of relieved laughs, everyone else filed out. As the door closed, Jack turned to Max. "Do you want to tell me how all this came about?"

Max looked longingly at the door. Then he pretended a cough. "Tell you about what, exactly?"

"Max, you know how our last conversation ended. You know what."

Blots of scarlet bloomed on his cheeks. "I didn't contact him, this time."

Jack slid his hands into his pockets. "Who contacted you?"

Max exhaled softly. "Browne's son-in-law. Kyle Bentsen."

Jack might have known… "Why did you decide to throw in with them?"

"I hadn't thrown in with them then."

Jack raised an eyebrow. "No? When? And why?"

"Some things had come up."

Jack folded his arms across his chest. "And?"

Max sagged in his chair. "Bentsen called me a few weeks after you and I spoke. Could we meet and talk about Prime? I thought he wanted my opinion. I was flattered."

"Your opinion?"

Max smoothed his palm across the cool glass of the table top. "Though I said I wouldn't be in touch with anyone from Cenotaph, I thought meeting to talk about Prime would be allowed. Only then at the meeting did he mention Chalcott House."

"And your response was…?"

"I almost didn't respond. I remembered our conversation and my promise not to be in contact with Browne." There was a long pause. "But Bentsen knew what to say to me." Max made a fist and put it to his mouth. "How did he know it was the money?"

Jack rambled over to stand next to Max. "Know about how you're in debt?"

Max eyes widened. "How do *you* know?"

"You've telegraphed it in so many ways. All those remarks about how you don't know how to pay for your kids' school, the divorce, and Cynthia wanting more. How could I not have figured it out?"

"Well then," Max said, turning on Jack. "Why didn't you offer to help me?"

Jack sighed. "Apparently, I have more respect for your pride than you do."

When Max remained silent, Jack added, "I'll turn that question around. Why didn't you ask me? Haven't we known each other long enough that you could have?"

"I was ashamed," Max burst out.

"So, because you were ashamed to ask me for help—I, who made you my highest paid employee— you put yourself in league with a man who you know is intent upon destroying the thing that is dearest to me. Isn't that right?"

Max's face whitened. "I didn't think of it that way."

"What exactly did Bentsen suggest to you?"

"He suggested…" Max's voice trailed off before strengthening. "It was just like you said. I would agree to vote my shares for his father-in-law and be paid an ungodly sum. My money problems would go away. But I'd get nothing unless I could—" He licked his lips, a plea for understanding glittering in his eyes. "If I could go to others and offer them similar large amounts of money to do the same, it would go even better for me."

"Did you go to anyone?"

"I looked around. The people here, their loyalty to you, the percentage of their shares amounted to nothing that would make a difference just like you said. But…" His face seemed to firm, suddenly defiant. "I did go to one person."

"Who was that?"

"Your mother."

CHAPTER FIFTEEN

"You contacted my mother?" A strange zinging sound popped in Jack's ears.

Max's chin went up. "I did. I thought I had an opportunity to…"

"An opportunity?" He was raging inside. "To do what?"

Max's gaze sawed left and right. "I knew she was insulted when you banned her from bringing her dog to board meetings. If I could sympathize with her, she would surely listen to me."

Jack reminded himself to curb his temper. "What was your next step?"

"I asked if I could drive down to visit her and if she would spend some time with me. She agreed. And so I did, one Saturday a few weeks ago."

"Ah. You felt it was appropriate to go behind my back."

"I did not." Max's voice raised in defense. "I didn't have to ask your permission to speak to your mother. You're not her keeper. If she didn't want to see me, she could have said so."

The gall of the man was stunning. "That's true."

Jack turned his back on Max and paced away. "You thought you could convince my mother to throw in with Robert Browne against me because I wouldn't let Monty come to board meetings? That's a fairly far-fetched supposition, don't you think?" His voice had grown still and soft while inside, his gut continued to churn.

"Your mum can be a bit dotty, Jack. So many women of that age... *You* know, and women in general. I reasoned it out. If you and your family together control ninety-two per cent of Chalcott House then it made sense that she would own something in the range of twenty per cent. It seemed a good place to start."

Jack squared his shoulders. He was almost done with Max Honeywell, but the noose was not as tight around the man's neck as he wanted it to be. "So, the math of the thing is what had you hopeful. Once you had my mother on your side—and therefore on Browne's side—at the next Board meeting, she would lobby for my sisters to do likewise?"

"Yes." He lifted his chin.

"For some, I suppose that would sound logical."

Max looked away. "Nothing came of it."

"How fortunate for me. How unfortunate for you."

"She said she didn't understand what I wanted her to do and then told me she was quite, quite busy, that she had to take *Monty*…" Max spit out the name of his mother's animal, as if saying it left a sour taste in his mouth. "…to be groomed. She dismissed me for a dog. And then when I was on my way home, I realized she'd been toying with me, that she made me drive all the way down to meet her and had no intention to do what I wanted her to."

"Do what *you* wanted her to?" Jack's voice bit sharp as the blade of a knife. "I would suggest you don't speak of my mother as if she were a puppet and you could pull her strings."

It was an illusion, perhaps, or perhaps not, but it appeared that Max was shrinking in on himself.

"What, may I ask, did Bentsen offer you, besides that ungodly amount of money, if you could get my mother or my sisters to vote their shares in his favor?"

"He promised me a role in the new company he would create once Browne got control of Chalcott House." There was an underlying tremble in Max's voice.

"So you would be set, then."

Max lifted a handkerchief from his pocket and mopped his forehead.

Jack took a step toward the door. "You would be compensated by Browne—"

"Nothing's signed yet." Wariness showed on Max's face.

"Your mistake, letting that detail get away from you. As your plan was to be compensated by Browne after what certainly seems like a very attractive offer, I'm quite sure you don't need to be compensated by me." Jack swung the door open and called, "Get me security, please."

He turned back to Max. "We worked together so well over the years. But now you've lost whatever credibility and trust I once had in you. You have a half hour to gather up your things."

Two men stepped into the conference room. They focused their impassive stares on Max.

"These two gentlemen will remain with you while you empty your office of your personal property. They will watch that you don't take anything that belongs to the company. IT will delete your access to the company server. As of this moment, you are no longer an employee of Anstruther Media Group."

Max took a hard, angry breath. His lips drew back in a sneer. "You're a fool, Jack. Oh, pardon. *Your Grace.*"

Jack gave his security men the eye, cautioning them to let Max go on.

"You could have saved Chalcott House for yourself and your family if you'd only listened to me. Without Marybeth—and you're a fool if you think she has the remotest chance of writing ever again— there's no way you can keep Chalcott House afloat."

Max rolled his shoulders, as if sloughing off a bother. "You think you've solved all your problems and when I'm gone you'll be safe, do you?" The words fell from Max's lips with spittle. "Think again. Browne is coming for you, Jack, and there's nothing you can do to stop him."

As the taller of the two security men took hold of Max's arm, Max shook him off. Giving Jack one last angry glare, he stomped out of the conference room.

Jack froze. That threat sounded too much like what Livvy had said, how her father would draw blood, if he had to, in order to win.

He shoved the thought away. Grabbing his phone, he keyed in the number that he had only recently become familiar with. Of everything Max had said—the arrogant attempt to turn Jack's mother against him, the comments about Chalcott House failing—that last thing was what gave Jack pause.

When Charlie answered Jack didn't bother with the niceties.

"I gave Max Honeywell the sack."

Charlie didn't wait on the niceties, either. "It's about time. You're well rid of the bloody prat."

"Max's parting shot, the words he used, were that Browne is coming for me."

"Ah. So the gauntlet is thrown."

"Correct." Jack paced around the table. "Max confessed to an attempt he made to help Browne get control of Chalcott House through a takeover of my board by, believe it or not, playing on my mother's hurt feelings."

Charlie made non-committal sounds as Jack told him the story. "As security escorted him out, Max said Browne wasn't through with me. That's a concern."

"Did he give you any indication what it might be?" The clack of computer keys said Charlie was typing.

"None, although it did seem he was pleased to threaten me."

"We know Browne doesn't play by the rules." More typing. Then, "From what little I know of him, there is every reason for you to be wary."

The typing ceased and Charlie said, "All right. I've put out some feelers. We have to assume there is something somewhere that will show us how to stop Browne. If it exists, my people will find it. I'll call you with what I find."

Jack didn't bother calling Stebbins to drive him back to Somerset Mews. He took the Underground instead, and then walked. The last thing he wanted now was to be distracted by Henry's non-stop chatter.

Despite the potential danger that Browne presented, it didn't keep him from feeling a warmth long missing. He had an ally and friend in Charlie Camville. As he walked up the last steps from the Underground, he permitted himself a little smile. He had other allies too. He pulled his mobile from his pocket.

The number he called rang and rang. He was ready to hang up when his mother answered. "Jack, how delightful. I didn't expect your call."

"Well, here I am."

"That's nice, dear."

"I called to say thank you."

"That's lovely. What exactly are you thanking me for?"

There was no question in Jack's mind that his mother knew exactly what he was thanking her for. A jot of coyness in her voice gave her away. "Mum, I know about your visitor, Max Honeywell, and how you sent him packing."

"Oh my." She made a tsking sound. "That fellow, I cannot say anything good about him. And really, did he think I was born yesterday?"

"You certainly can't be thought to have been. Although perhaps seeing you, he thought you were inexperienced in the ways of business because of your youthful looks."

The laugh she gave him was so unforced, Jack realized it had been a long time since he'd heard it. He'd begun to think of his mother as someone he needed to take care of, that care being something onerous. More shame him.

He turned the corner into Somerset Mews. "Earlier today, I gave Max the sack. He told me how he drove down to see you and how you told him to get lost. You shocked him. That's what I'm grateful for."

"What's a mother for but doing something for her much-loved son?"

Jack paused. For some reason, his mother's simple words "much-loved-son" sounded like armor against what he knew might come next. "Well then, I owe you an apology as well."

"Jack! You don't, although it would be lovely to hear what the apology is for."

He started again down the cobblestoned street toward his office. "It was after the unfortunate incident with Monty defecating in the board room. I was shocked, not that it's any kind of excuse and so I didn't offer you one when I should have."

"No apology necessary for that incident, as you call it. I should apologize. Monty's behavior was unacceptable and you were right to ban him. I, too, behaved badly. I'd had an overwhelming desire to defend myself and instead looked foolish."

"Even as arrogant as I was, I—"

"Not arrogant, dear. Just a bit haughty."

"Touché."

"Since we are speaking of apologies, I have a long-standing one that I must confess."

Striding on, Jack started up the steps to 10 Somerset Mews' front door. Hand on the knob, Jack paused. "Whatever for?

"I never told you this, but I never warmed to Freddie Camville. There was something glib about him I couldn't like."

Jack hadn't liked Freddie, but glib hadn't been the word he'd used. It was sleazy, more like.

"When your dad came into the dukedom, he saw immediately that the duchy's holdings were in a parlous state. I'm not sure you knew to what extent."

"I rather think I didn't, although I'm sure I thought I knew everything."

"You were a young man, Jack. Of course you thought you knew everything."

"One learns doesn't one," Jack snorted.

"Your dad felt it his responsibility to restore everything to its original state. It would take money we didn't have. Freddie offered access to a lot of money. He painted such a rosy picture. The scheme couldn't fail. And so your father committed us to disaster."

"Mum, don't—"

"Please, I've kept this bottled up for so long, I… I didn't blame your father for what happened. He was too trusting."

"Mum, really, you shouldn't—"

"I blame myself. I should have tried harder to keep him from making that commitment. But I didn't and if I'm being honest with myself, I think part of it was because, deep down, I wanted to believe in Freddie, because if he was right, our investment would have made us rich beyond anything. I have always felt that guilt."

Jack leaned against the doorframe. Closing his eyes, he exhaled a sore breath. "Don't flog yourself over it. There's no need."

"Still, I should have known."

"But Mum, you could have tried mightily. Who can say it would have helped?"

She sighed. "You're right. There's nothing more to be said for what's happened. I suppose even as I have admired you for how you have restored us all, I have been a little jealous thinking that your father and I were such failures—"

"Stop." His jaws were tight with emotion. "I will not let you finish that sentence. However successful I am it's because you and Dad gave me everything on which I built my life."

Her breath caught.

"I hope those are not tears I hear."

She sniffed.

"Mum, if you start crying I will, as well, and how will that look, me crying all over the entrance to my office?"

That had her laughing. "We won't speak of it again. Only one thing, Jack…"

"Yes?" He'd always done more than one thing for his mother out of a sense of duty. Now, if she wanted him to slay a dragon, he'd do it with a whole heart.

"You must follow your own advice. Learn to live in the present not the past. And now, my darling, I really must go."

Jack allowed himself a rueful grin. What he'd learned about himself today. He couldn't wait to get on a video call with Livvy to tell her.

As he pushed the door to his office open, Isabella looked up from her computer's display. "Good timing, sir. You have a call waiting."

"Do I?" He headed toward his office. "Who is it?"

"Kyle Bentsen."

Crossing to his desk, Jack snatched the handset out of its cradle. "Bentsen," he barked, no preamble. "It's not going to work. I've sacked—you Yanks refer to that as fired—your pawn."

"You mean Honeywell?"

Jack raised an eyebrow. "Just so. He was quite forthcoming about Mr. Browne's plan to wrest Chalcott House from me. Did you think you could get my *mother*…" The zing of temper came through in the sharpness of his voice. "…to betray me? I think you can assume your plans have been thwarted. The jig's up, mate."

Bentsen laughed. It wasn't the response Jack had expected.

"I told my father-in-law not to put too much trust in Honeywell."

"Good conclusion. Now that you've exhausted your underhanded efforts to take Chalcott House, I'm afraid I've rethought selling Prime to you. The moment this call is over, I plan on having a discussion with my attorneys. The subject will be whether and how to end negotiations for the sale of AMG to Cenotaph."

"Not so fast. What do you think? We give up so easily?"

A chill scudded across Jack's shoulders. In the back of his head he heard Livvy warning him that her father never quit. "There's nothing to give up."

Bentsen laughed again. "You think so? You think a man like Robert Browne wouldn't have a contingency plan? If that's what you've been thinking, that's sad. No, this time Duke, we have you. There's no way for you to get out from under this one, and you will sell all of AMG to us. Plus Chalcott House."

Pulling his chair back, Jack sat. "I wouldn't spend too much time entertaining myself with that nonsense."

"Nonsense? No. You see, we know how you've hidden a pretty big secret. Oh wait, it *was* a secret. Not any longer." Bentsen chuckled low in the back of his throat. "That's because now *we* know about that secret."

The hairs rose on the back of Jack's neck. "Get to the point."

"The point about how you could be king." Bentsen's sneer came right through the ether. "According to my sister-in-law."

Jack came out of his slouch.

"You're not wondering which sister-in-law I'm talking about, are you?" Bentsen went on. "It's the one who's living in that house of yours. The one you're sleeping with."

A band tightened across Jack's chest even as he had a stupidly errant thought that it was odd Bentsen knew he and Livvy were sleeping together.

"Let's see. What could we do with the information she gave us about your ancestors? Hmm…"

Jack heard Bentsen through ears deadened to sound.

"We could make some phone calls, be the unnamed source for what's bound to be a bombshell announcement."

Jack swiveled around to stare out the window behind him.

"You Brits love your gossip and the meaner it is, the better you like it. So yeah, I think we'd call the tabloids, and they could sic the paparazzi on you."

Jack's lungs caught. An illusion, he told himself. He could breathe. The vise tightened and he wheezed a small breath.

"Those bastards live to destroy people," Bentsen droned on. "I think it's awesome. But then I'm not going to be the one scared shitless about what might happen to my sister driving to the supermarket with a kid or two in the back seat, being chased by a swarm of guys on motorbikes, those big ass cameras all set to take shot after shot when she crashes into a pillar or something."

Leaning across the sideboard, Jack unlatched, opened the window, and took in a draft of cleansing, cold air.

"You there, Duke? I can't hear you," Bentsen said in a sing-song voice.

"What do you want?"

Bentsen laughed. "Shit, you know what I want."

The air, having done its job, Jack closed the window and listened to the drone of Bentsen's unctuous, false-friendly voice, until he said, "You haven't answered my question. How did you find out?"

"You don't mean how. You mean when, right?"

"Yes," he said, in a low, angry voice.

Bentsen laughed. "Why don't you ask Olivia about the phone call she made to her sister, Sheryl, just last night."

For Jack, it was, once again, last night. He was swimming up out of a deep sleep to feel her getting back into bed and curling up against him, her feet and legs icy to the touch. He'd asked her where she'd gone. As a joke. She'd spoken of worry about her father. But no mention of a phone conversation with Sheryl.

Somehow, he managed to say, "If I were you, I would tell your father-in-law that he should pray he doesn't have any skeletons in his closet. If he does, I will discover them and use them to destroy him. And you."

"You do what you do, Jack. We'll be right here." He hung up.

Seething, Jack stalked to the sideboard to Rose's punching bag. He placed his hand over its cone and dug his fingers into the cool leather until the skin over his knuckles turned white.

He took a step backward, bringing both hands up to rub his temples. He was not going to do it again. Think Bentsen spoke the truth. Jack made that mistake once before, believing Livvy only when it was corroborated by someone else, Bentsen then, as well.

He pressed a fist to the center of his forehead. She'd promised him she'd keep the marriage between Jessamine and Charles to herself. And he'd promised he would believe her.

"Think, Jack. Think." He growled. He tried to imagine her explanation because there had to be one.

As he threw one idea after another at the dartboard in his brain, the analytical person inside rejected each for a rationalization. After each attempt made, his heart sank further until it had nowhere to go. Livvy had to have done what she said she wouldn't.

But wait. He had to give her a chance to explain. He would confront—no, not confront. He would *ask* her, and he would listen. He would study her face. If she'd betrayed him, she wouldn't be able to hide it. Of all the things he knew about her, Livvy couldn't keep her thoughts from showing in her eyes.

He sat at his desk and called up his video conferencing app. When it opened, she appeared right away, smiling, her face alight with joy to see him.

Surely, that said something.

"I was wondering when you were going to call." She flounced around in her chair, drawing herself closer to her display. "Have you been busy? Do you miss me?"

He opened his mouth to speak and nothing came out.

She threw her fisted hands upward. "Oh, Jack, you won't believe it. I think I may have found a better end to the book. Do you want to hear what I came up with?" Her hair swung back and forth with her excitement. Her eyes sparkled. "I have to say it's better than the truth."

Better than the truth. He thought he would be sick.

Frowning, she turned her head to the side. "Are you all right? You look like you ate something bad."

"Did you…?"

Her frown deepened. "Did I what?"

"Make a phone call to your sister. Last night."

She gave him a nervous laugh, or at least he read it as nervous. "I meant to tell you. But we got busy with you-know-what and I forgot."

Jack's gut churned. "Did you tell her about the marriage certificate?"

Her head jerked back. "Jack, you know I didn't."

This was not what he'd wanted to hear. "No, I don't know that."

Her eyes went wide. "You don't? How can you not?"

He worked his jaw, trying for something to say, to ask how it could be anyone else when it was only the two of them who knew about Jessamine and Charles. With a steadiness he didn't feel, he said, "I got a phone call from Kyle. He and your father know about the marriage. They're blackmailing me, planning to go to the tabloids with the story."

She leaned forward, her face filling up his laptop's display. "I have no idea how he found out. He didn't find out from me."

"Tell me the truth, Livvy." He spoke each word like a bullet fired. "What did you say to Sheryl?"

"I said nothing. You know I wouldn't. It's what Sheryl said to me that I should have told you and would have— Oh." She thumped backward. Her eyes, so bright with desperate emotion, became guarded. Her color deadened to flat white. Her lips, always so ready to smile or broaden into a smile, flattened into a grim line. "After everything we've talked about on this issue of trust, you don't believe me. There's nothing I could say that would change your mind, isn't that right?"

Though his head told him she had played him for an unsuspecting fool, he wanted her to convince him he was wrong. He wanted to plead with her to convince him. "Convince me I'm wrong, then."

She placed her elbows on the table and leaned into the screen so there was nothing but her face filling it up, stern in implacable lines. "I can't. And hurray for you. You've done it. Killed it between us." She shoved hair that had fallen forward onto her cheek back behind her ear. "I'm a big fool if I thought you could ever change. Goodbye Jack."

His screen went black. He lifted his hand, halfway to get her back but then dropped it into his lap. By disconnecting, she'd proved it. She'd betrayed him. She'd laid him open to the most disastrous of Hobson's choices. Now, what did he do? Tell Bentsen to have at it and expose his family to pain and upheaval? Or did he cede control of Chalcott House, his father's legacy, to keep them safe?

Wasn't it irony of the worst sort that his father had been beguiled by a liar? He, it seemed, had been beguiled by one, as well.

CHAPTER SIXTEEN

She'd packed almost everything. The only thing left were her notes and her computer. She started to shove the papers into her suitcase when she stopped, mid-job. She should call him back. But no, he'd done it again. Assumed she would betray him. So, no. He didn't deserve a phone call from her. There was one she would make, though. To Sheryl.

The conversation was brief.

"Remind me. What did I tell you about Jack?"

"You mean other than to say he's hot? Nothing. And hello to you, too."

"That proves I'm not suffering from amnesia," she muttered.

"What amnesia?"

"Have you spoken to Kyle lately?"

"Other than seeing him for a moment that day he came to see Elliot? No, I haven't. Livvy, what's this about?"

"I'm coming home." She hung up.

Hugging her fury tight, she glared at the bed where she'd slept with him, and made love with him, not twenty-four hours ago. She looked away. She damn well wasn't going to picture herself making love with a man who didn't trust her.

Eventually, the anger wore off, replaced by grief that sank its hooks into her. She choked back the tears because crying over a man who was a lost cause was not in the plan today or ever.

But tears had a habit of not listening. When hers came, they brought her to her knees. It hurt in her throat and her chest, in her belly and in the fingers she clutched hard to her arms. She let the anguish pour out.

Afterwards, she clambered to her feet and swiped at her face with the back of her hand. Crying made her feel like crap. She refused to feel like crap when she was the wronged one. Besides, they stood in the way of her focusing on what she needed to do. Getting back to London so she could catch a flight to New Jersey.

Minutes later, she was dragging her suitcase and her backpack down the hallway. She slowed when she came to the library. Its doors were closed. She knew who had closed them and why, but it wasn't going to stop her. Before she left she would have one last look. She clasped one of the door's ornate handles.

"Please don't."

Livvy wheeled around. Madelyn stood at the top of the steps, a shuttered look on her face. "He told me I shouldn't let you in."

Livvy hadn't thought she could be any more sick at heart. In a thick voice, she said, "I'm not going to take anything."

Madelyn raised both hands, fingers fluttering with anxiety. "I work for the man, and he's given the order to be sure you leave. But I've gotten to know you, and I don't see what could be so wrong that he wants you to, so…" She stared fixedly away.

A small thing, but a relief. Squaring her shoulders, she opened the door and stepped in, her heart a lead weight in her chest. She loved this room. She loved the shelves. She loved the books now standing upright, books that she'd organized with precision and ruthlessness. She loved the ugly furniture, the tables, the chairs, even the chaise longue. She'd polished every surface she could reach in this room until all of it shone like it was the finest library in the world. She loved everything in this room, a love mingled now with the pain of separation.

Jessamine's diaries lay where she'd left them. She wouldn't look that way, though she wanted to cross over to them and touch them for the last time. She backed out and closed the doors behind her.

At the head of the steps, Livvy began to struggle with her luggage.

In a flurry of activity, Madelyn reached for the suitcase. "Oh, for goodness sakes, I don't know what's happened. All he said was he wouldn't have his family hurt again." She started down the stairs, the suitcase making clunking sounds as the wheels hit stone and echoed against the walls of the clerestoried hall.

Madelyn reached the bottom and turned around, eyes on Livvy, as Livvy followed behind, with her backpack. "How can Jack think you'd do something so terrible, when we both know you're in love with him and wouldn't hurt his family for the world."

To think Madelyn knew. To think she and Jack thought they were being careful… Livvy sighed and glanced up at the painting that enthralled her so, the painting of Charles making his only legitimate son, James, the Duke of Brompton.

With slow steps she passed under it into the seventh duke's monstrosity and whispered, "Goodbye."

At the front steps, the cab she'd called to take her to Lincoln's train station waited.

Madelyn reached for Livvy and hugged her tight. "Goodbye." Letting her go, she stepped back, lips trembling. "If you ever come back to England I hope you'll visit me, even if it's only for a cuppa."

"I will," Livvy whispered. She clambered into the cab. Refusing to look back, Livvy slumped down in the back seat. Out of nowhere, she remembered her sweater. It was draped over the chair in front of her makeshift desk in the library. She opened her mouth to tell the driver to turn around, but subsided in silence. Returning to the place that had become her home for the past few weeks would be too painful. Besides it wasn't the sweater she'd left behind. It was her heart.

The trip from Brompton Court to Lincoln's train station was a blur. By the time she stood on the platform, her brain had morphed into non-functioning gray matter. The simple task of dragging her luggage onto the train all but paralyzed her. She was saved by a girl wearing a hoodie. "Oi, you need help?"

This girl was half Livvy's size. A bubble of hysterical laughter rose in Livvy's throat. "If you don't mind taking the suitcase. Be careful, it's heavy."

The girl gave her a quick nod, and grasping Livvy's suitcase by the handle, lugged it onto the train and then disappeared before Livvy could thank her.

Livvy settled then, not just into her seat, but in her mind. Forget the poor-me thing she'd wallowed in. She was going back to New Jersey and her apartment next to the Hudson River with windows that did not face said river, but was home since she'd walked out of the house where she'd grown up.

She was going back to her old life. The job at the restaurant. Volunteering at the library. Writing her blog. Writing for the literary magazine, and oh yeah.

Finishing her book. What she wouldn't do was think of the man of her dreams, dreams become nightmare. So there. Only for a second did her heart serve up a yes-but before she shoved it back in its place.

Livvy kept busy during the trip to London. She pulled out her laptop and made a reservation at the Hotel Elgar. Next, she bought a ticket on the first available British Airways flight to Newark, which was the following morning at 11:15 a.m. She sent a message to Arlene Sawyer, head of the county's library service, telling her she was on her way back and ready to start on any project Arlene had for her. She sketched out ideas for her next few blog posts, when her computer decided to black itself out.

"Crap," she muttered. This blacking out thing was becoming more frequent. Her repair guy, who she would definitely see as soon as she got home, would tell her if she needed a new computer, which would suck.

What also sucked was her computer's little trick broke her train of thought and that conversation with Jack came flooding back.

She'd spent her entire life with people who had no faith in her. It had taken her years before she no longer cared that they didn't. She'd thought Jack had faith in her. Since he didn't—her throat closed up on grief—how could she love him?

Managing her bags when getting off the train in London was not a problem because by then she had herself, if not calm, at least collected. As her cabbie drove on through London's streets, she stared. When the man slowed and coasted past Club Chaos, Livvy's gaze sharpened. How different it looked in the light of day. There was no line; there were no ropes. It was just a building with no windows and a single, metal door marking the entrance, all its nighttime sparkle missing.

Moments later, the cabbie was idling in front of the Elgar. Livvy's heart stuttered. What was she thinking? There was no way she could stay here, not with all its connections to Jack. Leaning forward she said, "Can you drive around the corner?" There was a hotel there. It was small, but she was willing to take a chance there'd be a room available. If there wasn't, she'd ask the cabbie to take her to Heathrow. She wouldn't be the first person in the world to sleep at an airport.

Jack knew what the first thing was he needed to do once Livvy cut the line. He needed to save his family from Robert Browne. He needed to preserve their privacy. And their safety.

But one other thing first. Not caring what time it was in the UK or New York, he set up a conference call with the heads of both his British and American law firms. No one was particularly surprised that Browne, through Bentsen, thought the way to wrest control of Chalcott House away from Jack was through blackmail.

"We knew Browne's reputation, going in," said one of the attorneys from the American side.

"And if I hadn't wanted to get rid of *Daily Prime*, I wouldn't have considered their offer at all." Jack pressed thumb and forefinger to the tight skin above the bridge of his nose. "What an idiot…thinking I could do business with someone like Browne."

"Robert Browne is an amoral git," observed the head of the British firm.

"As soon as it can be done, I want him notified that I have pulled out of the sale. I don't give a damn what kind of legal remedy he brings against me or what trick he pulls out of his vulture capitalist handbook. No portion of AMG will ever be his."

Because it was the driver of the problem, Jack uncorked the secret of his royal forebear. Some of the attorneys, especially the Americans, were impressed that he had royal blood. More fools they.

They agreed it was better that Browne think he held the upper hand for the present. The consensus was they should tie up their counterparts at Browne's Cenotaph in legalistic minutiae until they figured out their next move.

As the call wound down, Jack said, "I need to speak to my family." He wasn't looking forward to it, but they needed to know what could come their way once Browne realized he was being thwarted.

After Jack severed the call, he held up his hand. Spreading his fingers, he stared. They were trembling. He made a fist. He was about to tell his family that once more their peace could be cut up. They would have to take precautions they hadn't in years because he'd dropped his guard for Olivia Browne.

He started the process setting up the conference call with his family and stopped. There was one more thing he had to do before he did and it only took seconds. He texted Pratt to cease all work at Brompton Court. He'd never had any real interest in the place. For all he cared, it could rot.

It took longer to set up the call than it ought to have. But once everyone was on the line, he spoke without preamble. "Robert Browne, who I'd been planning to sell AMG to, is threatening to disclose one of our family's secrets."

"Ooh," crowed Rose. "Is it a juicy one?"

Leave it to his baby sister to poke fun. "It depends upon your point of view."

"What's the secret, pray tell, Jack?" asked Diana. "I'm assuming you haven't done anything illegal."

"I have not. But you need to know that Browne's attack dog, Kyle Bentsen, called today to let me know they are going to force me to sell Chalcott House to them."

"Ah, the lovely Mr. Bentsen." Diana's words might be steady, but her tone was acerbic. "You did say he was a bent bastard."

"I did. And all of you, please remain calm. It won't do as I tell you the story if our conversation devolves into mass hysteria."

His mum sighed. "I reserve the right to be appropriately hysterical if what you're about to tell us demands it. Now out with it, please."

To Jack's relief no one interrupted.

"I suppose this means if things had turned out differently, we might have grown up in Buckingham Palace," said Alice, speaking into the silence. "How…quaint."

He rolled his eyes at her surprisingly off-hand reaction. "Quaint? No."

"But it will make an absolutely smashing story." Excitement filled Rose's voice. "I want to do it, Jack. I know my editors will say yes the moment I tell them. Just think how brilliant it will be, writing it first person as a princess of England."

Jack's eye widened. "This has the potential of putting you, your sisters, and our mother in the bullseye of paparazzi throughout the UK. It means being torn apart in media, perhaps even receiving death threats from crazy people on the fringe. So, no, Rosie-girl. You're not writing any story about our benighted history."

Ignoring Rose's just suppressed whinge, Jack said, "Now that I know what Browne's game is, I have something of an advantage. I can control the timeline. But at the end of the day, I've decided I will do what I must to keep him from opening up my family to the same kind of pain and upheaval we were forced to live with before. Though I won't sell him Prime, I will sell him Chalcott House."

"Darling boy," his mother said. "May I remind you that your sisters and I own shares in Chalcott House and we might not be in agreement with you making that decision?"

Of all of them, he hadn't expected to hear that from his mother. It was she, who had most acutely experienced the double nightmare of her husband dying under a black cloud and the holy hell that followed. "Mum—"

"I need to tell you something," Rosie said, talking over him.

"If it's about the nightmares, I know. It's a reason why I'm doing this."

"I hope you're not for me. Or my nightmares. Which I haven't had for years."

Jack blinked. When had *that* happened?

"And if you think to have one of your minders follow me around, think again. I don't want one."

"I don't either," Alice cut in.

"The last time the family was attacked, you did," Jack said with some heat.

"Good Lord," broke in Diana. "Do you think this is Groundhog Day?"

"She means the movie," said Rose, helping.

"Thank you, Rosie," said Diana.

"Please," Jack broke in, slapping a hand to his head. "Now is not the time for humor. Or to pretend to be brave."

"That's not what we—"

"Bleeding hell, are you—"

As they spoke over each other, Jack began to feel desperate. "Mum, girls, can you—"

"Jack," his mum broke in. "If all you're doing is calling to tell us what you've already decided to do without asking our opinions, I don't think I appreciate that."

With growing frustration, he said, "Sorry, Mum. But I must prepare for the worst. I can't think of another way to keep Mr. Browne from cutting up our peace."

"Whose peace are you talking about? I hope not mine," Diana said.

Jack exhaled sharply. "If my family can't remember what it was like then, the furor, the accusations, people looking at us with suspicion like we had committed murder, being followed by rabid reporters, let me remind you. It was awful, horrendous, months and months of you being afraid to go outside."

"Of course, I remember," said Alice, his most skittish of sisters.

"That's why I'm giving up Chalcott House so it doesn't happen again!" His heated shout was met by dead silence. "Have you lot got nothing to add?" he said, goaded.

"I have something," said Alice. "I'm against you giving up Chalcott House."

He opened his mouth. Nothing came out.

"I love you, dearest brother, and it warms my heart that you want to protect me—all of us really," Alice's words were drowned out by a chorus of yeses.

Rose picked up the conversational ball. "That's what I wanted to say before when you so rudely interrupted me."

There was a chorus of derisive laughter as Rose's sisters reminded her she was the baby and needed to be interrupted.

"You can say whatever you want," Rose spoke over them. "Even if my nightmares came back, they'd never be a reason for you to give up the thing you love perhaps more than you love us: your work."

"Rosie," Jack chided. "I don't love my work more than I love you." A smile flickered. "Not entirely."

More laughter broke whatever tension remained. When it died down, his mother said, "I think I can say we are all opposed to your plan for giving up Chalcott House. If you're worried about us, don't be, because you see, we are hardened veterans of the paparazzi wars. We know what to do if we're accosted by some unpleasant person with a camera in hand."

"Yeah," Rose said. "Arseholes…"

Jack glanced over at the sideboard and the picture of the five of them together for Diana's wedding, all three of his sisters with big smiles, his mother beaming. And he? Off to the side a bit, a little remote. Always on duty. Even at his sister's wedding.

He hadn't seen it. He hadn't thought to ask. But here it was. It seemed they could take care of themselves. They didn't need him to do it for them. "So is the consensus that I tell Browne to sod off?"

It was a unanimous yes.

His sluggish brain cells began to fire. "All right. Just a warning. It will get ugly."

"Then I think you better prepare well," said Diana.

As each of his sisters and his mum added their bit, Jack woke his PC. "We're dealing with tough and unethical men."

"So you have said. We expect you to be just as tough, Jack," said Alice, her soft voice firm.

"I'll keep you informed."

"You'd better," said Mum.

After they'd all disconnected, Jack sat back, stunned. It was extraordinary, really. It was as if someone had opened a door wide to reveal a home truth he should have long ago recognized. Caught in a hot beam of revelation, the cautionary tale he'd been telling himself all this time disintegrated into nothing.

When his mobile rang, he picked up, smiling. "Have you called back with advice, Mum?"

"I trust you to know how to go on without my advice. I do have a question, though. How did Mr. Browne find out?"

The euphoria that had buoyed him—knowing his family was strong—faded away. He felt Livvy's phantom presence, again, her absence, the steady but faint pain that wouldn't go away of a tooth needing attention. "He found out from Livvy."

The sound his mother made was a combination of shock and dismay. "How?"

Jack rubbed the top of his head. "She had a conversation with her sister and her sister must have told him. It turns out, Livvy was my Trojan Horse."

"That's a bit over the top, don't you think?"

"Over the top. Unfortunately, yes. It turns out that is exactly what she is."

It all came out then. He, who never spoke without forethought, or shared his feelings with anyone, shared with his mother all but the most personal of details about what had gone on between him and Livvy. "Why did she do it? It makes no sense."

Except he wanted it to make sense. He wanted her back in his life. But how considering the gulf that had opened between them?

"If this is so unlike what you know of Livvy, isn't it possible he found out some other way?"

"No, it's not possible, it's—"

Out of nowhere it came. The avalanche. How she'd told him she thought of herself as different from the rest of her family for as long as she could remember. The briefcase and the heart. The annulment her father forced on her and the humiliation afterward. Hadn't Livvy's father reminded her every chance he had that she was the family outlier? Why, then, would she have told her sister anything that could help him?

She wouldn't.

That awful expression—about heads exploding—he knew now what it meant. It meant he'd been wrong. Spectacularly, logically wrong. "Mum, isn't this a day for revelations? I need to go." He had an apology to make, the most important one of his life.

Grinning like a demented hyena, he knew what he needed to do. He'd tell Livvy he didn't know how it happened that Bentsen found out. It wasn't important. He believed her now. Not like before. This time, whole-heartedly.

Madelyn said Livvy had packed her bags and left Brompton Court for the train station in Lincoln, which meant she was likely here in London, perhaps no more than a mile or two away. He called the Elgar, thinking that's where she'd be staying. He could go to her and get this disaster resolved. But she wasn't at the Elgar. If she wasn't at the Elgar, she would stay at... He had a crackbrained idea to ask Isabella to assemble a team that would check every hotel in London where she might have reserved a room. He abandoned that as total idiocy.

Jack's next call was to British Airways because he made two assumptions. If she'd flown to the UK on BA, she'd be flying back to the States on BA, and given how these things worked, he doubted she would have found a flight out today.

No luck. It was against company policy to give him passenger information. He didn't waste more time trying to pressure someone farther up the food chain who could override policy. Instead, he called Charlie to see if there was anything he could do. There was no answer.

There was no point in remaining at the office. It was 8:30 and dark. On the long walk home—he preferred walking when he was at sixes and sevens—he tried Charlie repeatedly. Only as he was unlocking the door to his flat, did Charlie call back.

"Are you calling to congratulate me?" said Charlie.

With a genuine smile Jack said, "Are you a father then?"

"Just a half hour ago. I held her in my arms when she was just five minutes old. She looked up at me, dazed. 'What was that ordeal?' she might as well have said. I assured her she wouldn't have to do that again, as she was with her dad now. Oh, it's a girl."

Jack's smile grew into a grin. "Well done. How's the scrap's mum?"

"Doing very well. As spirited as ever. She kicked me out of the room when the baby began to come."

"I'm happy to hear that Annie is still Annie."

"Enough about that. You rang. More than once. It must be important."

"It is." Jack told him.

"So you want me to break into BA's manifest to see when Livvy is flying. Do we know it's British Airways?"

Jack assured him, as much as he could and was assured, in return, that Charlie would call back when he had something. But before he rang off, Charlie said, "I sense Livvy going back to the States is not what you expected, and I won't ask why. But I will wish you good luck in getting her back."

It wasn't a half hour later that Charlie texted him. Livvy was on a flight to Newark at 11:15 a.m. the following morning. Feeling ready to take on the world again, Jack told Henry to be at his flat to pick him up by 6:30. He would not take a chance missing her.

Before he fell asleep—although there wasn't much of it—he thought through what he'd say. He had to let her know he'd make it up to her if it was the last thing he did.

The next morning, Henry was waiting for Jack at the assigned time. Jack threw open the back door and slid in. "The airport, Henry. I intend to catch Livvy before she can board her flight."

"An excellent idea, Your Grace."

Henry proceeded to drive faster than ever. It seemed that bringing Livvy back was important to Henry, as well.

"Which terminal, Your Grace?"

"Terminal Five."

"Righto."

As Henry slowed for traffic, Jack drummed his fingers on his knee. He thought of a new anxiety. Had he left enough time to get to Livvy before she went through security?

He looked at his watch as Henry came to a stop. "Sorry, Your Grace. Don't worry. We'll make it through."

The accident ahead—two lorries, one overturned on the carriageway, and fuel that needed mopping up—meant a frustratingly long delay. Finally, Henry roared up to the terminal to deposit Jack at the nearest door on the departures level. "I'll ring you when I've got her." Jack bolted out of the car and slammed the door behind him.

The terminal was overflowing with people. Scanning the cavernous space, he sprinted toward security, stopping short when he got a good look at the length of the queue. It wound round and round stanchions, an amalgam of people of all sizes and colors and countries of origin, with hats, without, with children, without, with luggage, without. It would be a miracle for him to catch sight of Livvy. There was only one other thing he could do: ring her.

As people eddied around him, he pressed his auto dial and waited. After three or four rings, it went to voicemail. He re-dialed. This time it went to voicemail faster. With growing frustration, he dialed a third time. He got the same result and knew. She wouldn't take his call.

He looked at his watch. 9:45. There wasn't much time to waste. He called Isabella. She'd barely answered when he launched forward. "I want you to buy me a ticket." He gave her Livvy's flight number. "If that flight's booked, put me on any flight that leaves around eleven a.m. from any gate in that section of Terminal Five."

He disconnected and scanned the crowd until luck favored him and he caught sight of her as she stepped out of security into the protected part of the airport. He pushed his way to the security barrier, and shouted, "Livvy!" She looked around, mystified. "Livvy," he shouted again.

She faced him then, fully. Her face gave nothing away.

"Livvy, I'm sorry. I promise, it won't happen again."

She gave no hint that she'd respond.

"Oi, mate." Jack turned as a man in the security line beckoned him. He was a tall, skinny fellow with hair worn in a pony tail. He wore a wife beater that highlighted the spectacular tattoos inked across his chest and down both arms. "Go on with it, why don't you? Tell her you love her. It's what she's waiting for, isn't it?"

The fellow was right. It was what she needed to hear. He glanced around. So many curious eyes were on him. It chafed. He felt exposed. His heart was already beating triple time. But neither his time nor his heart mattered. He was losing her. He could see it in her eyes, even from the distance, and so he did what he'd never done before. Made himself the object of unwanted attention. Shouted the words he should have said on their last video call, not the ones he had. "I love you, Livvy!"

A whole section of the queue began to clap. His tattooed friend gave him a thumbs-up. Jack grinned and motioned for Livvy to come back out of the secure area. He couldn't wait to ask for her forgiveness, and then to hold her and apologize again and then again.

She continued to stare, until she turned and walked away. Jack's mind went blank. He sensed more than heard the groans and whispers from the crowd. The queue shuffled on and with it the man who had encouraged Jack to declare himself.

"Sir, you'll have to move."

A man wearing a lanyard and badge that identified him as being part of security frowned up at him. "You're not to loiter about."

Jack shook his head against shock and made himself respond. "Do you know how I can get through security?"

"Do you have a ticket?"

"Not at the moment. I have one coming." He pointed toward where Livvy had disappeared. "My fiancée is on her way to the gate. I must speak to her before she boards."

"You've got a mobile. Use it, why don't you?"

Jack knew if Livvy boarded that plane without

him pleading his case, it was going to be infinitely more difficult to get her to listen. His mobile buzzed. He looked down at the message from Isabella. Livvy's flight was overbooked. There were no other flights that left from that section of the terminal until after two p.m.. Did he want her to book him? He texted back yes. "Where's your Global Entry?"

It had been a while since Jack had accessed Global Entry at Heathrow.

The security guy pointed his chin. "The far side of this concourse."

Jack looked at his watch again. Though by the time he got to Global Entry he would have his ticket, there would be no time for him to make it before the gate closed on Livvy's flight. He made a snap decision. "Where's your supervisor?"

The man's face hardened. "You don't get my supervisor. All you get is me. Now, move."

"Look. It's important."

"It's important that I win the lottery, but that's not happening, is it?" Raising his voice, the man said, "Now that I'm thinking of it, I will call my supervisor and a couple of those lovely chaps with their lovely guns. They'll sort you, won't they?"

Stepping back from the barrier, Jack held up both hands, palms out. "No need to call anyone. I'm going."

As he began to walk away, the security man said, "I don't know what your problem is, mate. With the times the way they are, you should know. You'd not get through security without a ticket, even if you was to be the king."

Jack barked a humorless laugh. "And if I was?"

The man swelled up with righteous anger.

"Sorry. I'm going."

He called Henry. "I'll meet you at the same door where you dropped me off."

"Have you got our girl?" There was real excitement in Henry's voice.

"No."

"Oh, I'm sorry."

Jack held the mobile to his ear long after Henry had disconnected. He walked toward the door, gazing straight ahead. The turmoil around him might as well not have existed for the turmoil inside him. It flooded his brain with chemical reactions, destroying any possibility of him having a logical thought. When he exited the building he found Henry and the car at the curb, waiting for him. "This isn't the end, you know."

Henry pulled away. "I'm happy to hear you say that, Your Grace."

"I'm going to get her back."

As Henry returned him to his flat, Jack worked to regain his equilibrium. He'd been so sure he could fix what he'd broken. He hadn't reckoned with the depth of her sense of betrayal. Because that was what he'd done. Betrayed her.

How did one beg forgiveness for a betrayal?

CHAPTER SEVENTEEN

The plane was overbooked. Livvy was grateful for her middle seat, the last one to be had on the flight.

An older woman already occupied the window seat. Her all-white hair was yanked back in a knot at the back of her head. She wore a black dress with a white shawl thrown around her shoulders. Livvy wondered how long it would be before she hopped up and, Miss Clavel-like, brought order to the passengers trying to stuff oversize suitcases into already full overhead bins.

The aisle seat was empty. It remained empty until…

"Excuse me."

Livvy looked up to a see a man the size of an NFL linebacker with shoulders and torso that spanned the aisle, smiling down at her. He held a black computer bag in one hand and, on his black T-shirt, a message in white letters: *Pardon Me While I*

Buffer. With a fist that could have picked up Miss Clavel, and put her in the overhead bin, he stowed his bag above them.

Livvy suppressed a groan. As he prepared to sit, she prepared to get squished. But at some point in his travels, Gargantua must have figured out how to squeeze his girth into his allotted space without spillage into the seat next to him. "Sorry," he said in a soft voice.

Relieved, Livvy gave him a weak smile. "No worries."

Yeah, no worries, there. She had other worries. And misery. And the desire to lie down across all three seats in her aisle and sleep away the whole flight. If only there weren't Miss Clavel and Gargantua. If only she could get the picture of Jack, as she'd last seen him, out of her mind.

"*I love you, Livvy,*" he'd shouted. The self-contained, very private Jack Anstruther laid himself open to ridicule in front of thousands, and she'd walked away.

What did that make her?

Inside her heart, she cringed. She loved him. Looking down the tunnel of years to come, she couldn't see how she would ever stop loving him. But she'd spent the first part of her life with a man who had no faith in her. She'd walked herself out of his life, and now, excruciating as it had been, she'd walked herself out of Jack's for the same reason.

Sitting between alpha and omega, she told herself she'd done the right thing. She could not live with someone who didn't trust her.

As the pilot announced they were at thirty-seven thousand feet, she looked around, surprised that she'd missed the whole take off and cruising to altitude thing. Miss Clavel was reading a book. The linebacker had taken out his laptop. Stuck in the seatback pocket in front of him, all kinds of computer paraphernalia linked by wire to his laptop. Fascinated by the vision of a man the size of a house typing delicately on a tiny keyboard, she reminded herself she could be typing, too.

She powered up, in airplane mode, and her screen went black. She hissed a curse.

Her seatmate stopped what he was doing. "That happen often?"

"Too often."

"Have you been sure to save your work frequently?" Said like a nerdy IT guy, not a monster blitzing a quarterback.

"Yes," she told him. "To the Cloud."

"I'd be willing to look and see if I can find what's wrong. If you don't mind?"

The little black boxes that were dangling out of the seatback pocket blinked their orange lights at her. She glanced at his screen. On it was a graph with symbols and numbers that made no sense to her, which was when she decided. "I don't mind."

"My name's Frank." He folded his computer up, tucked it into the seatback pocket—the black thing-a-ma-jigs still dangling—and placed her computer on his table.

"I'm Livvy."

"Nice to meet you." Those were the last words Frank spoke before a whole lot of white letters and numbers and symbols came up on her display. His fingers flew. All those white characters flew with them.

After what Livvy thought was the longest computer diagnosis she'd ever witnessed—not that she'd been around for any—he stopped and stared at her. "Do you know somebody's installed a clandestine remote access client on your computer?"

They were over Iceland when Livvy concluded that her father had done it. After Frank explained what the clandestine thing was and what it could do—activate her microphone remotely and listen in on conversations, like the ones she'd had in the library where her laptop sat on a permanent basis—and how her computer guy could get rid of it. Frank could but he wouldn't feel comfortable taking her laptop apart on the plane, maybe losing some of its parts.

When the plane came to a stop at the gate in Newark, she thanked Frank for his help. As she made her way up the jetway, she couldn't decide what would give her more satisfaction: reading her father the riot act or telling Jack 'I told you so'. She was still playing how in her mind when her phone rang. She fumbled it out of her pocket to see Sheryl's number on the screen. "Hey, I just landed."

"Good. You're home. You can come to the party."

Livvy cuddled her computer bag against her chest and lodged her phone between shoulder and cheek. "What party?"

"The one for Hudson. This afternoon at five. Yours, too. Maybe you forgot but today is your birthday. Your thirtieth. Now that you're home, it can be a true family celebration."

Wow. Today was her birthday. She'd forgotten, not a surprise with how she was pretty much focused on her life falling apart. She sidestepped her way to the edge of the jetway. "Where will the party be? Who's going to be there?"

Sheryl laughed. "Wow. Does that mean you'd actually want to join the fun?"

"Knowing our family? Us getting together it's going to be fun. Where will it be?"

"At Stephanie's house."

At the Bentsen McMansion. Whatever exhaustion she'd felt withered away. "I assume Kyle will be there. What about Dad?"

"It's Kyle's house, so yes. Dad, too."

Here was her chance to unload her rage on the subject of that rage. "Okay, I'll come. I'll go home, park my bags and Uber to Stephanie's."

"It's settled. I'll let Stephanie know."

"Oh, listen," Livvy spoke before Sheryl could hang up. "If Stephanie hasn't gotten the cake yet, ask her to make it anything but chocolate."

Livvy hated chocolate.

Stephanie bought a chocolate cake. In the aftermath of the food coma inducing meal—pizza for the kids, for the adults, eggplant parm and chicken Marsala—Livvy sat at her sister Stephanie's mammoth dining room table in her fifteen-thousand square foot imitation of Versailles and listened to her sisters gossip. Staring at the cake's eight all-chocolate layers, the fat pink roses on top, she fought her jet lag and reminded herself she needed to stay sharp. She was here in the McMansion for a reason.

"...was the finishing touch on the pieces that I ordered to make Kyle's office perfect. Now the room looks put together."

Livvy blinked at what Stephanie had been saying. "Sorry, I missed that part. What are you talking about?"

Stephanie tossed her geometrically-cut shoulder length hair over her shoulder. "You never listen, Olivia. Not that anybody is shocked. What I was saying was Kyle found this stunning Persian rug in

London. It was outrageously expensive, but worth every penny."

Livvy had a quick thought that she should go look and while she was at it, take a couple of the kids with her hoping one of them would drop a glass of grape juice on it.

Speaking of which, the herd—her ten nieces and nephews—took that moment to thunder into the dining room from wherever in Versailles they'd been. Instantly, the cry for cake went up. Hudson, Livvy's favorite, threw himself on her lap. "I want a piece, Aunt Livvy." Plate in hand, he bunched up his face into a fierce frown. "Don't give any roses to Michael."

"What, you don't like your cousin?" The question didn't penetrate Hudson's animal brain, so fixed was it on the size of the piece Livvy cut for him, complete with the roses. He scuttled to the far end of the table, sat, and began to scarf away. "You're welcome," she said with a chuckle.

Her laugh faded as the men strolled into the dining room. First in line was Ben, Sylvia's husband, then Elliot, Sheryl's, and then Kyle, bringing up the rear.

"Here come the Masters of the Universe," Livvy said under her breath. Sheryl sent her a warning look, as in please don't make waves.

Livvy planned on making a tsunami.

The men took their seats across the table from where Livvy sat with her sisters. She had to give it to them. They were all good looking. And they all dressed to impress, even at a kid-centered dinner. Well, Elliot was not dressed quite as spiffy. Not that she cared. Elliot was the one brother-in-law she liked.

The men took seats across the table from Livvy and her sister, just as her father made his way to the empty seat opposite her. She stiffened.

He pulled out the chair and sat. Without any small talk he began. "I think we can all agree, Olivia, that your sister makes a very nice dinner."

Livvy eyed Stephanie who was supervising the distribution of second pieces of cake. "Yeah, there's no one who can place a takeout order like my sister."

He narrowed his eyes. "I'd hoped we could keep the cutting remarks to a minimum tonight."

"Really?" In a stage whisper, she said, "Did something change while I was away? Cutting remarks have always been the way this family communicates."

His black eyes flashed a warning. "This is supposed to be a happy occasion."

Not for her, it wasn't.

He folded his hands together in front of him. His gazillion dollar gold Audemars Piguet Royal Oak self-winding watch winked at her from his left wrist. "Did you learn anything in England to help you focus your thoughts on the life decisions you now have to make?"

He'd wanted to ask that question earlier, but noise at the table prevented it. "I just got off the plane. Can it wait?"

"You're thirty-years old, today. You need to stop thinking you can make a living writing books."

"Thanks for letting me know."

A look of disdain curled one side of his lip. "I do not appreciate your sarcasm."

Not bothering to lower her voice, she said, "I do not appreciate you putting a listening buggy kind of thing in my laptop."

As if it was a signal, her sisters left the table. None of them appreciated family battles.

Spots of color appeared on her father's cheeks. Kyle's shit-eating grin disappeared. Ben murmured an apology and got up to join the women. Elliot remained, his face impassive.

Livvy leaned forward. "What? You wanted to better your chances on the deal you already had with Jack's company?"

The color in her father's cheeks faded back to the marble-like white that was his normal skin tone. "Sometimes programs such as that serve such a purpose."

She'd expected an irritable answer, not an odd one. "I bet you were riveted by what you heard."

Her father said nothing.

"You do know if you go to the British tabloids with your blackmail, they're going to destroy Jack's family. Could you, just for once, not have gone for the kill?"

Robert made a dismissive sound. "We won't have to if he does what we want."

"And what's that?"

Robert loosened the clasp of his hands. "Sell us Chalcott House."

She squeezed her eyes shut against the pain lancing through her head. "Oh my God, Dad. Even Hudson knows Jack won't sell it to you."

He made a scoffing sound. "He will. There's a reason I'm buying Chalcott House."

Through gritted teeth, she said, "Unburden yourself. Please."

"I'll be able to publish your books, even if they aren't any good. You ought to be grateful."

"Do you really expect my gratitude?"

"Knowing you? No," he snapped. "I wouldn't have had to do any of it if you'd ever made the first attempt to get a real job writing in PR or advertising. Instead you've wasted your time on nonsensical blogs and reviews that pay you next to nothing and books no one will ever publish. That's why I've stepped in."

"Meddling in my life is standard operating procedure for you, right?" she shot back at him.

He pressed his lips together.

"When did you have the thing installed?"

"What does it matter?"

Her temper was a teapot at the boiling point. "Please answer the question."

He began to fiddle with his watch. "Before you left for England."

Not the answer she expected. "So was it meant to catch Jack saying something you could use later, or was it to…?"

For a nanosecond, his gaze wavered. "It was to keep track of you."

The piece of chicken she'd eaten earlier threatened to make a comeback.

Kyle winked at her. She told herself not to give in to the impulse to smash what was left of the cake in his face. "For what?"

"I needed to know you were safe." His jaw hardened.

"You were afraid Jack would put me in a dungeon? Just as a point of interest, he doesn't have one."

"Don't be ridiculous." He crossed his arms. "A father has responsibilities."

She kept her hands in her lap. They were clenched so tight her nails scored her skin. "Not to me, you don't."

An odd expression crossed his face. "I've never told you because you didn't need to know, but my father left my mother when I was two. I grew up without the guidance I should have had from him. I made up my mind I would guide my children as he never did."

He was right. Livvy hadn't heard this story. For the teeniest moment, her heart softened as she imagined what it must have been like for him growing up without a father. But then she'd grown up without a father, too.

"I'm sure it was difficult. Your way of compensating for it with me? It's not working. So stop."

Her father pressed his lips together. "I am not going to discuss this with you anymore, Olivia." And he got up and left the room. Elliot got up, too, but remained by the door, still frowning.

"Hey, Olivia."

She blinked her attention to Kyle, still sitting across from her. "Party's over," he sneered. "Time for you to leave."

"And spoil the illusion that we're one big, happy family?" She leveled the stabbing point of the cake knife at him. "Want me to cut you a piece of cake? Sweets for the sweet."

He held up a hand, palm out.

"Okay, no cake, then. So, what dirty part did you play? It must have been something disgusting."

"Shut up," he said, jaw clenched.

Hudson looked up from shoving cake in his mouth, the second piece Stephanie had cut for him. "Uncle Kyle, you should not tell anyone to shut up. That's very bad."

Kyle gave Hudson a look. Livvy decided if Kyle told *him* to shut up, she *would* throw the cake at him.

She held up a hand. "It's okay, I know the answer. You wanted to spoil things for me. Like get Jack to kick me out of Brompton Court."

He leaned back in his chair. "He did, didn't he?"

She didn't need to be reminded. "So did my father give you five gold stars for your efforts?"

"You don't think he appreciates my work?" Kyle's eyeballs shot out bolts of lightning.

"I think the only reason he so-called appreciates your work is because you're sleeping with one of his daughters."

"What a bitch you are," he ground out under his breath. "Without me doing my magic, he—" He stopped abruptly.

Elliot took that moment to clear his throat. Livvy gave him a fleeting glance, wondering why he hadn't left with everyone else. Well, other than Hudson who was still cramming his mouth with cake. To Kyle, she said, "What kind of magic?"

He slammed his hands on the table as if that would silence her.

Hudson's eyes grew wide. He stopped eating.

Livvy leaned toward him. "Hey bud. Why don't you take your cake and go eat in the kitchen?"

As Hudson scampered away, Livvy narrowed her eyes at Kyle. "Did you really need to scare the kid?"

He dismissed her question with a flick of his hand "When your father has something that needs doing but he doesn't want to dirty his hands?" His voice was a furious growl. "He calls *me*, Olivia."

"You do my father's dirty work?" She rolled her eyes. "I am so shocked."

"Kyle, I need you." Stephanie stood a few feet

away, one hand on one ample hip, a ticked-off look on her face.

Kyle got up. He leaned across the table, a smile on his face that was more a taunt. "That's the signal for you to go."

As Kyle followed Stephanie out of the room, Livvy looked down at her hands, clasped hard in her lap. She eased them apart .

"Olivia."

She blinked up at Elliot, who had moved to the seat Kyle had vacated.

He held up his cellphone. "Check your messages." That was when, finally, he left the room.

She said whatever goodbyes she had to. Once in the Uber back to her apartment, she took out her phone and read Elliot's message. She'd never been shocked by what she knew of her father's business practices, but this?

She stared out at the elegant houses set back from the gently curving streets of the upscale town in the upscale part of Bergen County that her sister and brother-in-law had chosen to live in. She was emotionally battered by the showdown at Versailles. Still, it would give her a serious sense of satisfaction to tell Jack about the so-called listening device, though it wouldn't change anything between them.

She looked at her watch. It was just after midnight, London time. She didn't care if she woke him. She began to thumb her message. Finished, she sat back, and waited. She didn't wait long. Her phone buzzed. There was only one word on the screen:

Yes.

It was the last thing Jack expected: a text message from the woman who only hours before, had walked away from his most private declaration of love in the most public way.

I have something to tell you. It's important. Will you take my call?

His heart leapt. Despite everything that warned him not to, he allowed himself to hope she was calling to accept his apology.

The video connection completed, one look at her unsmiling face had that hope dying. Still, he would keep the call as normal as possible.

"How was your flight?" He made fists of his hands so he wouldn't touch his laptop's screen, as if running his fingers across its cold surface would be the same as running his fingers across her cheeks and her lips.

"I sat next to a really interesting guy."

Jack pushed aside the sudden twinge of jealousy,

an idiot emotion, when what he needed to concentrate on was fixing what he'd broken. "Oh?"

"He was one of these geeky computer types. What made him interesting was what he told me. My computer kept going black because there was a listening thing in it. Once it's out, it'll work just fine."

Time stood still.

"You know what that means, right?" she prompted.

Blood cascaded through his veins. He knew what he should have known before. She'd told the truth. She'd *always* told the truth. And he'd paid her back with profound disrespect.

He cleared his throat so he could speak. "Can I assume your father's responsible?"

"You can assume that and you would be right."

Repulsive, but not surprising, considering the individual. "Why did he?"

"He wasn't looking for something he could use to make you give up Chalcott House, if that's what you're thinking. No, he was keeping track of me so if I did something foolish, he could swoop in and save me from myself."

That shocked him though he didn't think it was possible Robert Browne could shock him any more than he already had. "Bloody bastard."

"Yeah, well. We know that." Her jaw firmed. "And here's something *you* need to know. A little less than a year ago, Kyle took four million dollars from the pension funds of two companies Cenotaph controls. Some of the money went to cover business costs. But then he did something—I am willing to bet with my father's okay—he no way should have done. He took a chunk to build his new mega mansion, which my sister has redecorated in a way Louis XIV would approve."

Jack had an urge to laugh. If he had to guess, that was why Bentsen wanted a carpet like the one Jack had in his office at Somerset Mews. "That's an extraordinary piece of information. Who gave it to you?"

"My brother-in-law, Elliot. He's a forensic accountant. Straight arrow that Elliot is, I bet he's finally fed up with the way my father does business."

Jack already knew the Brownes were a picture-perfect example of a dysfunctional family. What the brother-in-law did then was no surprise.

"I don't care if Kyle gets caught up in the mess he's created. But my father?" A pained look crossed Livvy's face. "I don't like him. He infuriates me. But he's still my father. Isn't it pathetic that protecting him crosses my mind?"

It wasn't, and it said much more about the person Livvy was, better than anyone in her family. Not one of them deserved her, perhaps not even her sister Sheryl. Or Elliot, the accountant.

He exhaled a sharp breath. "Thank you. I know what to do with this information."

"Okay." She reached forward to disconnect.

"Wait." Before he let her go he had to tell her

what he'd learned about himself, unfortunately the hard way. "I'm an idiot."

She pressed her lips together.

"Things change. Life changes. I didn't. I hurt you. I hurt us. For that, I'm profoundly sorry."

"Jack…" Her jaw flexed.

He held up a hand. "I've just awakened to a reality I was never willing to admit to. I'm no longer the person who couldn't let his guard down in case there was a need to do battle against the enemies bent on hurting my family. My family doesn't need me for that anymore. I no longer need to fight and certainly not at the expense of love."

Her nostrils flared with emotion. "Please don't do this."

"Do what?" he whispered. "Ask for your forgiveness? Tell you I love you?"

She shook her head, back, forth, just once. "When you showed me how little trust you have in me, I knew. Without you having trust—or faith—in me, we can't have a life together."

She reached forward again. "Bye, Jack," she whispered. "Please say goodbye back, okay?"

The old Jack who had had to battle for so long, screamed 'No!' But the man he was knew. He had to let her go. She was in pain and he couldn't have that. So he gave her what she wanted. "Goodbye, Livvy."

She cut the connection and he sat back, staring at the blank screen but only for an instant. Though she wouldn't forgive him, she'd saved him. She didn't know she had, but she had.

He jumped to his feet. His heart jettisoned the heaviness that had weighed him down these last twenty-four hours. What she'd done was going to help him save his father's legacy. If that didn't say she loved him, it came damn close. Now, all he had to do was prove he had perfect faith in her and always would. He had a feeling he knew what it would take.

His legal teams went forward getting him out of the deal with Browne. They didn't bother to frame his decision not to sell AMG as a change of heart. Putting up a fight would be a mistake. Just in case Browne didn't get the point, they were to drop mention of pension fraud and time in jail into the conversation.

Four weeks later, Robert Browne and his company were out of Jack's life. That was when he sent his package. In it was the sweater she'd left in the library, the airline ticket he'd bought for her, and the other box, wrapped as carefully as he could. As big a heart as his Livvy had, he had wounded it. He could only hope this would heal it.

CHAPTER EIGHTEEN

"**S**tephanie just called me, hysterical," Sheryl said not bothering to say hello.

"What about?" Not that Livvy cared.

"Dad's gone ballistic because the deal he made to buy your duke's company has gone south and he's blaming Kyle."

Livvy allowed herself a smile. It had been almost a month since she'd given Jack Elliot's inside information. "Maybe our bastard brother-in-law is about to pay the price for being…well, a bastard."

Not that Livvy had been thinking much about Kyle getting what he deserved. That first week she was back, she spent it eating potato chips and ice cream. When she wasn't gorging herself on crap, she slept. Or cried.

The second week, after she was done boo-hooing, she pulled up her big girl pants and got back to living. She called Domenico at Faustino's and asked if he still had a job for her. 'Yes, and how soon can you be here' was his answer. She ramped up her blog posts. She started volunteering again at the library where shelving books was a little like being back at Brompton Court. A little. Not much.

Only her writing gave her comfort. Once she switched gears and decided that Jessamine's story would be a historical romance with elements of suspense, she allowed her imagination to take over. She resumed her schedule, sitting down at her laptop—blessedly free of black-outs—first thing in the morning, when her brain was most wide awake. She managed to write a healthy two to three thousand words most days. With her story falling into place, the writing went fast and she hurtled toward those magic words: The End.

No matter that her life seemed to have resumed its old rhythm, there was nothing about it that brought her peace. There were times when, empty of all her busy-ness, Jack came, unbidden, into her mind. That call between them…she'd been hurt, she'd been angry. And then she'd hung up. Maybe she shouldn't have. Maybe there was another something she could have done. She didn't know what. She solved the problem by not thinking about it.

On Friday afternoon at the end of the fourth week, she was getting ready for her shift at Faustino's when her doorbell rang, and she found herself signing for a package. The return address—10 Somerset Mews—made her heart lurch.

The box was light. She stared at it, turned it around, and put it down. She didn't open it. Every night she came home from work at the restaurant, she stared at the package but did nothing.

One week after she'd scrawled her name on the FedEx receipt, she told herself to stop being a baby. What could possibly be inside to make her life sadder than it already was? She sat down on the floor next to her bed, and scissors in hand, cut the package open. Three things slid out: a smaller box, an envelope, and her sweater.

She snatched up the sweater and buried her face in it, hoping if he'd held it in his hands, there would be a scent of him in its warp and weave. There was none.

Sighing, she dropped it on the floor and picked up the box. She shook it a little, which told her nothing except it was probably not a bomb. She set it on her knees and lifted the lid.

Her hands began to shake so hard she had to put the box down on the floor or risk dropping it and them: Jessamine Beresford's diaries.

When her heart rate fell back into normal rhythm, she reached into the box. She held them in her hands, not willing to put them down anywhere for fear of damaging them. "Get a grip. And start thinking," she muttered.

Beyond the fact that Jack Anstruther had officially gone insane sending her this most precious embodiment of his family's heritage by overseas mail carrier, she knew what this meant. He'd pulled out all the stops, done the only thing he knew he could to convince her to forgive him.

She set the diaries back in the box they'd come in. Her gaze fell to the envelope. She tore it open. Inside was an airline ticket to the UK. She squinted at the departure date and time and let out a scream. The flight, if she chose to take it, was at 6:40 this evening.

Would she take it? Oh, yes. But before that could happen, she had things she needed to do since the flight was leaving in four hours.

She called Faustino's and apologized for leaving them in the lurch. She called the library. Apologized there, too. She called Sheryl. No apologies to anyone, she told her sister, and then packed fast. She took only what she needed: her laptop, some clothing, her favorite shampoo and conditioner, her toothbrush...and the diaries. Anything else she needed? She crossed her fingers. She'd be buying it on the other side of the Pond.

Once he sent the package, Jack left for Brompton Court. He could do business from anywhere, couldn't he? He wanted to be where the memory of Livvy was strongest and so he set up his remote office in the library. The more time that passed when he didn't hear from her, he wondered if he'd done enough.

There were times each day when business flagged

and he could concentrate on Brompton Court itself. It hadn't taken long after Livvy left for him to realize his intention to let the place fall into ruin was ridiculous. He had a familial duty to the place. Because Pratt wanted him to understand exactly how much needed repair and reconstruction, he insisted Jack walk the entire court, top to bottom.

One afternoon, as the sun was setting, Jack climbed to what used to be the servants' quarters. The rooms were the size of large closets. The ceilings sloped down to accommodate the roof. No person of more than middle height could have stood straight in any room without knocking one's head on the ceiling.

Wiping off one of the dirt-caked windows with his sleeve, he peered out beyond the tree line to Moreham. The setting sun cast a warm, autumn glow across the land. His land. Its beauty took his breath away, beauty he would never have appreciated before, because he'd cast Brompton Court as the villain, the place that had killed his father.

Even if Livvy never came back to him—pain lanced through his head—he would always be grateful for her presence in his life. Because she'd hounded him to come to the court for her research, he'd had to see it again for himself.

That day when he'd brought her back from the hospital, he'd thought she was being more than a bit fanciful, describing what the library meant to her, as if she'd pitched her tent—so to speak—in it centuries before. As he walked the hallways to and from the duke's suite to the library and the kitchen, he'd begun to think she'd not been quite so fanciful. He felt the history of the place, too. Its ancient stones spoke of all the dukes who had come before him, the ones who were remarkable and the ones that weren't.

He angled his head downward. Below, was the evidence of Pratt's work on the landscape. The long grass was gone, ruthlessly yanked out of the earth. In its place, swaths of dark loam ready to be seeded. The overgrown flower beds had been cleared wholesale. The dead shrubbery had made way for new bushes that would sprout flowers in the spring. Where there had been a gazebo farther down the slope, lay piles of lumber, a sign that a new gazebo was about to go up.

Jack stepped back from the window and promptly hit his head. On a quiet curse, he bent and retraced his steps back into the hallway, and then down the stairs to the library.

Every time he entered, he thought of how she'd left it. It had needed to be patched and painted. The floor had needed a deep cleaning, and the carpet replacing. The four light fixtures, lovely in an historical way needed to go, or at least be upgraded if they were to produce real light.

He'd put off authorizing Pratt to start work in the library. He couldn't tell the man why. He could hardly admit it to himself. He didn't want the repairs to wipe away what Livvy had given this room before she'd left it: warmth. She'd brought it not just to the library, but to the entire, empty, sterile house. She'd brought warmth to *his* life, which he now realized had been as empty and as sterile as the house.

The day she was scheduled to depart Newark for London, he drove himself back to London, even though he hadn't heard a word from her after their video call. He found himself in a state of suspense. If sending her the diaries didn't bring her back, then he was at a loss to know what would.

Livvy made the flight with seconds to spare. Breathing hard, flopping into her assigned seat in first-class—she hadn't realized she was holding a first-class ticket until she got to the airport—she worked on calming down, which meant not breathing like her lungs were bellows.

As people around her settled into the privacy of their seat/beds, the flight attendant served cocktails. When she was a kid, Livvy had flown first-class. How else, her father would say? The Browne family deserved nothing less. Since she'd volunteered herself out of her father's orbit, she'd had to settle for economy and flying as a sardine. Livvy snorted a laugh, thinking first class definitely had its merits.

Soon after takeoff, dinner was served. After dinner, the lights turned down, Livvy tried to sleep. Like sleep would be possible with her brain banging around inside her skull.

Jack sending her the diaries meant…what? Did he want her to have them because he knew she'd obsessed over them for so long? Was he giving her permission to use what was in them to finish her book? Sending her the airline ticket meant he wanted her back, but how? Trust had driven them apart. Would the issue come up when they saw each other? It had to because it meant everything.

Hours later, as the eastern sky lightened, and she'd done nothing more than doze and fret, the plane began its slow descent into Heathrow, which was when she fell into a deep sleep, to be awakened, what felt like seconds later, by the flight attendant telling her it was time to rise and shine.

Gathering her stuff, preparing herself to meet the man she'd left so abruptly weeks ago, she wished she didn't feel like someone had poured maple syrup on her brain. It got only marginally better as she pressed forward up and down endless escalators and moving walkways to passport control and customs.

By the time she'd climbed the last escalator, she was a hot mess, because she hadn't thought about whether he would be at the airport to meet her. Of course he'd be there. He'd sent her the airline ticket, hadn't he? But maybe he wouldn't and she'd have to get a cab. Or a train. And where exactly would she go? Not knowing what or who she would see, her nerves vibrated hard enough to snap.

She stepped into the arrivals hall, only to be thrown by how jammed it was with happy people waiting to hug it out with their just-arriving relatives and friends. There was clapping. And shouting. There were balloons with messages printed on them.

Welcome home!

We missed you!

Happy birthday!

Someone jostled her and apologized. A loudspeaker brayed an incomprehensible message. Someone laughed in her ear.

There were the usual gaggle of limousine drivers in suits and caps, holding up signs with names on them. Her eye scanned the signs…until it lighted on the sign with *her* name.

Princess Leia.

Her heart leapt. And fell. It wasn't Jack holding the sign, but Henry Stebbins, who took the moment to step forward.

"Miss Browne." His eyes snapped with pleasure. "Welcome back. It's good to see you."

Seeing his driver and not Jack was a blow. She stiffened her knees to absorb it. "Thanks, Henry. It's good to be back."

He stowed the sign under one arm and relieved her of her backpack. "Now, I imagine I know what you're thinking. Where's the man I expected to meet me and why is an old fellow like Stebbins here in his place?" Henry waggled his eyebrows.

Livvy's moment of misery lifted a little. "Not that I don't want to see you, but I was wondering. Where is the duke?"

He winked. "He's nearby."

Sliding into the Tesla's super comfortable back

seat, Livvy realized how much she'd missed it, and said, "Why that name on your sign?"

Inching his way through the clog of vehicles at the airport, Henry looked over his shoulder. "His Grace knew you would ask."

He knew she would ask. Yes! "He did?"

"Yes, and he told me to tell you it's because it's not the name your father gave you. It's the name you gave yourself."

This sign with that name on it…it was a sign of another kind, a good one. "And nearby. What does that mean?"

Driving at his usual slow pace, Henry exited the airport. "Nearby, meaning London proper."

Livvy settled back, her brain trying to decide what kind of good sign the sign was. With all the names Jack knew her by: Olivia Sterling, Olivia Browne, Livvy, he'd chosen the one she'd named herself that night in Club Chaos. Did it to mean he accepted what she said about herself? It was a small piece of trust, and she'd go with it, until they got to wherever nearby was and she could ask Jack herself.

It turned out nearby wasn't as near as Henry said it was. It was miles. She tried to stay awake but all the hours she couldn't sleep on the trip had her paying a price. She jerked awake as they drove down a narrow road by a low-slung building that was surrounded by what looked like recently-constructed apartment houses.

She sat up, alert. This had to be Henry's nearby.

He held the door open for her, again, a broad smile on his face. Livvy wondered if the smile had left his face since the first moment she'd seen him at the airport. "We're here."

Livvy's heart began a slow thud. "Here" was where Jack was. At last, she'd know if the trip she'd taken so impulsively had been the right one.

Henry led her inside what looked to be some kind of lounge and then stepped back because there he was. The Duke of Brompton. Jack.

She'd forgotten how beautiful he was, how tall he was, how British he was. He was wearing a slim cut suit in a deep, navy blue. It accentuated his broad chest—a chest she knew well—and a trim waist. His trousers fit his long legs with almost a military precision. His shirt was crisp white, his tie, red and blue. She sensed Henry had left her backpack at her feet, which made no sense. Wouldn't they be getting in the car again to go wherever they'd be going? But she'd think about that later. After she knew what the rest of her life would look like.

He gazed at her out of watchful eyes and took steps that brought him closer to her. "Livvy. How was the flight?"

"Uneventful." She hesitated a fraction of a second and then took one small step toward him.

He gave her a rueful smile. "That's good."

Though dressed the proper English gentleman, he wasn't quite as put together as he'd seemed from a distance. He looked thinner. There were lines around his eyes and, of all things, considering her very proper Monk-Man, scruff on his cheeks and chin.

All inside her body, a fine trembling took hold. "You forgot to shave."

He lifted one hand to run it over his face. "It was dark when I got up." He smiled. Tiny lines bracketed the skin around his sapphire blue eyes.

Though it was an absurdity, she couldn't smile. Every word he spoke, every word *she* spoke was too filled with the potential for the miracle she'd hoped for when she'd left home.

He'd shown her a physical sign. She needed the one ultimate sign. She'd know it the moment she heard it. She took one small step toward him.

His smile faded.

"I wasn't ever coming back, you know."

He flexed one hand into a fist. "I know."

"Sending me the diaries, that was crazy."

"Not crazy. I wanted you to have them." He took another step. "I wanted you to use them to finish your book the way you wanted to."

That barrier that had stood between them for so long began to crumble. She had to clear her throat to speak. "You trust me with them? You don't think I'll hurt you anymore?"

His nostrils flared. "You would never hurt me."

The joy she hadn't dared admit to when she took the diaries from the box came percolating up. "You're right," she whispered. Her hand rose of its own accord to touch the little bit of cuff that showed from beneath his suit jacket. She stroked one finger over the stitching. "I wouldn't."

The guarded look on his face faded, replaced by a small, happy smile. "I have a new niece. She was born right after you left. Her name is Leonie. Annie and Charlie had a little girl, too. They've named her Abigail."

She gave him a genuine smile. "That's great news all around."

He closed the distance between them, stopping a hair's breadth away. "Marybeth is writing again."

"That's good." She matched his small step with another of her own. "It's good for Chalcott House."

Carefully, as if this was the most important thing he ever did, he took one of her hands in his. His beautiful eyes were filled with fierce, fixed attention. "I don't care if Marybeth never writes another word. I don't care if Chalcott House falls into oblivion. I don't even care if Somerset Mews collapses in a pile of eighteenth century brick and mortar."

With her focus on his lips and his beautiful words, she lifted her free hand to rest it over his fast-beating heart.

His eyes closed partway, until they opened again, the fierce look gone, replaced by a deep blue tenderness. "There's only one thing I care about. It's proving that the love I have for you is boundless and bottomless. But it's no greater or more important than my respect for what makes you who you are."

She swallowed hard.

"I love the girl who stood up to a family that didn't appreciate her for who she was born. I am in awe of how, with no help from anyone in her life, she followed her own path. I love the woman that girl became, the one who's had the strength to stay on that path despite all the slings and arrows tossed her way, especially the ones I tossed, I who should have kept them from hurting her…you. I want to say that man is no more. And hope you'll still might want the man who has taken his place."

A sob caught in her throat.

His gaze skimmed her face. "I just bought a new briefcase. For me, it's nothing more than an expensive piece of leather. One thing would make it precious: a heart carved on the inside flap with your name in its center."

Freed, at last, of the sharp, jagged edges of doubt that had been poking at her for weeks, laughing with delight, she threw herself into his arms.

He wound her tight in his arms. "I love you, Livvy. I love you more than you can imagine."

She lifted away from him and looked up into his dear face, his steady blue gaze, the tired lines around his eyes softening. "It can't be more than I love you."

He sighed and eased a hand beneath the fall of her hair.

She cupped his scruffy cheek. "You're not the only one with a confession to make."

He held her away, not much, but a little, and gave her one of his half-smiles. "You have nothing to confess to."

She placed a finger across his lips. "I do. All these years I've had this big-ass chip on my shoulder. About my name."

He kissed the top of her head. "Yes, the one that begins with O. The name I love."

"The one I didn't because I though O meant there was something wrong with me." She exhaled a soft breath. "It was never true."

He gave her a crooked smile. "If it had been, you would have been like your sisters. I didn't fall in love with your sisters."

She snorted a laugh at the thought of turning out like Stephanie, but then she grew serious again. "Jack, you looked inside yourself and saw how you needed to change. If you could do that, how could I not do the same?"

"Livvy, sweetheart…"

She took his hands and squeezed. "Let me say it. On the flight over, when I couldn't sleep, I started to think. I didn't have to walk away from you."

They both knew what she meant, how she'd walked away all those weeks ago at the airport. "I'd said horrid things to you. Of course you walked away."

She smoothed both hands across his chest. "And I didn't have to hang up on that video call when you accused me of betraying you."

He shuddered. "No matter how long I live, I'll never forgive myself for being so cruel."

She grabbed handfuls of his highly starched shirt. "And *I'll* never forgive myself for not telling myself to get over myself or something equally smart-assish."

He cocked his head to the side. "Is that another one of your made-up words?"

"Yes." She shook him a little. "I should have told you how, during that phone call I made to Sheryl, I said not one word about Jessamine and Charles's marriage."

He nodded and sighed. "If I hadn't been so distrustful, perhaps I would have heard you."

"Jack." She stood on her tiptoes. "Me getting all huffy and defensive has to stop, because if it doesn't, I'll remain that child who thought there was something wrong with her because her name didn't begin with an S. I'd feel like I had to lead with that chip on my shoulder. If I didn't change, if I didn't stop being so defensive, I'd lose the one thing I can't live without. That's you. I love you."

Jack picked her up and held her close in his arms, his face nestled against her neck and shoulder. "I'll take that," he said, voice muffled against her skin.

There was a riff of applause from somewhere, perhaps the small group of men whose presence she became aware of when she hadn't been before.

She knew they were making a spectacle of themselves and didn't care. Her heart was full to bursting. In just twenty-four hours everything in her life had changed from darkness to light. Life was good. It was the best.

Turning her head, she placed a kiss on the most accessible part of him—his ear. "About that briefcase. I have a better idea. When I carve my name on the inside of your new briefcase, how about if I carve Livvy loves Jack. Will that work?"

He lifted his head from her shoulder. His eyes glistened. His smile melted her heart. "My sweet, enchanting Livvy, it works."

He set her on her feet, took her hand in one of his, and lifted her backpack with the other. A roaring sound started up from outside of the building.

She jumped. "What's that?"

He gave her a wide grin. "Don't you remember when I said use it or lose it? I've decided using it is so much better. Come with me."

He led her out through a glass door onto a platform by the Thames, and there before her, a helicopter its engine running, its rotors circulating lazily.

"Is this your famous helicopter?" She had to raise her voice to be heard.

He held onto her backpack and with the opposite arm, pulled her hard against him. "It is. I thought I'd use it to fly far away to be alone forever if you wouldn't come back to me."

"That's silly. I'm here, aren't I?"

"Yes, you're here. And as you know, there are times when I believe in moving fast. It just so happens that I have a place in Lincolnshire that's waiting for us to make some serious renovations, inside and out. Shall we go and get started?"

She hadn't thought she could be any happier. She was wrong. "Awesome thought. Let's go home."

EPILOGUE

Text, Jack to Livvy

Now that you've written those wonderful words, The End, I'd like to introduce you to an agent. Her name is Maisie Helfgott. She will shepherd you through the process. She's your kind of Yank and will get you the best possible book deal.

Text, Livvy to Jack

I haven't met her and I already love Maisie. I want to be her when I grow up.

Text, Jack to Livvy

Gif: wide-eyed, sweating man biting his nails

Text, Livvy to Jack

Give me a break.

Text, Jack to Livvy

I hope you'll consider letting Chalcott House publish Jessamine's and Charles' story. After all, you keep reminding me that she was my grandmother.

Text, Livvy to Jack

That's true, but I'm a businesswoman now. I don't say yes to just any handsome man who treats me well in bed.

Text, Jack to Livvy

What's that expression of yours? I live to make you happy. Speaking of which I was finally able to make the reservation.

Text, Livvy to Jack

At last. I was beginning to think you wouldn't get me to the church…anvil…on time. Meet you at the car.

***

Group text from Rose Anstruther to her mother and sisters:

I have news! Jack and Livvy have decided to forego a big wedding with bridesmaids and flowers and thousands of guests as would befit the maybe king of England and his consort. They went to Gretna Green and took their friends, Charlie and Annie with them—and their baby girl—as witnesses. Who knew my brother was such a romantic?

The End

ACKNOWLEDGMENTS

I used to think if you couldn't write your book without help, you weren't an author. Not until I saw My Cousin Vinny and heard Mona Lisa Vito (Marisa Tomei's character) tell Vinny he was just going to accept that he would keep on winning case after case but only with others' help did I realize how wrong I was.

To write this book I had wonderful help from some wonderful people. Paul Janowitz who filled me in on the business elements of Jack's life. I'm sure he thought I was a business dunce and he wouldn't have been far wrong. Thanks also to Ilana Scandariato, doctor extraordinaire who one day at a family dinner described concussions to me and how quick recovery was possible. Brian Higgins, former chief of the Bergen County Police and current head of a security firm, spent one lunch with me patiently describing how high-profile people protect themselves. Thank you to Arlene Sahraie retired director of Library Services at Bergen County Cooperative Library System, who told me lots about how libraries work and where Livvy might have found all she learned about Jessamine. Big thanks go to Ewan Watson, new friend, who was willing to spend time with me making sure I had as many British colloquialisms right as possible. Any usage that's wrong is on my head. I'd also like to thank the internet for everything else I've learned in order to write this book, including how to care for old books and how to navigate Terminal Five in Heathrow Airport from gate to customs.

I'm grateful to two brilliant professionals: Gina Ardito for her fabulous content edit and Paula Gardner, phenomenal proofreader. And finally, as always, my gratitude to my critique partners and friends, Jen Wilck, Lisa Verge Higgins, and Nancy Herkness. Without their patience and brilliance over the long process of birthing this book, it never would have seen the light of day.

To my husband, Andy, for his incredible patience and understanding, making runs to Shop Rite and Trader Joes, making dinner, washing dishes, keeping the TV turned down, and being so understanding of all my writing tics, I couldn't have done it without you.

ABOUT THE AUTHOR

Award-winning author **Miriam Allenson** writes about smart-mouthed women and the men who love them. (She's been told she's a little smart-mouthed herself.)

Miriam took a dog's age and then some to publish her first book, FOR THE LOVE OF THE DAME. She cut the time to write her next book, A DUKE FOR DESSERT, in half and she reduced it by half again in writing WHEN THE DUKE FINDS HIS HEART. She apologizes for being so slow.

When Miriam is not working on a book—which is almost never—she's in the kitchen baking something, gardening on her "huge" 8'x4' deck, or adding one more character to her 400+ Pez collection. She likes licorice but not chocolate, polenta more than pizza, and baseball any day over football.

Miriam lives in northern New Jersey with her fabulous, supportive husband, Andy. One day they're going to take a cruise around the world. She'll still take her laptop with her.

Visit Miriam at miriamallenson.com or her Facebook account, facebook.com/msallenson.